The Chosen Prince

The Chosen Prince

Diane Stanley

HARPER
An Imprint of HarperCollins*Publishers*

For Ann², Judy, Lauren, Margo, Marisol, Marj,
Marty, Molly, Nancy, and Sue

The Chosen Prince
Text and map copyright © 2015 by Diane Stanley
For information address HarperCollins
Children's Books, a division of HarperCollins Publishers, 195 Broadway,
New York, NY 10007.
www.harpercollinschildrens.com

Library of Congress Cataloging-in-Publication Data
Stanley, Diane.
The chosen prince / Diane Stanley. — First edition.
    pages cm
    ISBN 978-0-06-224897-8
    Summary: "Prince Alexos, the long-awaited champion of the goddess
Athene, follows the course of his destiny through war and loss and a
deadly confrontation with his enemy to its end: shipwreck on a magical,
fog-shrouded island. There he meets the unforgettable Aria and faces
the greatest challenge of his life. Based loosely on Shakespeare's *The
Tempest*"— Provided by publisher.
    [1. Princes—Fiction. 2. Fate and fatalism—Fiction.] I. Title.
    PZ7.S7869Ch 2015   2014022042
    [Fic]—dc23   CIP
                                                              AC

Typography by Adam B. Bohannon
14 15 16 17 18   CG/RRDH   10 9 8 7 6 5 4 3 2 1
❖
First Edition

Be not afeard. The isle is full of noises,
Sounds, and sweet airs, that give delight and hurt not.
Sometimes a thousand twangling instruments
Will hum about mine ears, and sometime voices
That, if I then had waked after long sleep
Will make me sleep again; and then in dreaming
The clouds methought would open and show riches
Ready to drop upon me, that when I waked
I cried to dream again.

—William Shakespeare, *The Tempest*

Athene

FOGBANK
ISLAND

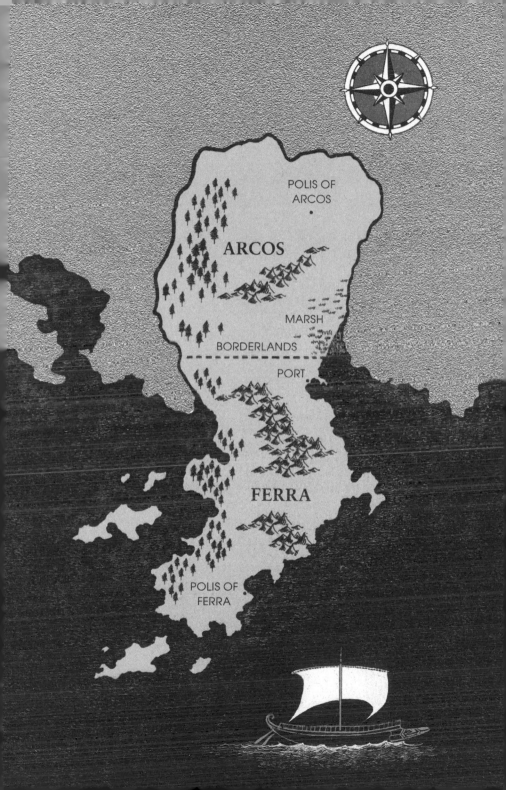

The Procession

THE NEWBORN PRINCE ALEXOS is asleep in his father's arms. The king does not hold his son tenderly. He isn't a tender man. But he's all the little prince will ever have in the way of parents. Alexos will have to make do.

Strictly speaking, he also has a mother. But having brought him safely into the world, the queen can do no more for him. She is helpless even to care for herself, prone as she is to irrational fears and fits of depression. And though she will live another eight years and bear another son before dying of childbed fever, she'll spend her days in solitude, tended by nursemaids and visited only by the king. Alexos won't remember her at all.

Considering what lies ahead for him, that's probably just as well. Kindness and affection would soften him, and he will need to be tough. Even now, as the sun rises on the first day of his life, his destiny is unfolding its great, dark wings.

Alexos is carried in solemn procession out of the palace, along the royal road, and into the city, then up the wide ceremonial way that leads to the temple of Athene on the hill. Early though it is, word of their approach has spread throughout the city. A crowd has gathered; they line both sides of the road, waiting.

They are not a handsome people. The ancient justice of Olympian Zeus is written on their faces and their bodies. They are short and scrawny, their clothing shabby. The children are wan and listless—and those are the healthy ones. The others, the fortunate few who fell to the summer sickness and survived, lean on crude wooden crutches, their legs imprisoned in makeshift braces wrapped with dirty rags. Even here in the great *polis* of Arcos there's never quite enough of anything. It is worse in the countryside.

The crime committed by their ancestors, which so enraged the gods, is long forgotten now. But the punishment lingers on. The kingdom of Arcoferra was split in two—Zeus, the king of gods, did this himself with the flash of his thunderbolt. Then the newly created Arcos and Ferra, on the north and south of that line, were condemned to fight an endless civil war.

They must fight through fierce winter blasts, through floods and droughts and punishing heat; on empty bellies when the crops wither in the fields; and with broken hearts when their children die of the dread new disease that comes every year in the summertime. To make this even harder to bear, Zeus decreed that neither side could ever win. This is the fruit of Zeus' righteous anger.

But Athene, patron goddess of Arcoferra, promised that once her father's rage has cooled, she would send a champion to deliver them. The people have been waiting for a very long time.

And so, on this cool spring morning, like their parents and grandparents before them, they watch the solemn procession with a tiny spark of hope. They kneel as King Ektor passes by, but their eyes are on the bundle in his arms. They wonder: Will he be the one?

The chancellor walks behind the king with a coffer of gold, a tribute for the goddess. Poor as the people are, they don't resent this. If the riches of Arcos will please Athene and remind her of her promise, they will have been well spent. Some have even added gifts of their own. The broad marble steps leading up to the temple are littered with small, shiny objects, the humble offerings of those who have almost nothing to give—rings, coins, copper spoons, precious objects passed down in their families from the old time, before Arcoferra's fall from grace. No thief would dare to touch them.

The procession enters the temple now. It's dark and cold inside. The chill of stone stings their bare feet as they proceed down the cavernous aisle, moving through gloom toward the brilliance of silver lamps on silver stands that surround the sacred image of the goddess. She looms above them, white as mountain snow, tall as the tallest tree, stern and serene. Beautiful.

The chancellor steps forward and holds the coffer up before the image.

"O wise, good, and most splendid Athene," he half speaks, half sings, "our patron and defender since ancient times, we bring you this humble gift of worldly riches as thanks for your unfailing kindness." He sets the coffer down on a corner of the dais, then steps back and kneels, his hands folded.

Now King Ektor comes forward and holds the infant high. "I offer you this blameless child, my newborn son and the heir to the throne of Arcos, to be the instrument of your mercy. If you accept him, I pray that he may be worthy, that he may strive to earn at last the forgiveness of the immortal gods and most especially your great father, Zeus."

The augur steps forward to join the king. Together

they climb the steps of the dais and kneel at the feet of the goddess.

The augur has done this many times—here before Athene and at other temples, too. There are always pressing questions to ask the immortals. But the one they ask today is altogether different. The fates of Arcos and Ferra hang upon the answer. And the augur is afraid of making even the smallest mistake.

His hands tremble as he spreads the pure linen cloth at the feet of the goddess, smoothing out the wrinkles with gentle strokes. They fumble as he pulls open the leather pouch, withdraws eight small golden amulets, and begins to lay them out on the cloth one at a time, in the form of a circle. He takes special care with this. Each amulet has its own particular meaning and its own assigned position. When he is satisfied that he has done it properly, he turns to King Ektor and nods.

The king unwraps the child's swaddling cloth and lays him in the center of the circle. The baby's skin is red and wrinkled, his little umbilicus swollen, wound-like, tied with a golden cord. In this magnificent temple, at the feet of the goddess, he seems a poor offering indeed.

They wait.

Naked and cold, the little prince stirs in his sleep.

But other than that, he doesn't move. The king looks to the augur, who responds with the slightest movement of his hand: *Be patient.* So they continue to kneel in silence, listening to the child's soft snuffling breaths and the muted sounds from the city below.

Finally, when the augur feels they have waited long enough, he reaches into his pouch again and brings out a vial of sacred oil. He pulls the stopper and pours the golden liquid over the baby's chest. The oil is cold; the child wakes. His squealing cry echoes off the marble walls.

And at last he is in motion.

The king and his augur lean in to watch as a tiny arm swings upward, sending the first amulet flying. It's a good one, *strength*. There follows a brief moment of joy before the arm comes down again, striking *foolishness* this time.

Strong and foolish, the king is thinking, *an unfortunate combination,* when the other arm jerks out and two more amulets are chosen. They are the opposites of the first two: *weakness* and *wisdom*.

This can't be right. The king shuts his eyes, sick with disappointment. He'd had the strongest presentiment that this child would be the one. But it seems he was mistaken. His son will just be one of those worthless boys who swings with the wind, turning first one way, then the other. He will never be dependable, will never amount to anything. His strengths will all be canceled out by his weaknesses.

He hears a gasp from the augur and opens his eyes again. The child is still moving. With his left leg he makes a decisive kick, choosing *virtue*. Then two heartbeats later he raises his right arm high over his head. His little fingers scrabble at the cloth, searching.

Ektor sucks in a breath and holds it, afraid to move. He knows what this amulet means. Like its opposite, it is placed so as to be difficult, if not impossible, to reach. It's too important to risk being chosen by chance. There must never be the slightest doubt.

But there will be none, no doubt at all. For the little fingers find what they are looking for and grasp it in a tight fist. Then, with a grace and assurance impossible for a newborn child, Prince Alexos lays the golden prize directly over his own beating heart.

He is finished now. He sighs as his arm drops drowsily to his side; his eyes close and his breath slows. Once again he sleeps. And on his chest, in a pool of amber oil, glittering in the light of the lamps, is the amulet for *greatness*.

The goddess has spoken.

Part One
The Kingdom of Arcos

1

ALEXOS HAS BEEN SUMMONED by his father. As usual, the king is occupied. So the prince waits in the anteroom, trying not to show that he is nervous.

There are two attendants standing guard at each of the doors—the one from the hall and the one that leads to the king's reception chamber. They are too well trained to stare openly at the prince, but they watch him out of the corners of their eyes.

Alexos is tall for his age, taller already than his father. He's slender, all muscle and bone, with the long, brown legs of a runner. His narrow face is well proportioned, his eyes large and dark, his bearing princely. The attendants exchange discreet smiles when they think he isn't looking.

Alexos is used to this. He is known—or suspected,

or believed—to be the future champion of Arcos, the long-awaited hero sent to win the forgiveness of the gods. It's only natural that people should be curious about him. So Alexos, knowing he will always be watched, has learned to keep his feelings to himself and behave with dignity at all times. As he is doing now.

He wants to cross and uncross his restless legs. He wants to shift around on the bench, to fidget away his growing tension. But instead, he sits calmly, hands folded in his lap, staring at the mosaic on the anteroom floor.

While he waits, he counts the number of times he's been called to his father's chambers. There haven't been many; King Ektor is rarely at court. He lives and rules his kingdom from the borderlands, returning only once or twice a year. Ektor is a warrior-king and his place is with the army.

Alexos curls a finger to record each meeting he can recall. He stops at nine. He may have left out one or two, but he doesn't think so. Visits with his father are hard to forget.

The door to the inner chamber opens and the steward comes out.

"Prince Alexos," he says with a smile and a respectful bow from the waist. "Your father will see you now."

The prince rises without haste in his natural,

graceful way. He acknowledges the steward with a nod, then, doing his best to conceal his dread, enters the lion's den.

Ektor is sitting at his desk, a scroll in his hands, apparently engrossed in reading it. This is what he always does. He makes Alexos wait.

Finally the king looks up at his son and heir, whom he hasn't seen in almost a year, and notes that the boy has grown.

"You're very tall," he observes.

"Yes, Father."

"I expect you'll be taller still."

"I expect so."

"That's good. A man ought to be tall."

Alexos has nothing to say to this.

"You may sit," Ektor says, carefully rolling up the scroll, tying a ribbon around it, and setting it down. He isn't scowling exactly. It's more his usual expression of impatience.

"I have good reports from all of your masters," he says. "That's as it should be, of course. Much is expected of you. You cannot afford to fall behind."

"I won't, Father."

Every time Alexos is called into Ektor's presence he is warned *not to fall behind*. He's thoroughly grasped the concept by now. Why must his father keep repeating it? But he hides any hint of annoyance.

"However, I am disturbed to hear you are not well liked by the other boys, that you keep apart from them and refuse to join them in their games. This will not do, Alexos! You will need their support when you become king. It's crucial that you earn their friendship now, while you're young—which you cannot do by being haughty and aloof."

Alexos' face has flushed hot. "That's not true," he says. "The situation is very different from what you describe." He speaks quietly and in a respectful tone, but he senses that he has still managed to offend his father.

"Really? Then perhaps you'd care to enlighten me."

"I would." Alexos has unconsciously balled his hands into fists. He releases them, though his body remains as tight as the skin on a drum. "It's my classmates who keep apart from me. Apparently they don't feel natural in my presence, because of who and what I am."

"Well, they *might* if you didn't lord it over them! Truly, you have no reason to disdain those boys. They may not be your equals, but they're the sons of the highest nobles in the kingdom."

Alexos gasps, shocked by the unfairness of this accusation. "I *don't* disdain them," he says. "And I don't lord anything over anyone. I'm always polite and kind to my classmates. I praise their accomplishments and am modest about my own. Can I help it if they stop talking when I walk into a room? It's not my fault that I'm a prince, and heir to the throne, and all the rest. Surely it must have been the same for you when you were a boy."

"Not in the least; I was well liked. I had many friends. You'll just have to try harder, Alexos. Tell a few jokes, have a bit of rough-and-tumble. And it wouldn't hurt to smile now and then."

This last bit hits home. Alexos resolves to work on smiling.

"I especially arranged for you to be schooled with those boys, not privately tutored as your brother is, so you could make them your friends. They will be your lieutenants someday, advising you and helping you carry out your plans. You'll need every ounce of their devotion—for believe me when I say that being king of Arcos isn't the roll in the grass you think it is."

Alexos grits his teeth. He thinks nothing of the sort. He is perfectly aware that ruling a kingdom while fighting a war is hard.

"And King Pyratos of Ferra is a most formidable adversary. These past ten years have been hard going, even for a seasoned commander like me. I've needed all the help I can get. It's well that my men worship me as they do—why, they would walk on burning coals if I asked it of them! You had better make sure *your* men feel the same about you. For without their full support, Pyratos will have crushed you like a worm beneath his heel within a month after I am dead."

Speechless, Alexos nods.

"See if you can be a bit more accommodating and a good deal less solemn. Make an effort. Be a *boy*, for heaven's sake, not a dreary old man."

Alexos feels a hot stinging rising in his eyes, and it terrifies him. This conference has been unpleasant enough already. He cringes to think how much worse it would be if he should actually shed tears. So he quickly orders his mind to think about something else—mathematics usually works; that's what he chooses now—and manages at last to recover his composure. By then the king has moved on.

"Good," he says. "Good. Now, on a happier note, I also hear you have wings on your heels."

This change of subject takes some readjusting. "Running, you mean?"

"They say you are marvelous fast."

"I . . . yes. I like to run and I give my best effort to everything I do."

"Then you'll be glad to know that now you've

turned twelve you may race on festival day."

"Oh!" Alexos cries. "Father, *no!*"

The king's smile vanishes. "And whyever not?"

"I'm too young. For me to compete at such an age would make me look ridiculous. And it wouldn't sit well with the other boys. They'd laugh at me behind my back."

"They'll stop laughing soon enough when you win the race."

"But I *won't* win, Father. I couldn't possibly! I doubt I'd even make the final twelve."

"You needn't worry about that. I've reserved you a place."

"You mean I *won't even compete in the trials?*"

"Of course not! You're the crown prince of Arcos; it would be unseemly. And it's not as if you're some pathetic weakling. Everyone knows you're more than good enough."

Alexos buries his face in his hands. "Father, I beg you—"

"Oh, stop being such a child. I have my reasons."

Alexos is trembling now and can't control it. "May I at least know what they are?"

"I suppose."

A sniff of annoyance, a bit of toying with the scroll, a drumming of the fingers.

"You are the chosen champion of the goddess Athene. But unfortunately, as victory in war is forbidden under the decree of Zeus, there's little scope for winning fame and glory on the battlefield. And even if there were, your masters say you lack the spirit of a warrior, and while you are more than competent with the sword and the lance, Leander and Titus both excel you. Clearly we must look elsewhere."

"*Fame and glory*, Father?"

"It *has* to be running, don't you see? That is your goddess-given gift. But it won't mean much if you win the crown at the age of eighteen. You must show yourself to be a prodigy. Why do you look at me like that?"

"Athene didn't choose me to be a *hero*. I am not Achilles. That's not what she wants from me at all."

"How do you know the mind of Athene?"

"I have spoken with the priests. I sacrifice a white heifer to her every year on my birthday and they are there to help me with the prayers, to make sure I do everything properly. I have asked them often what is expected of her champion. Never once have they mentioned fame and glory. Quite the opposite, they speak of submission and sacrifice, purity of heart, forbearance."

There follows a terrible silence. Ektor is stone-faced,

rigid. He has no good answer to give his son, but he won't and he can't back down. "Then," he finally says, his words heavy with irony, "you will submit to me with purity of heart and run the race as I have asked. Athene will blow a fair wind at your back and you will win the crown."

Alexos knows he's beaten, that to protest will only make things worse, but he can't let this lie go unanswered.

"No," he says coldly. "That's not how it is. Athene doesn't make things easier for me. She puts obstacles in my way to make things harder."

Ektor ignores this completely. "You may tell the other boys that I made you do it, if that will be any help. Be humble, say you expect to fail."

Alexos shuts his eyes, begging Athene to please, please, *please* let this meeting be over soon. Apparently she is listening.

"That's it, then," the king says. "I have things to do."

2

"I HAVE BEEN INFORMED by your lord father, the king," says the master of arms, "that you will be racing for the laurel crown this year." He speaks in a booming voice, as if addressing a crowd.

"Yes," Alexos says.

He's been dreading this moment. Now that it has come, it's even worse than he'd imagined. The other boys whip their heads around and stare. Alexos is too embarrassed to meet their eyes.

It would have been so much kinder and more courteous of the master to have had this conversation in private. Alexos has to assume, therefore, that he has done it on purpose: because he disapproves of the idea, considers it unfair and unwise (which of course it is), and probably judges Alexos to be a puffed-up prince who doesn't know his limits.

"I assume you'll want to step up your training, then," the master says. "Put aside your work with the sword and the javelin and concentrate on running. I can set up a training program for you. We'll also need to discuss strategy and so forth. Would that please you, my lord? We can begin today if you like."

"Of course," he says woodenly. "Whatever you think is best."

"Well then, I think you oughtn't to waste any time. You're a fine runner, my lord, but the festival race will be a challenge, even for you. So let's take advantage of the two weeks we have. I expect you'll make significant progress in that time. I know you'll push yourself. You always do."

Alexos wants to explain that this was not his idea, that it's been forced upon him, but he doesn't know how to say it. He can't just blurt it out. And he doesn't want to sound pathetic: *my father made me do it!* He's searching for the right words when Leander interrupts.

"Excuse me, Master," he says, taking a couple of steps toward them, coming near enough to join the conversation without seeming to intrude. "But the trials start in seven days. Not two weeks."

"That is correct, Leander. Thank you for pointing

it out. But the prince will not be running in the trials; he already has a place." The master's voice is completely devoid of any expression. He can't even *try* to pretend he thinks this arrangement is fair.

"I see," Leander says, and the silence that follows is excruciating. Alexos feels his cheeks flush with shame.

"It wouldn't be appropriate," the master continues impassively, "considering his position."

This doesn't help, of course. Really, nothing could. For while it might be regarded as bold for Alexos to enter the race at such a young age, to *push ahead of the others because he's the king's son*—there's no way that could be made acceptable to anyone.

"Excuse me?" It's Leander again, now with the addition of his most dazzling smile. "I was wondering, since Prince Alexos will be running, if I might enter, too."

"Certainly you may. Anyone in the kingdom may enter, so long as he is male and at least twelve years of age."

"Well then, I wonder if I could join in the training—for the first week at least. Until the trials begin."

"That's entirely up to the prince, Leander."

Alexos doesn't know whether to be heartsick or glad. He's relieved to have one of his classmates also trying for the laurel crown. It will make him seem less ridiculous. People will think they decided to do it together, on a lark or out of boyish competition. But oh, that *Leander* should be the one—that's hard! Handsome and athletic, confident and funny, Leander is the kind of boy that other boys like. Wherever he leads, they will follow. Wherever he is, the sun is shining. In short, he is everything Alexos is not.

The room has fallen silent. They are waiting for Alexos to respond. And really, there's only one possible answer.

"Of course," he says. "I would welcome it."

The master tells them to run a single lap as hard as they can go, as if this were the day of the race. But neither Alexos nor Leander is fooled by this. The master already knows how fast they are; he wants to study their form.

"Good," is the verdict, "but not good enough."

They nod respectfully, panting a little, and wait for more.

"My lord Alexos, you are a beautiful runner. It's a pleasure to watch you in motion. But your head and upper body are too far forward. Your shoulders should be over your hips. Do you understand?"

"Yes, Master."

"Show me, then."

"Now?"

"Yes. Leander, watch and learn."

"A whole lap?"

"*Yes*, Alexos."

So he sets off again around the track, alone this time, concentrating on his shoulders and head, feeling awkward. Running is something he's always done by instinct. Once he starts thinking about his form, it throws everything off. But soon he gets the feel of it, imprints the new stance into his muscle memory. When he rounds the bend and returns to the master, he is smiling.

"Better?"

"Much."

"Good. Now, Leander, did you learn anything from watching the prince?"

"He moves his arms more than I do."

"That's true. Anything else?"

"He's more graceful."

"Also true. But what about his stride?"

"I . . . I didn't notice."

"Really?"

"No, Master. I was . . . I didn't."

"Alexos," he says with an exaggerated sigh, "would you demonstrate for Leander? And yes, a whole lap, please."

Alexos laughs out loud. He's not sure why he thinks this is funny, but he does. He's feeling strangely elated. Off he goes, running gracefully, moving his arms, keeping his shoulders over his hips, smiling the whole way. He's breathing somewhat harder when he stops this time.

"Thank you, Alexos. Leander?"

"His strides aren't as long as mine."

"Very good. Is that because you're taller? Are your legs longer than his?"

"No, Master. We are the same."

"And what do you deduce from that?"

"I deduce that my strides are too long, for if his were too short, you would have mentioned it."

"Well, high marks for logic. I'd rather you thought about it from a physiological perspective, however. Tell me, what happens when you take those big, long strides?"

"I was always under the impression that I went faster that way. But I'm guessing that is not correct."

"Demonstrate for us, please. Notice how your forward foot lands."

Alexos watches intently. He's raced with Leander a thousand times, but has never really *looked* at how he runs. And yes, his upper body is too tight; his arms don't swing free from the shoulders. His strides are very long—and he lands on his heel with every step.

"I come down on my heels," Leander says when he returns.

"And what do you suppose that does?"

"It forces me to recover from every step."

"Because?"

"It slows me down?"

"Exactly."

"I am astonished. I was actually *trying* to do the wrong thing."

"That's not so unusual, Leander. Now as to the arms . . ."

Soon they progress from stance and form to the strategy of racing. As before, this is first discussed, then practiced on the track. They have to learn to pace themselves, not to wear themselves out in the beginning. They need to know how to cut over to the inside edge and stay there, because that's the shortest route. To do this, they must slip effortlessly through the gaps between the other runners, never at too sharp an angle, as that adds steps and wastes time. To practice this, the other boys are recruited to race with them.

Every day they have increased the distance they run in the training session. Today Alexos will be going the full six miles, the same as in the actual race. But

Leander will stop at twenty laps. The first qualifying round is the following morning and the master doesn't want him to tire himself.

This is the last time they will run together like this, just the two of them. Alexos looks over at Leander and notes that he doesn't seem the least bit anxious. He's fresh and eager, jogging in place as they wait to begin, flapping his arms like some large, demented bird, working out the kinks in his muscles, loosening up his shoulders. He shoots a bright smile at Alexos, who responds as everyone does when smiled at by Leander: he feels a sudden surge of elation; then he smiles back.

"Runners, get ready," the master calls.

The boys position themselves for a quick start.

"On your marks."

Stance adjusted, muscles tense, they fill their lungs with air.

"Go!"

And they are off, legs flying, arms pumping. Within seconds, Alexos has forgotten Leander and his smile. He has moved to the calm center of his mind where there are no distractions, there is no goal, there is only running. He monitors his posture, the placement of his shoulders, the angle of his head, the fluid movement of his arms—and then forgets them. He looks at the track, not his feet, leans into the turns, gripping the sand with his toes.

His rhythm is light and fast. He feels the air moving as he streaks through it. He is thrilled by the speed, drunk with the pleasure of it, completely unaware of the crowd that has gathered on the grassy verge to watch. He doesn't hear the master as he calls out the laps or notice when Leander leaves the track. He just runs, and runs, and runs, faster and faster.

And for this brief spell of time, Alexos is transformed into the boy he might have been had he been born to some other father, if he had not chosen the amulet for greatness on the day of his birth: unburdened, free, and full of joy.

For however long it takes to run six miles as fast as he can, Prince Alexos is at peace.

3

FRESH FROM THE BATHS, his muscles released from the strain of running by hot water and a brisk massage, Alexos leaves the gymnasium and cuts through the agora, headed in the direction of the palace. But he leaves the path as he nears the broad, grassy lawn that slopes down to the river, hoping the lady mistress will finally have relented and let his brother come out.

Alexos has known her all his life. Long before she was put in charge of Teo's nursery, she had care of Alexos. But she was a different woman then: younger, more energetic, and completely subservient to the king. Anything Alexos wanted to do, any childish comfort or luxury he desired, was forbidden because "your father wouldn't approve." The lady mistress always seemed quite sorry to refuse. But her marching orders were clear: Alexos must not be pampered. He mustn't be spoiled with sweet words and motherly attentions. He must grow up to be strong and independent.

All these restrictions flew right out the window when Teo came along. No one cared whether he was spoiled or not. Teo wasn't heir to the throne; he wasn't the chosen one. He was just a sweet little boy who'd been abandoned by everyone except his brother (and the women of the nursery, of course). So whatever the lady mistress had been forced to withhold from Alexos, she has lavished on Teo.

But in her new motherly guise, the lady mistress still tends toward excess. So every time Teo sneezes, he must be wrapped in blankets and put to bed like an invalid. And judging by the length of this latest disappearance, he must have sneezed twice, perhaps even three times.

Ah, but there he is, waiting at the edge of the river with his favorite nursemaid, Carissa. He spies Alexos and runs to meet him, arms upraised. Alexos catches him on the fly and up Teo goes. He's flipped in the air, swung in circles upside down, righted, and hugged. Then they take hands and join Carissa by the river.

She is all smiles, as usual. Carissa is pretty and she knows it.

"Your Grace," she says, "Prince Teo very much

wants to go fishing. But I told him you may not have the time for it. I didn't promise him anything."

"Of course I have time for it. I've missed him like mad. Where have you been hiding, you little rascal?"

"Lady Mistress said I had a fever. But I didn't really. Just a watery nose."

"As I suspected. Carissa, you can go back and assure the mistress that Teo is in excellent hands. We'll be back in time for supper, which I perfectly well remember is uncommonly early, and you may set a place for me."

"Yes, Your Grace," Carissa says with another pretty smile and a graceful curtsy. But already the boys have turned away from her.

"Shall we stay here or take out the skiff?"

"The skiff!" Teo says. "Oh, please!"

Alexos doesn't really have the energy for rowing after running six miles as hard as he can go. But he can't disappoint his brother. So they put their gear into the boat and cast off, heading for the usual spot, the section upstream where the river widens. The current is slow there, the water almost glassy smooth. It's a bit of work to get there, but after that it's all floating and fishing.

While Alexos rows hard against the current, Teo stares lazily at the passing landscape, which is not in the least picturesque. Everything is brown and dry.

The crops are withering in the fields and half the trees are dead. It hasn't rained in months, not since the spring floods. Now, day after day the sun beats down on hard-packed earth, causing it to crack and split. The winds, when they come at all, catch the dust and spin it up into the sky. It has been the worst summer Alexos can recall.

It occurs to him with a stab of sorrow that his brother has never seen a bright green forest. Alexos himself can barely remember how it used to be. Suddenly his sadness turns to alarm. Why, after hundreds of years, have things gotten so much worse so quickly? It has to mean something. It's bound to be important. But he's afraid to explore the subject any further, afraid of what he might find.

"Alexos?" Teo says, interrupting his thoughts. "Did you see me there this afternoon? Carissa took me to watch you practice."

"What? No. I hardly even noticed there was a crowd. I'm sorry, Teo. I would have come over to see you."

"That's all right. It was very exciting."

"That's good, then. I'm glad you enjoyed it."

They've arrived at their fishing spot. Alexos ships the oars and starts baiting Teo's hook.

"Carissa says you're going to run in the festival race."

"That's true."

"And I get to go this year. I just know you're going to win."

Alexos sighs and hands the pole to his brother. Teo takes it and carefully drops the baited hook into the water. Then Alexos starts on his own.

"Don't get your hopes up, little man," he says. "You'll just be disappointed."

"No, I won't. Carissa says you're the fastest thing on two legs."

"Teo, look at me. I want to explain something."

"What?"

Alexos drops his own pole in the water. "I'm a good runner for a boy my age. But I'm not 'the fastest thing on two legs' and I can't seriously compete with experienced athletes twice my age. So when someone I love expects more from me than I can possibly deliver, that doesn't make me happy and proud; it makes me sad. Don't you see?"

Teo squints thoughtfully and furrows his brow.

"All right then, what if I said: 'I am absolutely sure you can row this boat up the river all by yourself'— how would that make you feel?"

"But you know I can't do that."

"There you go. My point exactly. And now let me tell you something else: I don't want to run in that race. Father is making me do it. And I'm afraid I'll fail horribly and make a fool of myself in front of all those people. So that's hard for me and I don't really want to talk about it anymore. All right?"

Teo nods and frowns, so serious. Alexos leans over and raises his pole, which is dragging in the water.

"I wish we could do this all the time," Teo says. "Just be like this together, you and me."

"So do I."

"But you have important things to do."

"Yes, but nothing I care as much about as being here with you."

Teo gives a happy little sigh. "I know."

A boat passes them, headed downstream. They've seen this particular fisherman before and he clearly knows who they are. He smiles at them and bows from the waist as he rows by. Teo waves.

"Alexos?" he says after a while. "Let's talk about when you're king."

This is an old game Alexos started ages ago—or it feels like ages anyway, though it can't have been much more than a year. It embarrasses him now, but Teo loves it.

"Remember, you said I shouldn't be the royal fisherman, because that wasn't important enough for a prince? You said I should either be your chancellor or the commander of your army."

"Of course I remember."

"Well, I've decided to command the army."

"Why? You seemed so keen on being chancellor. And you could stay here in the palace and not have to sleep in a tent and be cold all winter."

"But you'll be down at the borderlands and I want to be there with you. We could share the same tent."

"Oh, we would, definitely. But maybe I won't have to go there at all. Maybe things will have changed by then."

"Because you'll go up to Olympus and talk to Zeus and make him be nice to us again? That's what Carissa says."

"Oh, dear gods!" Alexos is horrified. "Let me tell you something, man-to-man: Carissa is a very pretty, kindhearted girl—but not everything she says is true."

"Oh."

"And while I'm flattered that she thinks so highly of me, she's really just spinning a lot of harebrained fantasies. So whenever she tells you something like that—that I'm the fastest runner in the kingdom of Arcos or I'm going to fly up to Olympus and admonish the gods—you might want to ask me first before you start believing what she says. All right?"

"All right." Then after a brief, thoughtful moment,

"So it's not true about the goddess either?"

"I don't know, Teo. What did she tell you? I can only imagine."

Teo blushes.

"As I expected. Look, we got a late start, and I'm tired, and the fish aren't biting. Give me your pole and let's head back; I'll tell you about it as we go." Teo reluctantly hands over his pole and Alexos stores them both away and puts the oars back in the water. He could just float downstream now, but it's easy rowing with the current, and he did promise to get back in time for supper.

"So here's the real, true story, little man. Long ago, on the day I was born, Father and the priests and the augur took me to the temple of Athene, as is traditional."

"I know that part. Carissa— I mean, I've heard it before."

"Of course. Everyone has. And everyone thinks that while I was there, the goddess gave me all sorts of magical gifts. But she didn't, Teo. She just gave me a big, hard job to do. And I have to do it all by myself, without the help of special powers. To be honest, I'm not exactly sure what it involves; I expect Athene will tell me when the time comes. That's not very exciting, I'm afraid. Absolutely no flying to Olympus or magical wings on my heels."

Teo shrugs. "She still chose you. That's exciting."

"I suppose it is. And now that I think about it, there is one other thing. I'm only guessing, since I was a little baby at the time and can't remember anything at all. But I see how things have been arranged in my life, and it makes sense."

"What?" Teo has perked up again.

"Well, the goddess Athene is, as you know, famously merciful and kind. And I think she must have looked down on me that day—so tiny and defenseless, you know, with all that hard work ahead of me—and felt pity in her heart. So she changed her mind and gave me one gift after all. What do you suppose it was?"

Teo cannot imagine.

"It was you, Teo. The goddess gave me you."

"Oh," Teo says with a contented sigh. "That was very nice of her."

"Yes, I think so too."

4

THE MORNING HAS FOLLOWED the usual schedule: mathematics, literature, poetics, then music. But in no other way has it been routine. The boys are inattentive; the masters are distracted. They all keep glancing at the door or gazing out windows as if expecting news to arrive at any moment. This is pointless, of course. They aren't likely to hear anything till midday at least. And since this is the final round, there will probably be some formalities afterward—speeches of congratulations, instructions on where and when to assemble for the race, how they will enter in procession—which will take even more time.

But the formalities would only apply to the eleven winners, the ones who will run on festival day (Alexos, who already has his place, being the twelfth). So the longer they wait for Leander, the better the news is likely to be.

And no one wants Leander to succeed more than Alexos does. But his reasons are complicated, a web of dark and light, genuine good wishes woven with his own deep fears: What if Leander fails to win a place, and after his brave struggle and well-earned glory, he has to sit in the stands on festival day while Alexos gets to run? Far worse, what if he comes in *twelfth*— but *too bad*, that place is already reserved this year?

This thought is so appalling that Alexos has been seriously thinking about arranging some kind of accident, conveniently breaking a leg and thereby opening up that twelfth spot. The more he thinks about it, the more appealing the idea becomes, regardless of how Leander fares in today's trials. It would be such an easy way out of an impossible situation. Why did he not think of this before?

He'd have to plan it carefully, though; it mustn't look suspicious. And it would have to be a serious fall, enough to do real damage without causing his actual death. He's mentally working out the details, not paying the least attention to his classmates (two of whom are trying, in an unfocused sort of way, to play a duet on their lyres), when his thoughts are rudely interrupted by the music master's voice.

"Markos! Timon! *Stop!*" The master has covered his ears and is scowling as if in physical pain. "You offend the very gods with that disgusting noise—I will not dignify it with the name of music."

Markos and Timon fall silent as ordered. They know their playing wasn't that bad. It's just the master's way of breaking early for the midday meal. He, like everyone else, is too nervous to concentrate today.

In summer they eat outside on the covered porch, the whole class at a single long table. For Alexos this has always been the hardest moment of the day. Sitting together like this, free of masters, free to talk, the boys at their ease, he is made keenly aware that he really isn't part of the group. When they speak to him, it's always with forced politeness. But most of the time they don't.

It's even more uncomfortable now that they talk of nothing but Leander and the race. Alexos is never mentioned; you'd think he wasn't running at all. So he sits quietly in his usual spot at the far end of the south bench, tearing off bits of bread and putting them in his mouth. He isn't the least bit hungry.

"What should we do if he makes the finals?" Titus asks. "Throw him into the horse trough?"

"Don't be stupid," Delius says. "We carry him

around the track with a chamber pot for a crown."

"No, I think Titus is right. We should throw him in the trough."

"But what if he doesn't make the cut?" Felix says.

That brings the conversation to a halt. It's not that they haven't considered this possibility. But by the time Leander made it to the finals, it had come to seem inevitable that he'd go all the way. It would be bad luck even to suggest otherwise.

"I say we throw him in the trough anyway," Titus says.

And then Delius spots Leander far in the distance, ambling across the field at an easy pace, looking down at his feet as he goes. He seems to be in no hurry, kind of thoughtful, lazy, perhaps even a little bored. When he's near enough, they see he isn't smiling.

This is exactly how Leander would act if he had lost: casual, easy, dignified. He wouldn't have the heart to joke about it, but nor would he show them his pain.

"Oh, no!" Gaius says.

"Don't jump to conclusions," Markos says. "He's probably just tired from the race."

"Yeah, probably."

Alexos feels sick. He's back to thinking about falling down stairs.

The master of arms takes a step forward. The boys

hadn't heard him come out onto the portico, hadn't even known he was there. He'd probably been standing nearby all along, waiting like the rest of them. Now the other masters emerge from various doorways. Together they watch his approach.

At last Leander reaches the porch and flops down on his end of a bench. He is red-faced and slick with sweat. He looks around at the shocked, expectant faces, raises his brows, shrugs, and gives a brave, false smile. "Oh, well," he says.

There is a deep silence in which all of them search for comforting things to say, then wonder if some sort of joke might be better, more in keeping with Leander's style, less humiliating. They gaze down at the table, at their hands, at their feet. They nod silently, in a sad, "Oh, well" sort of way.

But Alexos continues to look directly at Leander. So he is the only one to notice when Leander starts to lose control. There's a twitching at the corners of his mouth, a pursing of the lips. And now Alexos is leaning in, drilling him with his eyes, *daring* him to keep it up, knowing he can't do it.

"You made the finals, didn't you?" he shouts. "You absolutely did!"

Leander breaks into a spectacular grimace of shock and wide-eyed amazement, then jumps off the bench and dashes away as the others are up and running after him. He barely makes it to the grass along the side of the portico before they bring him down, pile on him in a heap, screaming, "Horse trough! Horse trough! Horse trough!"

An hour later, having doused their champion and sent away the masters, they sit in a companionable circle, laughing and slapping their thighs at the wonder of it all, while Leander gives his highly colored account of the race.

He had come in ninth. And of course he makes a huge drama of that, with the Giant of the North (of whom they've already heard) playing a strong supporting role— dogging Leander's heels, frothing at the mouth, grunting and growling.

"And wait till you hear the best part," he says. They wait. He leans into the center of the circle, looks left and right, and drops his voice. "You'll never guess."

"That's *right*, you toad," Titus says. "So tell us!"

"Oh, I'm wounded." Leander pretends to be wounded. Then there's another long pause with lots of feigned scowling. "All right," he says, relenting. "So. Here it is. Among the final eleven—plus Alexos, of course, who makes twelve—there are several from the royal city. We've seen them around, but I don't know any of them by name. There are also several of the type you'd expect—country gentlemen's spawn, shining and earnest."

"And the Giant of the North."

"No, sadly, the Giant didn't make the cut. I would *so* have loved for you to see him."

"Shall we throw him in the trough again?"

"No, please. I'm almost dry."

"Tell us the amazing thing, then—or in you go."

Leander cocks his head, grins wickedly: *"And then there is Peles of Attaros."*

"What is that?"

"That is a man—or rather, a youth; I'd guess he's sixteen, seventeen."

"But where is Attaros? I've never heard of it. All the great houses, even in the—"

"He doesn't live in a great house, Delius."

"Where does he live, then?"

"In a hovel, you boulder-for-brains! He's a *peasant.* He lives in a hovel and pushes a plow."

"No!"

"Yes! Peles of Attaros is a genuine, humble peasant—a bit greasy, kind of stringy, and none too clean. But he's in the final twelve for the festival race and you shall see him for yourselves."

"A peasant and a twelve-year-old in the very same year—that's too amazing! It'll go down in the records."

"Two twelve-year-olds," Leander says. "Don't forget Alexos."

"Oh, right—and a prince, too!"

"Is he fast?"

"Who?"

"The plowboy."

"Well, *of course* he's fast, you thick-wit. I don't know why I even talk to you people."

The afternoon slides away; the shadows of the buildings creep slowly out onto the empty track and the training yard. As the sun sinks, the wind drops. In an hour or so the day will settle into the thick, oppressive stillness of summer nights.

The boys have worn themselves out in their revelry. They have said everything witty or rude they can think of, and soon they will be expected back at their fathers' houses. They stretch and yawn. There are little silences. The party is breaking up. Alexos, who has said next to nothing all this time, now clears his throat to get their attention.

"May I say something?" He glances from face to face, as if this were an actual question, as in: Did he have their permission to speak?

They are stunned. These boys might be rowdy in a school yard setting, but all are sons of great families; they have good manners when they choose to use them, and a thorough knowledge of court protocol. And for the crown prince of Arcos to ask their permission for anything is so surprising that for a moment they do not answer. Then there follows a chorus of polite voices: "Of course, of course!"

"Thank you," Alexos begins. "I have wanted to explain to you about the decision to race for the laurel crown, but I could never quite find the right time or the right words. It seems appropriate now, and it will make me feel better." He pauses, marshaling his thoughts. "I never wanted—and still do not want—to run in the festival race. But my father insisted. It was also his decision that I not run in the trials, but be given an automatic place. I spoke strongly against both decisions and was overruled. I tell you this with his permission, by the way. And I tell you because I can't bear any longer for you to think less of me than I deserve.

"I also wish you to understand that I am quite aware of the difference between me and Leander—and I don't mean that I am a prince and he is not."

This draws a laugh and Alexos is encouraged.

"The difference is that he won his place fairly, while I was given mine. I am in awe of that, Leander. And envious, too. However things turn out at the festival race, you will long be remembered for what you've already accomplished, what you earned by your own merit. I am honored to race at your side."

There is a brief silence while everyone waits to see if there is more. When it's clear that Alexos has finished, the circle breaks into loud applause, punctuated by hoots and cheers. Alexos smiles, and blushes too, quite cheered by this display of affirmation.

"Oh, and something else," he says, a bit giddy with new hope and good feeling. "I would like to thank you, gentlemen, for just this once not being *so annoyingly polite*!"

Now they're roaring and pounding him on the back. For a moment Alexos is afraid he'll be the next one in the trough. But they do have to draw a line somewhere.

All the same, this is new. This is good. It's wonderful, in fact. And really, how hard was it?

Not very hard at all.

5

THE PROCESSION TO THE temple begins at dawn. Alexos has been up for hours, performing the act of purification and dressing in his sacred robes. Now he walks in the place of honor beside his father. They are followed by Ektor's chief counselors and the priests of Athene. Altogether, they are about twenty.

Early though it is, the day is already muggy and hot. Alexos feels it as never before. He's ragged, too, having slept poorly the night before, worrying about the race and the part he must play this morning.

He's been rehearsing his temple speech for days, afraid that in his nervousness he might get tangled, or miss a word, or forget the whole thing. When he'd finally fallen asleep last night, he'd gone on reciting the speech in his dreams. Now, between the exhaustion and the heat, Alexos feels almost sick. He tries earnestly to hide it, telling himself not to slouch, to walk with dignity, to keep a solemn expression on his face.

They climb the wide marble steps, proceed through the gateway into the sacred compound, then stop in front of the altar. The four white heifers are already there, tied to iron rings, waiting placidly. Alexos has heard that sacrificial animals are usually dosed with special herbs to assure that they will die well. Certainly these heifers seem exceedingly calm.

Alexos has never liked sacrifices, but the gods apparently do, and it is important to please Athene on her festival day. So he stands, quiet and dignified, as the priests say the appointed prayers; as one after another the white throats are slit, their blood startlingly bright against the marble of the altar; as one after another their bellies are cut, their livers studied, and the omens declared to be good. The thigh bones, especially favored by the immortals, are removed from each carcass and burned on the altar. The smell of roasting meat floats skyward, a tempting gift for blessed Athene. The rest of the meat will be carried away. They'll feast on it at the banquet tonight.

Usually the smell makes Alexos hungry. But today it makes his stomach turn—that and all the blood. His father and the masters were right. He'll never make a warrior.

The sacrifice complete, they enter the temple. The alcove in which the image stands has been draped with swags of laurel. The goddess herself is dressed in cloth of gold. Smoke and incense hang heavy in the air.

They have brought many gifts—golden goblets, wine bowls, statues, coins. In pairs they climb the steps of the dais and set their offerings before the goddess. When the last of the gifts has been presented, the priests begin their prayers while Alexos and his father lie prostrate on the floor, their arms outstretched in supplication.

"O great and compassionate Athene," the priests chant in unison, "wisest of all the immortals, we honor you this day with our humble gifts and heartfelt praise. We are as beetles and worms in your august presence. We are undeserving of your notice. But we dare to come before you . . ."

The cool stone is soothing against Alexos' body. But even here in the temple the air is stagnant and heavy with moisture. He has heard the stories of the old days, before the Time of Punishment. Back then summers in Arcoferra were fair and mild, a season of flourishing fields and wildflowers in the grass.

No one alive can remember those days; it was

much too long ago. Yet Alexos senses it now as he lies sprawled on the temple floor, his arms reaching out toward the feet of the goddess, his cheek pressed hard against stone. He can almost see the fields and flowers, feel the fresh wind in his hair, hear the carefree laughter of children as they run in the grass, unafraid of stalking pestilence. Because, in that other world and time, the summer sickness doesn't exist.

"We are most heartily sorry, and penitent, and ashamed of the grievous sins that have brought disgrace upon our kingdom," the priests are chanting, "calling down upon our heads the wrath of all who dwell on Olympus, most especially the great king of the gods. Meekly we submit, and humbly we accept the righteous retribution they have seen fit . . ."

Alexos is no longer *sensing* this vanished paradise; he is seeing it clearly in the eye of his mind. The trees are so intensely green, so shiny and clean, it's as if someone has taken a cloth and polished every leaf. There are no dead branches; the trees are all perfectly formed: dream trees, like something the gods might have made. The grass is as soft as kitten fur. Alexos strokes it in his mind, noting the perfect little white and yellow blossoms that nest among the silky, green blades. There is a delicate mist floating across the landscape. Alexos can feel it, moist against his skin:

cool but not cold; just right.

He sees a man and a girl sitting in a wild country garden. Flowers are everywhere, a riot of color. Like the trees, they are also perfect, every petal fresh and new, every leaf immaculate.

The man and girl seem to be peasants, judging by their clothes at least. But their faces aren't ravaged by hardship. Alexos thinks the man must be old, since his hair and beard are turning white. But his arms and shoulders are as strong and firm as those of a much younger man. His skin has the sheen of youth. And really, he doesn't seem peasantlike at all. He's—how to describe it? Serene. Confident. Almost regal.

How very odd.

The girl is remarkable too. Had it not been for the shabby dress she wears, he might have taken her for a goddess. Her skin is fair and creamy smooth, like Teo's: baby skin, breathtaking, flawless. And her hair, which has been hastily gathered up in a messy pile on the back of her head and fastened with a wooden comb, is the color of summer wheat. It shimmers like fine gold. It takes his breath away, just looking at such perfection.

The two sit at the edge of a grassy lawn as the father draws figures in the dirt with a stick. The girl leans over and points. Alexos, who floats above them unseen, studies the marks and is startled to see something quite familiar: a triangle with squares attached to each of its three sides. Now the man writes the formula and the girl, who can't be more than eight or nine years old, seems to understand it. She nods and smiles at the neatness of the theorem, just as Alexos had when the master first explained it.

This peasant man is teaching his little peasant daughter—*geometry*! How truly astonishing.

Alexos is dimly aware that the priests are no longer praying. The king is on his knees now and has just finished speaking. It's Alexos' turn to address the goddess now.

Dragging himself away from the vision is horribly wrenching. He doesn't want to go. Leaving that place and those people feels like a personal loss, like the death of someone he loves. And it's physically painful too. It's as if his spirit had somehow left his body and has now returned to find it a ruin, broken and bleeding. It takes all his strength just to rise to his knees.

He tries to calm himself as invisible hands begin to touch him. They squeeze at his throat, they form a tight band around his head, they suck the breath from his chest and grip his belly. He's afraid he's going to be sick. And this terrifies him most of all, for to vomit at the feet of the goddess would be the worst kind of sacrilege.

Also, he has completely forgotten his speech. For a moment he just kneels there, swaying, frantically trying to think. And then it comes to him that neither the beautiful vision nor his current torment is a natural occurrence. They are goddess-given, sent for a reason. And with this flash of understanding, the words come. They are not the words his father gave him to memorize; they are what the goddess wants him to say.

"O great Athene," Alexos cries in a startling voice, so full of anguish that the king turns and stares with alarm, "I submit myself to your will this day, and every day of my life, wholly and unreservedly. I put myself in your hands, trusting in your wisdom and goodness to guide me. I ask no pity for myself, whatever I must endure, but only for the suffering people of Arcos and Ferra. For them, I humbly beg your mercy and your blessing."

Somehow he manages to rise and leave the temple, descending the great marble staircase and continuing down the hill toward the palace. The road is lined with people. Some are from the city; others have come from far away to attend the festival. They are animated, smiling. They stare at Alexos, the embodiment of their hope. He hardly sees them.

Only now is he aware that his father has a firm grip on his arm. It must be obvious how unsteady he is; the king is afraid he will fall. But the grip is not friendly. Alexos can feel the anger in it. And he suspects he'll feel a great deal more anger when they reach his father's chambers.

"You are supposed to be so clever," Ektor says, his voice as cold as ice. "Yet you couldn't learn a simple speech, given to you well in advance. Or was it too much trouble, not worth the effort? Was that it, Alexos? You just decided it was easier to make something up on the spot? Because you *didn't think it mattered*? Well, let me tell you . . ."

Through it all, Alexos is strangely calm. He's still in his fog, but it's become more transparent now. He can hear his father's words; he can see the handsomely appointed room they're sitting in—the tapestries, the mosaics, the finely carved chairs and tables. He can smell the rank air and feel the oppressive heat.

The king has stopped shouting. His son's composure has unsettled him. It's an unnatural response to such a scolding, certainly not what he'd expected. And he begins to wonder if perhaps the boy—who is, after all, the chosen one—knows something he does not. His mouth goes slack. He leans forward.

"Well, then," he says. "Tell me."

Alexos meets his father's eyes directly. As before, the words do not come from conscious thought; they are already formed on his tongue.

"The goddess is ready for me now, Father. And I have accepted."

6

THE CROWD HAS BEEN gathering since midday. Already the commoners' stands are full; those who came later sit on the grass. Many have walked great distances to get here; tomorrow most of them will head back home. But they will be able to say that they've been to the great *polis* of Arcos. They can say they've seen King Ektor in person, and the famous crown prince Alexos, the chosen champion of Athene. They will have witnessed the sacred procession and the festival race and dined at a royal banquet. Stories will be told about this day for as long as they live. They feel it was more than worth the trouble.

There has been a performance over in the theater—a play, or maybe it was poetry with pipes and a lyre, something like that. Apparently it has just let out, because the men of rank are coming in now, their ladies on their arms. They take their places in the stands reserved for them. They are quieter and more dignified than the common folk, but just as excited.

When everyone is settled, the first fanfare sounds. They all rise as the runners come onto the field, two by two, and go to stand on the grass in the shade of a special canvas awning. Moments later, the second fanfare announces the arrival of the king, his councilors, his greatest noblemen, and the priests of Athene.

Everything about their entrance is majestic, just as it should be: flags flying, musicians playing, sunlight dancing off the gilt threads of flowing capes and robes, and sweet little Prince Matteo, as solemn as a priest, walking behind his father, dressed in purple linen and wearing a tiny crown on his head.

"Is that your baby brother?" Leander asks, hand to heart, a huge grin on his face. He and Alexos stand together at the edge of the little knot of elite runners.

"That's Teo, yes."

"But he's *too adorable*! Can I have him?"

"No, Leander, you can't."

"I'll trade you two of my brothers and throw in my father for free."

"No."

"Selfish!"

"Absolutely."

Alexos had joined the other runners at the last minute, just before they marched in (Ektor had insisted, on the grounds that a prince "does not wait around"), so he hasn't had a chance to study them till now. They are, as previously described by Leander, the sort of men you would expect: noblemen's sons from the *polis* or great country estates. Several could still be described as boys—seventeen or eighteen—and a few are vaguely familiar. The rest are full-grown men with beards.

But Alexos isn't interested in them. He's looking for the famous greasy peasant from Attaros. Leander has refused to point him out, assuring Alexos he'll know him when he sees him.

"It's going to be all right," Leander says.

"What?"

"The race. All you have to do is run really fast."

"I'm aware of that, Leander."

"Apologies, my lord. It's just that you were looking very flushed, that's all. I thought perhaps you were nervous."

"It's hot. Haven't you noticed?"

Leander starts to reply, then bites his tongue.

Alexos has found his man now. And, as described,

he looks like a peasant, not a prodigy, with the sun-blasted skin and lean, ropy muscles of one who labors in the fields. His face is all angles; his wiry, short-cropped hair gleams with oil and sweat. His hands are brown and calloused, dark half-moons of dirt wedged beneath the fingernails.

It's not completely unheard of for a commoner to enter the race, but it is extremely rare. And usually they're eliminated in the first round. To have made it this far is remarkable. Alexos tries to imagine this hollow-cheeked country lad actually winning the laurel crown. He finds the thought surprisingly appealing. For as amazing as it is that Leander is here—by his own merits, when he is only twelve—how much more astonishing is the path this peasant has taken?

Running for the laurel crown is a nobleman's sport, not the sort of thing a plowboy thinks of. Yet somehow this fellow *did* imagine it; then he presumably trained for it in his rare free time—racing down country lanes after a long day of grueling work, fueled only by the pathetic scraps that must constitute his diet. And now here he is: one of the final twelve on Athene's festival day! For these few, brief hours, Peles of Attaros has earned the right to stand beside noblemen and a prince as their equal. Nothing Alexos has ever done remotely compares with that. It moves him so deeply that tears well up in his eyes.

"Touching, isn't it?" Leander says. His eyes crinkle and Alexos can't tell whether he means it or not.

"Yes," Alexos replies, no expression in his voice. "I rather hope he wins."

A sudden blast of horns startles them. The high priest of Athene comes out onto the field; they kneel as the prayers are sung. Then King Ektor formally announces that the race will begin: runners, make ready.

The surface of the track has been packed smooth, sand spread over clay. It's dazzlingly white and hot under their feet after the cool of the shaded grass. They make discreet little hops as the sand stings the tender skin of their insteps. The sun is brutal. Already they are glistening with sweat. Alexos closes his eyes and fills his lungs with warm, damp air and lets it out again in a rush.

His assigned place is near the right edge. He'll need to make a lightning start and stay ahead of the pack just long enough to work his way across to the far left side. If he misses this chance, he'll have to wait till the mass of runners has started to spread out, which could take a while, perfectly matched as they are.

This strategy is mostly used when running on an oval track. But while it doesn't exactly apply here, where the course meanders through the city and out into the countryside, the track will eventually make a wide turn to the left nearly a mile long, and the runners on the inside lane will have an advantage. So it's worth the effort, the master had explained; the smallest thing can make a difference in a contest like this.

They are all on their marks now, tense and waiting. Then comes the final blast of horns and they are off. Alexos' toes grip the sand and hurl him forward, his strides measured and graceful, his body straight, and his arms pumping. He shifts to the left a heartbeat before the man beside him moves up to block his way; then he slides left again.

Now he's running beside Leander and can't get past him. They race side by side like a pair of oxen pulling a plow, until Alexos puts on another burst of speed and crosses two more lanes. But it doesn't come easily; it's like running through steam. His legs ache as they've never ached before, his lungs can't get enough air, and his head is pulsing with pain.

Alexos has run greater distances than this and done it with relative ease. He can't think why, so early on, he seems to be nearing his limit. It makes no sense. It's alarming.

At least he's finished with strategy; that's something,

anyway. The field is spreading out a bit and he has the inside edge. Leander is right behind him, huffing and grunting as he runs. He's doing it on purpose, of course. Leander never grunts. He's trying to make Alexos nervous. But it has the opposite effect. It makes Alexos want to laugh. It lifts his spirits.

The miles fly past. They've left the city now, out through the east gate and into the drab, sun-baked landscape of the countryside, making the long turn back toward the finish line. Alexos has a good position. Now the time has come to put those famous wings on his heels.

He pushes everything out of his mind—Leander, the other runners, his exhaustion, the headache, the pain in his legs. He becomes a racing animal, as natural as a soaring hawk or a leaping deer. Sweat runs down his forehead and into his eyes; he blinks away the stinging salt and keeps on going. This is how Alexos runs, how he does everything—not to win, just to do his best.

There are four or five in the lead now, clustered loosely together. Alexos pays no attention to them, doesn't even bother to notice who they are. He's racing only for himself, just running as fast as he can.

But there really is something wrong with his legs. They're trembling, unsteady; he's half afraid they'll suddenly refuse even to hold him up. He feels himself slowing down, just a little. He decides that's probably wise. He doesn't quite trust his balance anymore. Better to lose speed than to lose control.

Then someone passes him close on the right, startling him and putting him off his rhythm. Alexos stumbles, and for a horrible moment he's afraid he might actually fall. But he doesn't; he recovers his stride. Only now the man is directly in front of him on the inside lane.

It's Peles of Attaros, and he is a wonder.

He runs as little children do, for the joy of it. No one has forced him to come here and compete with noblemen's sons. No one has taught him technique or strategy. And certainly no one expects him to win. He's just here because he wants to be. And he runs as simply, naturally, and beautifully as the wind moves across a meadow. Watching him, Alexos is struck by the sudden knowledge that *this boy*—who probably sleeps on straw in a one-room wattle hut—is freer than Alexos himself will ever be.

Alexos has completely lost his concentration now. He's overwhelmed by the troubling symptoms he's mostly managed to ignore till now: his burning cheeks and stinging eyes, the rising nausea, the throbbing pain in his head, and the terrible, aching unsteadiness of his legs.

He's falling behind. His form is terrible. He lurches from side to side as more runners pass him—two, three, four of them, including Leander.

He can't concentrate at all anymore; his mind is heavy, as though he was just awakened from a deep sleep. His legs are still moving, but haltingly. Three more runners pass him, gasping for breath, putting on speed as they near the finish. Alexos can hear the screams of the crowd and is vaguely conscious of the pavilion up ahead, where his father and Teo sit in regal splendor, expecting him to win this race.

But Alexos is only trotting now—stumbling, almost. His face is on fire; he feels as if he will melt onto the track like candle wax. He's not sure he can even finish the race.

A huge roar goes up from the crowd: the winner has crossed the line. And from the amazed exuberance of the shouting—it goes on, and on, and on—Alexos is pretty sure he knows who it was.

Was-buzzzz, buzzzzzzzz. His mind is buzzing, as though flies have crawled inside his head. He listens, inert. He can't see much of anything. It's all blurry, the world around him. Like fog—hot, stifling fog. He wants to lie down somewhere cool. Grass would be nice.

And then, from deep inside his consciousness, he wills himself to stop drifting and come back to the race. He looks lazily down at his feet and is startled to see that they aren't moving at all. He's just standing there, bleeding sweat onto the track.

The shock of this clears his mind—not completely, but enough to understand that he has failed to a degree that was unimaginable till now. He has failed his father, he has failed the goddess, and he has failed Teo. The shame of his performance will dog him for the rest of his life. But at least, *at the very least*, it will not be said that Alexos didn't finish the race.

So he hobbles the rest of the way, staggering like a drunkard. He feels the eyes of the crowd burning into him—for they have fallen silent now, and it's a silence of horror and pity. *Don't think about it,* he tells himself. *Just take another step and then another after that.*

It goes on forever. He is hunched over, staring down at his legs, so ungainly, so very weak. And then he steps across the chalk line, smeared now by the eleven pairs of feet that have run across it. And there he stops.

Alexos watches his father with something akin to awe. How does the king maintain such incredible control? He sets the laurel crown on the oily, sweaty brow of a peasant lad who has just defeated a host of young aristocrats—and does not look amazed. His son and heir, the future savior of Arcos, has publicly shamed and disappointed him—and he shows no anger or despair. Teo is weeping and making a scene. Ektor ignores him. He goes through the ceremony of praise to the goddess in a calm and dignified manner. He acknowledges the cheering crowd of commoners, delirious with pride that one of their own has won the laurel crown, and guides young Peles of Attaros to his proper place for the procession back to the palace.

Never once does he show any feeling at all.

Never once does he look at his son.

Alexos sends a message saying he's unwell and cannot attend the banquet. The king does not reply. The next morning he is gone, back to the borderlands. Father and son have not exchanged a single word.

7

DAYS FLOW SEAMLESSLY INTO nights, and days, and nights: fever dreams broken by fitful wakefulness, both soon forgotten, all of it much the same. It is always dark. Lamplit faces hover over him; the servants speak in whispers. He is bathed, arranged, changed, massaged, examined. Drops are administered, damp cloths, sharp-smelling unguents, powders. Someone combs his hair.

On the fourth day, Alexos wakes, truly aware for the first time. He can't tell if it is night or day; the shutters are closed, so the room is dark. But a lamp is burning on the table by his bed. His skin feels dry; it itches. And his back aches from lying so long in one position. The room is too warm and smells of sickness: sweat, medicines, urine, too many people. His first conscious thought is, *Will someone please open a window?* Then he sees Suliman, the court physician, standing over him.

"What happened?" he says. His voice sounds strange to him. It's breathy and the words are slurred.

"You've been very ill, my prince."

"How long . . . ?"

"Four days. But the fever is down. You're on the mend now."

Alexos doesn't feel like he's on the mend. He feels like he's been trod upon by horses, then left to rot all night in a bog.

Extra servants have been brought in, among them Teo's nursemaid Carissa. They all seem to be wearing sad faces, as though someone has died, or is dying.

"Where's Teo?" he asks, suddenly alarmed.

"He's perfectly well, my lord."

This isn't an answer to the question Alexos asked, but it's a relief. The sad faces must be for *him*, then, not Teo.

"I'm sorry, Alexos, but I can't allow your brother into the sickroom. There are some physicians who maintain that disease travels from one person to another through the patient's polluted breath. And I have observed often enough how sickness spreads through families. Better not to take the chance with Teo."

Alexos nods. *Please, yes, keep him away.*

"I have sent a message to your father informing

him of your illness. I expect he'll return as soon as he gets the news. But it could take a week, perhaps longer. There is considerable distance to travel, first for the messenger and then for the king."

Alexos closes his eyes. His father. Only now does he remember. "He won't come."

"Why do you say that? Do you think he will stay away because of what happened—?"

"*Yes.*" It comes out rather more sharply than he intended.

"But, Alexos—you were severely compromised, already burning with fever! Most people would have collapsed on the track. Truly, your conduct was greatly to your credit. The king will understand that once he learns of your illness. So will everyone else."

This seems too good to be true: his shameful failure instantly erased, his father's anger assuaged, and his reputation magically restored. Life, in his experience, is never like that, at least not for him. When things go bad they generally tend to get worse instead of better.

"He'll come," Suliman says. His fingers play idly with his long, black beard; he rolls the hairs together as a spinner winds wool. It's an old, familiar habit of his, something he does when he's thinking. And Alexos can guess what's on Suliman's mind: he's starting to have doubts as to whether Ektor will come after all, and wondering how the prince will bear it if he does not.

"But for now," Suliman says, "we must try to build you up again. You've had nothing but water these past four days and not very much of that. It would be a terrible shame if you survived the illness only to die of starvation." He raises his dark brows, clearly hoping for some response, perhaps even a smile at his little joke. But when none is forthcoming—Alexos really doesn't have the energy—he pats the boy's arm and goes on in his soft, deep voice. "I've ordered you some nourishing broth. I know you won't be hungry, but you must take some if you can."

"All right," Alexos murmurs, though the thought of food is mildly repulsive. His gut feels as though it's been turned to stone, or has died, or withered away. He can't imagine putting anything in there.

"Then let me prop you up so you can eat more comfortably. Hesta, bring me the bolster, if you will." A young servant Alexos has not seen before quickly produces the bolster. "Slip it behind his back. That's right; just so."

Alexos allows himself to be arranged like a rag doll. He lies passively as Hesta drapes a cloth over his chest, then sits on a stool beside the bed and begins to feed him, rewarding him with a smile for every mouthful.

Does she take him for an infant, he wonders? He scowls at her and she blinks, surprised. She hadn't meant to offend him. "Just give me the soup," he says softly.

Then he flinches suddenly as a sharp spasm grips his calf. He tries to shake it off, to raise the leg and pull up the foot to stretch against the cramping muscle, but he can't. The pain is terrible. He lets out a moan, clutches at the sheets, arches his back.

In an instant Hesta and her bowl are gone and Suliman is there, throwing back the covers, massaging the muscle. Alexos stares, panting, desperate for the cramping to stop. He tries to slide over the other leg to get it out of Suliman's way, but it might be made of wood and not attached to him at all, just a thing someone left in the bed.

"What's *wrong* with me?" he wails. "My legs won't move!"

"It's a feature of the illness," the physician says, not looking up, continuing to work the muscle.

"What illness? You never said!"

But Suliman doesn't respond; it's as if he hadn't even heard the question. He just goes on pressing his thumbs into the belly of the muscle, moving down the length of it, kneading it like dough. As the cramping begins to ease, he rubs with a brisk, quivering motion.

The skin and muscle are soft now, loose; they flutter under Suliman's hand.

When he is satisfied that the event is over, Suliman lifts Alexos, pulls out the bolster, and settles his head back on the pillow again. He tugs at the sheets to smooth out any wrinkles, then arranges the covers over the prince's legs and chest.

"There," he says.

The whispering servants all seem to have disappeared; it's as if they had melted into the walls. Alexos doesn't remember Suliman telling them to leave, but then Suliman has very expressive gestures. He could send them away with a subtle jerk of the head, a roll of his eyes.

But why clear the room at all? So they could be alone, of course. So they could talk privately. So Suliman could answer the question he'd ignored before, because the time wasn't right. And the answer will be hard for Alexos to hear.

Suliman is sitting beside him now. It's strangely quiet all of a sudden, as if they weren't simply alone in this room, but the last two people in the world.

"I asked you a question, Suliman, and you didn't answer."

"I was attending you, my prince. I couldn't give you my full attention. But you have it now."

"You told me I had a fever, but I know it's worse than that. Tell me the truth. It's the summer sickness, isn't it?"

"I never lie to you, Alexos. I said your fever is down, which it is. Fever is one of the symptoms of the summer sickness. I'm so sorry."

It's not as if Alexos didn't suspect this, especially after he couldn't move his legs. But to have it confirmed is a blow, a boulder pressing on his chest. Now he will have to rethink everything. He has been transformed into a different person, a broken, ruined person.

"Will I be like those children you see in the streets with their braces and crutches? Will I have to be carried around in a chair?"

Suliman lays a gentle hand on the prince's shoulder, another old habit of his: the consoling touch. Alexos has noticed that it often does more good than all the medicines combined.

"I would say no to the chair, Alexos. But it's too early to tell how much damage has been done. The illness must run its course. That said, you were remarkably strong and healthy to begin with, and that is a great advantage. You have survived the crisis. And the cramping you experienced just now was actually a positive sign; it means the muscle has not been entirely destroyed."

Entirely destroyed?

"There will be some impairment. I'm afraid you must be prepared for that, because there always is with the summer sickness. . . ."

I will never run again, never feel the thrill of speed and grace anymore. I may not even be able to walk. I'll have to be helped in everything I do. My legs will be ugly. People will pity me. They will find me repulsive. I will forever be separate from everyone else, more even than I was before.

". . . but I expect you will be one of the lucky ones. You'll work hard at your recovery, because it's your nature to do so. And whatever the outcome, I know you will face it with courage and dignity . . ."

I can't possibly be king now. It would be laughable. And the champion of Athene—more laughable still. I will be useless, nothing but a sickly prince rattling around in his private rooms, being waited on by servants.

". . . because you are a remarkable boy, Alexos—so serious, always striving to excel, willing to do whatever . . ."

Please, will you help me out of bed? Please will you wash me? Please, will you carry me to the privy? Please, will you help me put my tunic on?

". . . is asked of you. You have always done this in the spirit of service, for someone or something else: your father, the kingdom, Athene. Now you must use that strength to heal yourself. You will rise above this, Alexos, as you have so many other things."

Suliman seems to have finished. He seems to be waiting, and of course he *is* waiting, because that's what he does—he gives Alexos time to absorb and respond. And it's a good thing he's such a patient man, because Alexos just stares up at those large, dark eyes, so full of expression, and says nothing at all.

But he is thinking. His mind is awake now, though not in a good way; it's agitated, anxious, confused. All these random thoughts are running around in circles, shouting, each trying to drown out the others. And the loudest thought keeps screaming over and over, *Why? Why did this happen?*

So finally Alexos asks, "Why did Athene allow this to happen to me?"

Suliman sucks in breath. Alexos is impressed; it's hard to startle Suliman.

"Are you sure you want to have this conversation now, my prince?"

"Yes, I'm sure. I want to know. She could have protected me; she's a goddess with enormous powers and I am her chosen champion. But she didn't lift a hand to do it. So, why? Did I fail her in some way? Am I not needed anymore? Because I'm useless to her as I am now."

"Oh, Alexos! Do you think Athene needs you to run races for her?"

"I don't know what she wants."

"Nor do I. But assuming that nothing is accidental where the gods are concerned, I would guess that this is part of her plan."

Alexos is shocked by this. It flies in the face of everything he's ever assumed about his role as champion. "Are you saying that I'm supposed to suffer? *That's* what the goddess wants from me?"

"That's a surprisingly simplistic question coming from a clever boy like you."

Alexos shrugs. It had seemed like a pretty straightforward question to him.

"All the heroes were tested. Think of Heracles cleaning out the Augean stables, washing out thirty years of cow dung in a single day. And poor Odysseus—all he wanted to do was get home to Penelope—but no! First he must wander the seas for ten years, be tempted by the Sirens, attacked by cannibals, imprisoned by a one-eyed monster—and you think the champion of Athene isn't supposed to *suffer*?"

Alexos laughs, as Suliman meant him to. It clears the air.

"We cannot see into the minds of gods, Alexos. But we know from experience that hardship, challenges, and great disappointments help to form us as feeling, loving human beings. As I said before, the way you respond to a blow such as this—*that* is what's important. To show courage in the face of adversity will impress Zeus far more than being fast and strong."

Alexos isn't sure why this helps, but somehow it does. This new understanding won't give him back his legs, but it gives him back his purpose.

"Have you ever watched a blacksmith at work? Humor me, Alexos; I *am* making a point."

"No, Suliman, I have not."

"The blacksmith takes shapeless lumps of iron and turns them into useful things—a sword, for example. But to change its form, he must soften it over burning coals. Then, when it is red-hot, he shapes it on his anvil with a hammer. The iron must go from the fire to the anvil and back again many times before the process is complete.

"The iron was always strong, Alexos, and a thing of great value. But it was of no use to anyone until the blacksmith transformed it."

"Is that me you're talking about?"

"You are the instrument of Athene. She is forming you on her anvil."

"Well, it hurts."

"I know."

8

IN THE HALLWAY OUTSIDE the sickroom, directly across from the door, there is a large ornamental chest. It rests on feet carved to look like lion's paws. Beside it, wedged into the corner where the chest meets the wall, sits Teo, his legs drawn in close, his arms wrapped tightly around his knees. He is trying to be invisible and it seems to be working. Servants come and go from the room, yet no one has noticed him yet.

Teo wants to see his brother, but they won't let him in. Whenever he asks why, they say that Alexos needs his rest, which makes no sense at all. How can he rest with all those people bustling about? And besides, Alexos would much rather be with Teo than with any of them. So why can they go in when he cannot?

It isn't fair.

But the answer is clearly never going to change, no matter how often he asks. So Teo is doing the next best thing. He waits in secret outside the room, hoping at least to catch the sound of his brother's voice.

The lady mistress, back in the nursery, doesn't know where Teo is. She's sound asleep in her comfortable chair. Of late she's taken to sending the other nursemaids away in the afternoons and putting Teo down for a nap. She does this not because he's sleepy at all, but because the lady mistress, no longer as young as she used to be, is completely worn-out from looking after a little boy. So as soon as Teo hears the dragon snores begin, he creeps from his bedchamber, tiptoes past the chair where the lady mistress sits—her arms hanging loose, her head lolling back, her mouth agape—and slips out into the corridor.

This has been going on for quite some time and Teo is getting very good at it. He can tell by the sound of her snores when it's safe to leave and has a good sense of how much time he has before he needs to run back.

The sickroom door opens again and this time Carissa comes out, carrying a chamber pot. She stops for no discernible reason, facing in Teo's direction. He scrunches farther into the crack between the wall and the chest. But he can still see her, so it follows that she can also see him—or she could if she weren't scanning the walls instead of looking down at the floor where Teo is hiding.

"What was that?" Carissa says, as if talking to herself. "I thought I heard a little mouse. I guess I'd better call the rat catcher."

"No!" Teo whispers.

"Or maybe not. The mouse is probably just visiting, hoping to hear how Prince Alexos is doing. The palace mice *would* be eager to know that, I suppose. It's perfectly reasonable."

She ignores the stifled giggle from behind the chest.

"Well, I assure you—wherever you are, little mouse—that the prince is growing stronger every day. His fever is gone and he's eating again. But he *does* miss his little brother most terribly. He asks about him every single day."

There is a joyful little gasp, which Carissa also pretends not to hear.

"And," she goes on (still talking to the wall—which is really very strange, since mice are usually to be found on the floor), "King Ektor is coming all the way back from the war to visit Alexos. Isn't that exciting? He should be here very soon."

She turns to go (she has to empty the chamber pot

and wash it clean) but pauses again just for a moment. "I should also remind the little mouse that the cat is likely to wake fairly soon, so he might want to scurry back into his hole."

As soon as Carissa has gone, Teo dashes down the hall, turns the corner, and runs up the stairs to his nursery.

The cat is still asleep.

9

"THE BRACE WILL KEEP his leg in its normal position," Suliman explains to the king. "It will allow him to rest his weight upon it without creating deformity at the ankle or the knee."

"And the other leg?"

"It has regained some of its function, though it's still very weak. We've been working to strengthen the unaffected muscles, to compensate for those which have been lost."

"I see. He'll walk with a cane, then—always?"

"I'm afraid so, Your Majesty."

Alexos sits in silence on the edge of his bed, taking no part in this conversation. His legs are bare and on display, the right one imprisoned in a metal cage that reaches from his thigh to below the ankle, a leather strap running under the instep of his foot. The humiliation is unbearable and Suliman seems to sense this. He reaches over and rests a consoling hand on Alexos' shoulder.

"The prince has shown remarkable courage throughout this whole ordeal."

"I would expect nothing less," says the king.

Alexos stays in his rooms for weeks, allowing no one to visit. He isn't ready to show himself in public yet. He has tried telling himself that the awkwardness, the pitying looks, the embarrassment of the brace and the cane, are all marks of his noble suffering. But he's a boy of twelve who has been damaged for life and even Alexos finds this daunting. He just needs a little more time. Also there is the question of how he will get around.

"It will be easier if you walk with crutches," Suliman says. "Your right leg can bear your weight, reinforced as it is with the brace. You will have stability and can move fairly quickly, though stairs will be a problem."

"No, Suliman. I'd rather use a cane."

"Certainly that is your choice, my prince. But it will be harder; and first you will have to strengthen the undamaged muscles in your left leg."

"I understand."

"Well, then, I will bring some linen bags filled with sand—we will begin with a light one, then increase the weight as you get stronger. But it will be painful, Alexos. You may be surprised by how much it hurts."

"I don't care. Just show me what to do."

Suliman smiles, something he rarely does. It's the kind of smile that makes its own light. It fills the empty place in Alexos' heart where hope had been before.

"I'd like to start right now."

"I wonder what you will think of this," Suliman says one morning. He has brought a long tunic for the prince. It is the sort of garment worn by men of distinction who are past the age for showing their knees. This one is particularly handsome: whisper-fine chestnut-colored wool trimmed with sage green, a bit of gold embroidery at the neck.

"It's . . . nice," Alexos says guardedly. "You think I should wear that to hide my legs?"

"No," the physician says. "But you seem self-conscious about the brace. I thought it might free you from any such concerns. And it would make you look more dignified. I have worn long robes myself since I was not much older than you."

Alexos nods.

"There is one other thing to consider, my prince. You have suffered a terrible injury and everybody knows it. What you do now, how you comport yourself as you return to the world, is of the greatest importance. You must seem to say to all you meet, 'Yes, I have been wounded by fortune, but I am Ektor's heir and will one day rule this kingdom. My legs are of no consequence. Let us move on to serious matters.' They will respect you for it."

"Better than whining?"

Suliman chuckles. "Much. And if you will forgive me for saying so, my lord, I believe you are ready now."

"Ready for what?"

"For the rest of your life."

"Let me try it on," says the prince.

With all the dignity he can muster, Alexos leaves his rooms for the first time in over two months. He is dressed in chestnut wool and clutching a handsome gold-headed cane. He goes alone by choice. He wants, for once, not to be hovered over, protected, treated like an invalid.

He makes his way down the corridor at a stately pace until he reaches the stairs. Here he stops for a moment, reviewing his strategy. Then carefully he sets the tip of his cane on the first step below, bending his left leg so he can step down with the right, stiff in its metal cage. That done, he quickly brings the left leg down beside it. He pauses briefly on each tread to make sure of his balance, then continues on to the next.

It wouldn't do to fall.

At last, a bit breathless, he reaches the bottom of the stairs and crosses the entry hall, leaning forward just the right amount so he won't rock side to side. At the door, a porter waits, holding it open for him. He bows as Alexos passes. "Your Grace," he says.

It is strangely warm for autumn; the sky is cloudless and uncommonly blue. Alexos is astonished by it, cannot remember such a day, not for years and years. Or maybe it's just that he's been cooped up in the sickroom so long, he's forgotten what it's like to be outside, how glorious it is to feel the sun on his back, the soft breath of wind on his cheek.

The rest of my life, he thinks. *It begins now, on this glorious afternoon.* He feels an unaccountable surge of happiness.

He turns onto the gray stone walkway that leads to the Queen's Garden, so named not for his late mother but the consort of some long-ago king. The palace gardeners keep it clipped and tidy, see to the roses, and rake the leaves, but it's rarely used anymore. Ektor will occasionally walk here when he tires of being inside and needs to stretch his legs, but as he is generally busy and rarely in residence, it's almost always empty.

Alexos doesn't really like the Queen's Garden. It's too formal for his taste, too small; and what natural charm it might have had in the old days has since been ruined by an excess of statuary and ornamental ponds. But Suliman had suggested he come here for simple, practical reasons: it's an easy walk, not too far from the palace, there are no steps, and the ground is flat. Also, it's a private place with an abundance of marble benches where Alexos can practice, unobserved, the newly complicated art of sitting down.

He enters through a trellised arch and continues down the gravel path. The garden is rather like the palace, he thinks, with hallways and rooms, except that here the walls are high boxwood hedges and the rooms are open spaces with ponds or fountains in the middle, furnished with benches instead of beds, tables, and chairs.

He wanders a bit, looking for a room that's more peaceful than garish. Which demented ancestor was it who chose those hideous statues, anyway? The thought makes him laugh, and again he's startled to realize that he is actually happy. It's wonderful to move his body, to feel the blood flowing, to breathe air that isn't stale, and look at something different for a change, however dreadful. Really, why was he so resistant to going out before? He might have done this weeks ago.

Having considered all the possibilities and pretty well worn himself out, Alexos decides on a round room with a round pond and a stone dolphin in the middle. There are three benches to choose from, all of them curved to fit the curving walls. He picks one at random, backs up to it, and begins the now familiar series of motions: leaning forward, positioning his cane just so, reaching down to release the latch that allows his brace to bend at the knee. Then—using the strength of his right arm, which grips the gold-headed cane, and the delicate muscles of his left leg, more powerful now from lifting sandbags over and over a thousand times—dropping as gracefully as possible onto the bench.

It doesn't go well. The bench, it turns out, is lower than the chair in his room. *Well, consider that a lesson learned—at least there were no witnesses.* And for now he's content to rest and enjoy the sunshine.

It's incredibly quiet. There is no sound but the rustling of dry leaves overhead, the occasional chirp of a bird, the distant plash of water from a fountain in one of the other rooms. And then, faintly, there are boots crunching on gravel and the soft voices of men in conversation. They come closer and closer, till they stop almost directly behind him on the other side of the hedge. Alexos knows exactly which room it is—rectangular, with an enormous birdbath in the center and a marble Apollo against the far boxwood wall. He hears the delicate rustle of clothing, the little grunts as the two men sit down.

Ektor has a carrying voice—an excellent trait for a warrior king, except on those occasions when he doesn't wish to be overheard. Like now.

"It can't be helped," the king is saying. "A lame king will be seen as a weak king. Pyratos will only redouble his efforts. The boy couldn't possibly handle it."

Alexos feels a prickling all over his skin: tiny hairs standing at attention.

The other man's voice is more difficult to hear. He says something about the army, and "could do it just as well."

"No. The decision has been made."

"But, Your Grace," the other man says, clearly treading carefully, "Athene chose him."

"So it seemed at the time. But we must have been mistaken. The amulets were contradictory: he would be strong but also weak—remember?"

"Yes, sire. But he *was* strong, and now he *is* weak.

That supports the truth of the rest. Was he not also destined to be virtuous and wise?"

"*And* foolish."

"We are all foolish sometimes, Your Highness. And he grasped the amulet for greatness. There was no doubt about it—quite impossible for an infant to do unless the goddess guides him. As your chancellor, and I hope also your friend, I strongly advise you to reconsider. Who can tell what Athene intends?"

"Have you seen him?"

"Alexos? No, Your Majesty. He has not yet appeared in public."

"Well, if you had, you'd know I am right."

"But Athene—"

"We *made a mistake*, blast you! We even sensed at the time that something was wrong. But we wanted *so badly* for him to be the one that we turned a blind eye to the inconsistencies. Now I'm not going to compound that mistake by making another one."

There is a silence. Alexos, frozen, holds his breath.

"It'll break the boy's heart, you know—after all he's been through."

The king grunts.

"Perhaps if you waited a while, gave him a chance to fully recover—"

"No! I've given it more than enough time and

thought. I told you, it's done. Teo is my heir." There is a long pause. Then, "I sometimes think it would have been kinder if the boy had died."

"Oh, Your Highness!"

"You think I don't grieve over what's happened to him? Of course I do! He was such a strong, handsome boy. Now he's ruined. And as I have another son who is perfectly sound, it's the only reasonable decision. It's best for the kingdom."

"Prince Matteo is very young. What is he, four?"

"Every heir to every throne was once very young. He'll have a regent if he inherits before he comes of age."

Another long pause.

"When will you tell them?"

"This afternoon. Then I have to get back to the army and Teo must start his training. He's a terrible baby for a boy his age. All he wants to do is fish. I'll see that Antonio takes him in hand."

"And Alexos?"

The king heaves a deep, carrying sigh.

"He will just have to take it like a man."

10

TEO STANDS AT THE window of his sleeping chamber
gazing down at the grassy slope below, the shade trees
on the bank, the river, the little skiff that is always tied
up at the bank—and all of it reminds him of Alexos.
He misses his brother so much!

Everyone says he's better now. So why won't he
come out of his rooms or let anyone in?

The dragon snores have already started, but Teo
has learned to wait until they've grown more regular,
without the occasional waking snorts that tell him
she's still settling in for her nap. It'll be soon, though.
Then he can sneak out.

Below, a figure has just come out onto the lawn.
He walks with a cane, moving with an awkward, jerky
motion. He's dressed in an ankle-length tunic, the

kind old men wear, but Teo doesn't think this person is old. His hair is black, not gray. And he wears it long, pulled back and tied with a ribbon at the nape of the neck, a young man's style.

Teo holds his breath. The fellow is moving too fast; he's going to fall. And sure enough, he almost does, but then he manages to catch himself in time. He stands for a moment, trying to compose himself. Then he looks around, probably to see if anyone noticed. And for the first time Teo catches a glimpse of his face. . . .

He races down toward the river, his heart nearly bursting with joy. He runs so fast that he trips and goes tumbling down the slope. But he just laughs, picks himself up, and keeps running till he's reached the fishing place.

Alexos is sitting on a tree stump facing the river, a gold-headed cane across his knees. He is very still. Teo decides to surprise him. He circles around and with a joyful leap suddenly appears before his brother—arms spread wide, a bright expectant smile on his face.

But how strange! The boy he sees before him, while he looks very much like Alexos, is at the same time altogether different: gaunt, wizened, brooding.

"Alexos?" Teo asks.

"More or less, little man."

"Carissa says you're better now—but you look sad."

"Do I?" His voice sounds empty.

"Yes. You look different."

Alexos turns his head away.

This isn't at all what Teo expected. It's probably his own fault. He should have said how much he'd missed Alexos, how he'd waited outside the sickroom all those afternoons, and how glad he is to see him again. That would have been so much nicer than saying he looks different and sad.

"We could go fishing," he tries, thinking that might cheer his brother up. "We can take the boat out." When Alexos doesn't move, just continues to stare at the moving water, Teo skips over and climbs into the skiff. The poles are already there, as they have been since the last time they went out on the river. There's no fresh bait, but Teo hasn't thought of that. He just looks longingly at his brother. "Come on. It'll be jolly."

He hears a little groan then—or was it a sob? Teo doesn't see any tears, but his brother's face is all twisted up, as if he's about to cry. But at least he's moving now, leaning on the cane, hauling himself up into a standing position. It looks hard. It looks like it hurts. But he's coming, that's the thing.

Alexos struggles down the sharply sloping bank, then continues unsteadily along the water's edge to where the skiff is tied. Only then does Teo truly grasp that there's something terribly wrong with his brother's legs. Can he even climb into the boat? Of course—*that's* why he's so sad!

Alexos leans down, one hand gripping the cane, the other fumbling with the rope. It would have been easier with both hands, but he manages to undo the knot. He pauses for a moment, still holding the rope, staring at Teo, who sits there waiting, confusion on his small, round face. Then Alexos flings the line into the front of the skiff and pushes hard against the bow.

The boat slips backward till the current catches it, spins it around, and starts to carry it downstream. Alexos continues to stand on the shore, watching. His face is so contorted with anguish, Teo wonders if he is dying.

11

AN ODD ASSEMBLY IS waiting in the room when Suliman arrives. Besides the usual house servants, there's a gardener, the side-door porter, a pair of humble laboring types, and one of the grooms. Suliman can feel the burning heat of their excitement: that blend of elation and anxiety, so common in moments of crisis.

"Oh, my lord physician!" the gardener cries as Suliman comes in. "Such a tragedy!" He claps a meaty hand to his chest to express the depth of his emotion. "I was the one who found him. And I didn't know what else to do but carry him back to the palace—with the help of these fine lads here—and then to send for you. He isn't dead, my lord, but he's quite insensible."

Unwilling to take the man's word for this, Suliman

makes his way through the crowd, picks up the prince's wrist, and feels for a pulse. He finds one, slow and steady. Then, satisfied, he returns his attention to the gardener.

"Where was he?" Suliman asks. "Please describe the circumstances."

"Down by the river, my lord. Right at the edge of the water. He was still breathing when I came across him, so I knew he was alive. But he wasn't as he ought to be, neither. He wouldn't open his eyes or speak a word, no matter how much I talked to him."

"Did it look to you like a simple fall? Anything else you want to add?"

"Probably just a simple fall. There wasn't any blood."

"Was he lying facedown?"

"He was."

"Not in that position, then—bent over as he is now?"

The gardener looks at the figure on the bed and considers the question for a moment.

"I guess you're right, my lord. He wasn't *exactly* facedown when I found him. His legs were sticking straight out, but he'd sort of twisted and bent over from the waist, same as he is there. And when we brought him up here and put him in the bed, we set him down on his back. But he's curled up again, like before."

"He moved then, of his own volition?"

"He must've done."

"Thank you. That was very helpful. Now, you have served the prince most admirably, but I'm afraid I must clear the room so I can examine him."

The men seem reluctant to leave. They'd evidently hoped to stay and see how it all turned out. But the physician's expression, calm but implacable, makes it clear that this is not to be. When they've all filed out, followed by the chamber servants, Suliman shuts the door.

Alone with Alexos now, the physician begins his examination. He sets the back of his hand to the prince's cheek, but detects no sign of fever. If anything, the boy is chilled from lying in the wet. His reflexes are unchanged, his breathing fine. Suliman runs his fingers through Alexos' hair, probing for wounds or signs of injury. He finds nothing, not so much as a scratch or a pigeon-egg lump.

"What *happened* to you, my prince?" Suliman whispers, touching the deep furrow between the straight, dark brows, feeling the clenched jaw muscles, and especially noting the tortured, curled-up posture. People lie in this way, as an infant lies in the womb, when they are frightened or sad. It is diagnostic, suggestive not of concussion but some emotional trauma. "What was it?" Suliman whispers again. "You were so confident this morning, so determined and proud. You were ready to face the world. And now . . ."

Alexos hears everything Suliman says; he feels the gentle touch of his hands. But he can't respond because his body and his spirit are no longer connected.

His body lies on a princely bed, trying to draw itself up into a protective ball, the way a wood louse does when it is threatened. But the knees won't rise to meet the chest, so the pose is incomplete. Whatever comfort it might have given his body to curl up smaller and smaller, as if hoping to disappear, is denied him.

The real Alexos is far away. It feels as if he's fallen into a very deep well; now he lies at the bottom under the dark, cold water—just him and the memory of the inexplicable, unforgivable thing he did.

He relives that moment again and again: his hand on the bow of the little boat, the sudden shove, the alarm on his brother's face as he floats helplessly away. It's like walking into a firestorm to see if it will hurt. And always it does. It washes over him like a hot wave of agony, the terrible, scalding knowledge that Teo, the best, most innocent soul who ever lived, the person Alexos loved most in the world, is gone forever. There is no taking it back. Teo is dead because he, Alexos, killed him.

And because Teo died alone on the great, dark sea, no coin was set on his tongue to pay the boatman. So he will spend all eternity wandering the shores of the River Styx, unable to cross into the Underworld and dwell in the paradise where virtuous souls are sent.

Alexos wants to die too, but his body won't allow it because that would be too easy; it would bring him forgetfulness and end his pain. So the heart keeps stubbornly pumping away in his chest, the lungs move air in and out, and the mind never sleeps.

Alexos has drifted so far away now, has become so utterly confounded by the fog of his misery, that he's lost all sense of time, all awareness of his body, or the room in which it lies, or anything Suliman says or does. Untethered from his corporal self, he rises into the dark beyond, where there is nothing but emptiness.

And then the king arrives. His voice can be heard from the anteroom; then the door is flung open and he crosses the room with heavy steps. Everything Ektor does is loud when he is in a mood.

Perhaps it's the sudden break in the silence that jerks Alexos back into his body, or more likely it's the natural terror his father has always inspired in him. But whatever the reason, Alexos is in the room again.

"I have to talk to my son!" the king shouts, as though Suliman were hard of hearing. His breath is labored; he must have run up the stairs.

"The prince has collapsed, Your Majesty. As you see, he is not well."

"I don't care. I have questions I need him to answer."

"He hasn't spoken since they found him, Your Grace. But perhaps in time—"

"Alexos!" The king is at the bedside now, shaking the prince's shoulder. "Stop this nonsense. I mean it! Look at me! Alexos!"

Suliman stands, helpless, as the king shakes and slaps his son in an effort to wake him. It goes on for an unbearably long time. But finally even Ektor sees that the boy cannot respond.

"What's the matter with him?" he asks. "Is it the summer sickness again?"

"No, Your Majesty; there are no symptoms to support a relapse. We do know that he fell, and he may have a mild concussion, but there is more to it than that. I don't have an answer yet. I'm sorry."

Ektor sucks in air, then huffs out a great, theatrical sigh. "I'm at the end of my wits," he says, more quietly now. "Are you aware that Prince Matteo has disappeared?"

There's a moment of dead silence. "*No*, I had not heard that, Your Majesty. But surely he's off playing somewhere, probably here in the palace."

"Oh, gods, Suliman, how I wish that were true!" Ektor belches out a sob, an extraordinary display of feeling for a man whose emotions run generally in the narrow range between irritation and anger.

But the king trusts his court physician as he trusts no other. He considers Suliman almost a peer—he is a prince, after all, the younger brother of a sultan. But even more important to Ektor than Suliman's pedigree are his intelligence, dignity, discretion, and wisdom. And in truth, he has come here not only to speak with his son but to ask the advice of his physician.

"When that *blasted, incompetent* nursery women discovered that Teo was missing, half the palace went searching for him. One of the porters said he'd seen the boy running toward the river, over by that big willow where the boys liked to go fishing. So a gardener was sent to look for him. But he found Alexos instead—lying right beside the post where the boat is always tied up. And, oh, Suliman—*the skiff is missing!* Can't you see the implications? Do you understand now why *I must* speak with my son?"

"Yes," Suliman says. Alexos hears the weight of that single word.

"I must know what happened down there!"

As usual, there is a brief pause; Suliman thinks before he speaks. "Your Highness," he says at last, his voice remarkably calm, "I've been trying to put it all together and I have some thoughts. Would you care to hear them?"

"I would," the king says.

"Alexos went out this afternoon for his first time since the illness. I knew he was doing this. He insisted on going alone. He said he would walk in the Queen's Garden."

A gasp from Ektor. It doesn't go unnoticed by the physician.

"But let's suppose he changed his mind and went down to the river instead. It's one of his favorite places. And let's further suppose that Teo spotted him crossing the lawn from the nursery window. Not having seen his brother in a very long time, he would naturally want to run down and see him."

"I figured that much out already," the king says. "I want to know what happened after that."

"Well, what if Teo climbed into the skiff, thinking they would go fishing together? I doubt he knew how damaged Alexos was, that even walking over to the boat, let alone climbing into it, would be difficult for him. So Teo might have untied the skiff, expecting his brother to jump in right away, and the current caught it before Alexos could get there."

"Then why wouldn't Alexos call for help?"

"He probably did, but he was far from the palace. Maybe no one was close enough to hear. And in his effort to rescue Teo, Alexos may have fallen and, unable to rise without assistance, was forced to lie helplessly on the riverbank as his brother floated away. It would explain everything: Teo's disappearance and Alexos' mental collapse."

"*Mental?* You mean there's nothing really wrong with him?"

"On the contrary, my lord. There's a great deal wrong with him."

"With his *mind*."

"His body, his mind, and his soul."

Ektor moans. "I suppose you *also* haven't heard that I'd made Teo my heir. I signed the document this very day."

"I did not know that either, Your Grace."

"Now Teo's almost certainly lost—he couldn't manage the oars, he can't swim—and my one remaining son is not only lame, he's *mad*! Gods, what a disaster!"

"There's still a chance that Teo's all right. The skiff may have drifted into the reeds. And if not, the people along the bank would surely have noticed a little boy alone in a boat. Someone would have gone out and brought him in to safety. I assume you have men out searching the river and the shore."

"Of course I have. And I pray to the gods that you are right. But too much time passed before it was noticed that the skiff was missing. And even after I was informed, it took a while to organize the search. They won't find him, Suliman. Not likely anyway."

The king rises abruptly. "I have to go. Send for me if he wakes, night or day."

"Yes, Your Majesty."

"Though I don't suppose it really matters anymore *how* the accident happened. Teo is gone and Alexos is all I have left. I'm too old to make any more sons. So heal him if you can. He might still be a decent king with a ruined body—but not with a ruined mind. Take care of him, old friend."

"I will, Ektor. I promise."

12

WITH THE KING GONE, the room falls unnaturally still. There is only the sound of Suliman moving softly about. Then he is at the bedside again. With one hand he turns the prince's face and, with his thumb on the chin, opens his mouth. Alexos feels the drops as they fall onto his tongue— one, two, three. He recognizes the flavor of honey and aniseed, then the bitter aftertaste.

The physician stays for a while, waiting for the sleeping drops to take effect. Soon Alexos feels his muscles start to release. His breaths come more slowly now. He is conscious of the gentle rhythm of his own beating heart. Through the peaceful mist that fills his consciousness, he hears a soft puff of air as Suliman blows out the lamp. He hears gentle footfalls as the physician crosses the room, the rustle of robes and the creak of wood as he sits down. Soon they are both asleep.

Darkness and silence, like the end of the world. It goes on and on and on.

And then Alexos feels the touch of a hand. It lands on his shoulder, soft as falling silk. And there it seems to melt, to become insubstantial, until he almost forgets the hand is there; he can only feel the consoling warmth of it.

Then the fog opens and brings him a dream.

He is hovering in the air above the river, looking down. The day is calm. The skiff, with its flat bottom, hardly rocks at all as it drifts with the current. Teo sits frozen on the bench, gripping the edge of the plank with his little hands. On the bank, people stare as he floats by, but they do nothing. Nor does Teo call for help. He is paralyzed with fright.

Gradually the daylight begins to fade. A breeze rises, cool against his sunburned face. Somehow, in the dream, Alexos knows that Teo is thirsty. *There's fresh water all around you*, he whispers. But Teo can't hear him.

Or maybe he does. Stiff and sore from sitting so long without moving, he slides down into the bottom of the boat. Then, bit by bit, he starts shifting to the side, waiting after each little scoot to see if the boat will tip, and when it doesn't, moving a little more. At last he's close enough to reach.

Gripping the gunwale with one hand, he dips the other into the river, holding his fingers together to form a cup. Most of the water spills along the way, but a few drops fall onto his tongue. Encouraged, he does this again and again until his thirst is quenched. Then he scoots back to the middle of the boat, curls up on the floor, and falls asleep.

When Teo wakes, it is night. Low clouds cover the moon and stars, but he can see well enough to know he's not on the river anymore. Dark water stretches away on every side. For the first time he whimpers, just a little. Then he lies back down and sleeps again.

Alexos watches from above, his heart aching. This is even worse than walking into the fire, because he wants so desperately to save Teo but he doesn't have the power to do it. *I am going to watch him die*, he thinks.

When Teo wakes the second time, he is allover wet. Water has puddled in the bottom of the boat. The waves rock him back and forth, back and forth, slapping the sides of the skiff. He scoops up some of the water and drinks; but it tastes of salt, old wood, and fish. He tries to go back to sleep, but he can't. So he just lies there, curled up in a ball, afraid.

The hours pass; a storm builds. Rain comes down

in big, heavy drops: wet, bruising blows against Teo's face and arms. There's a lot more water in the boat now; it sloshes around as the skiff pitches in the churning sea.

"Oh," Teo cries, "help me! Please help me!" But his small voice is swallowed by the wind.

Exhaustion pulls him under and he sleeps once more.

Dear goddess, O great and wise Athene, Alexos prays in his dream, *protect my innocent brother. For I have put him in harm's way and now I cannot help him. Punish me however you want, but please don't let him die!*

It's still dark when Teo wakes for the third time. The sea is calm now, the rain has stopped, and straight ahead a dark mass is slowly emerging from a thick bank of fog. It's an island, rather small, with a mountain in the middle. All along the coastline, jagged boulders rise out of the water, waves crashing hard against them. And the skiff, which now seems to have a mind of its own, is heading straight for that perilous shore.

Helpless to stop it, Teo abandons himself to his fate, waiting passively as the boat draws closer and closer to the rocks. Then he sees it: a break in the ring of boulders, an open channel that leads directly to a broad, white beach. Alexos watches, his heart aching with joy, as the boat enters this safe harbor, scrapes against sand, and comes to a lurching stop.

But Teo is still afraid. There's water all around him and it's too dark to see how deep it is. So he stays where he is, wet and shivering, gazing longingly at the beach ahead.

Now slowly the skiff begins to rise, as if the sand itself was lifting it. Teo gasps as water streams away on either side of the boat and forms a little pond far behind him. The boat is on dry land.

Come, the air sings to him. *Come onto the island. You will be safe here.*

Teo swings his legs over the gunwale and drops onto the sand. The water keeps its distance. Encouraged, he takes a deep, shuddering breath and runs as fast as he can till he reaches the soft, dry sand of the beach. Then he runs farther still, through the brittle, honey-gold grass that grows at the edge of the shore till he comes to hard-packed earth. Only then does he stop and turn around.

He sees the skiff perched on a wide shelf of sand. But it's settling now, slowly sinking back into the rising waters. For a brief time the waves seem to play with the little boat, pushing it toward the beach and drawing it out again; then they let go. Teo watches as the skiff floats gradually out to sea, growing smaller and smaller until it's lost in the fog and the darkness.

Only then does he turn away and head for the shelter of the forest. It's as if a door has closed in a corner of his mind. Behind it is his old life: his former home and all the people in it, and most especially his brother and the terrible thing he did.

Somehow Alexos knows all this and he fully understands: Teo will not remember him, not even the good things, not even the love they shared. But that's the bargain he made when he begged Athene to save his brother. And she has done it admirably. She has brought Teo across the River Styx with no need of a coin for the ferryman. And because he lived a pure and blameless life, brief though it was, he will be blessed in the Underworld.

In his dream, Alexos thanks the goddess.

Teo walks deeper into the forest. He senses that he is thirsty. And the moment the thought forms in his mind, he hears the rippling of water and looks down to see a clear stream running close beside him. It wasn't there before; he's sure he would have noticed it, for even under the canopy of trees on this foggy, foggy night, the air glows with the light of a thousand fireflies. But he doesn't ask himself why any of this is so. He just drops to his knees, makes a bowl with his hands, and draws the water, cold and sweet, up to his mouth.

When he can drink no more, he sits down on a nearby rock. It's the perfect height for a boy his size and is smooth and flat on top, almost as if it had been specially made for him to use as a stool. Only a formless sadness still lingers in the now-empty space where his memory used to be—a sadness and a new awareness that he is very hungry.

Overhead, he hears a rustling of leaves, as if the wind has risen. But the air is perfectly still; there's not a hint of a breeze. He looks up to see a fruit tree, its smooth, heart-shaped leaves gleaming in the glowing light, so shiny you'd think someone had polished them. And the branches of the tree don't merely droop, as heavy-laden branches do. They actually reach down, as if to ask: *Won't you have some? Take as many as you like.*

He's never seen fruit like this before. It's not a peach, an apple, or a pear; and it's nothing at all like a fig. But it looks delicious. Teo bites through the fruit's smooth, delicate skin and finds it moist but not runny, tender but not soft, sweet without being cloying, and just a little tart. It's altogether new and the best thing he's ever tasted.

I know this place, Alexos is thinking now. *It's the enchanted country the goddess showed me on festival day.* It had seemed a paradise then. It seems so now.

Teo eats three of the fruits. Then he picks two

more. When he's finished the last one and is quite satisfied, he looks up at the tree and thanks it. The tree shivers its leaves as if in reply and stands up straight again.

Teo's muscles don't ache anymore and the desolation that filled his heart has been replaced by something like hope. Also, he is very, very tired.

As it happens, there is a mossy hollow at the foot of the tree and it's just Teo's size. He lies down in it and curls up small, as he did earlier in the boat. But this is not hard and wet; it's soft and warm. As he drifts off to sleep, a gentle breeze rises and covers him with a blanket of leaves. The air fills with sweet music. The wind is singing a lullaby.

Now two figures emerge from the fog and stand over Teo. Alexos recognizes them too: it's the man and the girl from his vision. The man kneels by the mossy bed and takes Teo into his arms.

"What sort of creature is it?" the girl whispers.

"Oh, for heaven's sake, Aria!" says the man. "It's a little boy."

"A human child?"

"Yes."

"But where did it come from?"

The man does not answer. "Let's go," is all he says. Teo sleeps as he is carried out of the forest, back to the welcoming beach, then up a long, steep, winding path to the highest point on the island. Nor does he wake as he is laid on a down-filled pallet, then a blanket is draped over him and pulled up to his chin. But he feels the girl's tender kiss on his cheek. He can smell her breath: fresh, like clover.

"He's very sweet, Papa," the girl says.

"They generally are," the man replies.

13

THE HAND LIFTS FROM his shoulder as softly as it fell. Then gradually, like a flower unfolding its petals from the bud, Alexos opens again into life. At the shock of it, he gulps in air and opens his eyes.

It's still dark in the room, but it must be morning now. Light bleeds in at the edges of the shutters where they meet the window frame. Across the room, Suliman wakes when he hears Alexos gasp.

Wordlessly he rises and goes to him. He pulls up a stool beside the bed and sits down.

"So," he says. It's almost a whisper. "You have returned to us."

"I didn't want to." This is the truth. "I wanted to stay there forever."

"Where?"

"In the Underworld."

Suliman sits up straighter. *"You crossed the River?"*

"I must have. It was a perfect paradise. I saw Teo. He'll be happy there. He has a kindly death-father and death-sister to love him and look after him."

Suliman doesn't speak, just studies him through half-closed eyes. Alexos feels the depth of his scrutiny; it makes him feel exposed, vulnerable, transparent.

"Shall I open the shutters?" Suliman says.

Light comes into the room along with a gust of cold air. It's autumn now, Alexos remembers; soon will come the bitter winds, the sleet, and then the snow. Suliman arranges the covers to keep the prince warm, then sits again and waits. Ever the patient man.

"I heard," Alexos says. They have things to say to each other. This is the best way he can think of to begin.

"What did you hear?"

"My father, what you talked about, everything."

Suliman looks down at his hands, folded in his lap. "And what did you think of it, Alexos?"

"I'm not sure. It's complicated."

"So it is. Would you like for me to prop you up? You look uncomfortable as you are."

"Yes, please."

Alexos feels his vertebrae shift as Suliman moves

him. He lets out a little moan, but Suliman takes no notice. He just goes on arranging the pillows and covers in a brisk, professional way. Alexos senses the disapproval in his manner and knows he'll have to do a whole lot better than "I'm not sure. It's complicated."

"Will you take some water? Say yes, Alexos."

Alexos nods and accepts the drink he is offered. And *that*, he realizes, is all the prologue there is going to be. Now it's time for the main event.

He closes his eyes and tries to think. "I heard what you said, what you guessed might have happened to Teo."

"And?"

Alexos struggles with what to say next, because it really *is* complicated. Suliman's account of Teo's death had been remarkably close to what happened, almost to the end. And that version—an unfortunate accident—would be infinitely more comforting to the king and better for the kingdom than the ugly truth. Obviously it would also be better for Alexos, because if his crime is revealed, he will be ruined. What exactly will happen to him, he doesn't know—execution? banishment?—but there is no doubt it will be terrible.

On the other hand, he could lie. He could say to Suliman, "Yes, that's exactly how it was," and he would be magically washed free of blame so far as the world was concerned. He could go on as before, his reputation unsullied. He could even be king.

Alexos shoots Suliman a pleading look but Suliman just gazes back, still as stone. *You have to do this yourself,* he's saying. *I can wait forever if I must.*

"You know, don't you?" Alexos says.

"I think so."

"Then you must despise me."

Suliman pulls in a deep breath. He makes Alexos wait.

"No," he finally says. "I don't despise you. But I don't understand it either. It goes completely against your character to do willful harm—and *to your brother,* Alexos! How is that possible, when you loved him so much?"

"*I don't know!* That's the truth. It just happened somehow. My hand was on the bow; I meant to get into the boat. That was truly my intention. But then . . ." His voice breaks and he can't finish. Still, he's satisfied that he's done what was required. He's confessed his crime when he might have evaded it. Every word he said was true.

Tears are streaming down his cheeks now. He takes shuddering breaths, wipes his eyes and nose, tries to get control of himself. "I don't understand it, Suliman. I really don't."

Once again there is silence. Then, with admirable calm, "I think I have some idea, Alexos. May I tell you?"

"Please!"

"For all of us, there are moments when we 'forget ourselves.' In moments of overwhelming emotion we sometimes lose connection with our higher nature, our ability to reason and act according to our values and beliefs. We are reduced to our animal natures; and in that state we do irrational things. We kick a door and break a toe. We throw a precious cup against a wall. We say cruel words we do not really mean. This is a well-understood phenomenon, Alexos. Even our laws acknowledge it, punishing 'crimes of passion' more leniently than those committed 'in cold blood.'

"In this case, of course, the harm you did was much worse than a broken toe or a shattered cup. So let's consider what led up to it."

"Nothing," Alexos says. "Nothing at all. Teo was his usual, wonderful, sweet self and I—"

"Please listen, Alexos. Let me finish. I have spoken in the past about the weight of responsibility you've carried since your earliest years. You were never allowed to be a natural child—or really a child at all. You handled it with remarkable courage, as I have also told you before.

"But these last few months you've been tested almost beyond endurance. Think, Alexos: the pressure and humiliation of the festival race, the disapproval of your father, the grave illness that might have killed you, and the resulting paralysis that has robbed you for life of the normal use of your legs. Then on top of all that, your father takes away your life's purpose and makes Teo his heir instead. He was in the Queen's Garden at the same time as you—am I right? And you overheard him?"

"How did you know?"

"The king gasped when I told him you had planned to walk there."

"He said it might have been better if I had died."

"That was very cruel."

Alexos shrugs. "Maybe not. If I had, then Teo would be alive."

Suliman gives him that deep look again. He is turning it over in his mind.

"It was hurtful to hear all the same. And you were already strung as tight as a bow just before the arrow is loosed. When a bow is drawn as far as it will go, then pulled a little bit more, it can snap—from the pressure, you understand."

"Are you saying I'm not responsible for what happened? Because I 'forgot myself'?"

"No. We are all responsible for the things we do." He lets this hang in the air for a while. He strokes his beard and gazes out the window.

"Suliman?" Alexos says. "Last night, after Father left and you gave me the sleeping drops, then went to sit in your chair—did you rise again and come over to me and lay your hand on my shoulder?"

The physician blinks, clearly astonished. "No," he says slowly, looking directly into the prince's eyes. "I slept without moving till I heard you wake."

"Then who—?"

After a long pause: "Who do you think?"

Alexos draws in breath to speak, then lets it out again without a word.

"The goddess Athene was here in this room," Suliman says. "She looked into your heart and saw the depth of your sorrow. Then she forgave you. She must have, Alexos, else she wouldn't have taken you across the River, where living mortals never go, and shown you that Teo is safe and happy there. It was a kindness, was it not?"

"Oh, yes. You can't imagine."

"I can, actually. And now you must thank her and accept her forgiveness. You will find that hard to do, I would imagine."

"How can I possibly, when I can't forgive myself? I don't deserve her mercy."

"That's true. But mercy is, by its very definition, an undeserved gift. And it's not your place to question the goddess and her motives."

Alexos droops. He is exhausted, body and soul.

"There's something else you need to keep in mind, going forward," Suliman says. "Grief and guilt are two entirely different things. The guilt you cannot bring yourself to put aside, which you hold so fiercely to your heart like some poisonous darling—that's all about *you*, Alexos. But the grief is for Teo. So accept Athene's forgiveness, and in doing so think less about yourself. Just grieve for your brother, purely and sincerely, as he deserves. Do you think you can do that?"

Alexos isn't sure. "I will try," he says.

"Good. Then take up your burden again and continue your life of service. Fulfill your duty as a prince and the champion of the goddess."

"But my father—"

"Yes, well, I have considered that. And I don't think it would be kind to tell him the truth; nor would it be good for Arcos. Why don't we just leave things as they are? You've done harm enough already."

"Suliman?"

"Yes, Alexos?"

"What would you have done if I had lied, if I'd said your version of the story was true?"

He gives this a moment of serious thought. "Would

I have exposed you—is that what you're asking?"

"No. I mean, what would *you* have done?"

"I'd have packed up my things and left the kingdom and never returned. Because you would have broken my heart. But you didn't lie, Alexos, even though I gave you a big, wide door to walk through."

"Was that a test?"

"I hadn't thought of it that way, but I suppose it was. And in that at least, you proved to be the boy I always believed you to be. So you also have *my* forgiveness, for what it's worth. And I shall stay and guide you and help you become a whole person again. I will be at your side for as long as you want me, Alexos."

"Is that it?"

"No. I want you to sit up and eat. After that, we shall see."

14

ALEXOS RETURNS TO HIS classes late and unan-
nounced. He waits till the boys are seated and the
master of mathematics has started his lecture. Then
he slips in and takes the back bench, which is always
empty.

But he hadn't considered the noise he makes—the
tap of his cane, the click when the brace is released,
the thump as he sits down—or the startled expression
on the master's face. His classmates turn as one and
stare at Alexos. And at first they seem unable to speak
or move. So much has happened since the last time
they saw him, that terrible day of the festival race. And
none of it was good. What can they possibly say?

They hardly recognize him now, this boy in the
long black tunic, a brace on his leg and a cane in his

hand. He is shockingly thin, with bruiselike shadows beneath his eyes. And he has cut off his hair in mourning for his brother, as women do. He looks older, wounded, sick.

After a long, awkward moment, they get up from their benches and move warily in his direction. This is something they are required to do out of courtesy, but there are no rules to guide them. How does one greet a boy who nearly died, was forever damaged by his illness, then lost his beloved brother—all in the space of a few short months? They have no idea.

So they gather around him politely: the boys standing, Alexos still seated, because getting up would be such an embarrassing production that it would only make things worse. They mutter condolences: *Oh, Alexos, so sorry, what a bad time you've had, it must have been awful.* Not once do they allude to his cane and brace. Nor do they mention Teo, who is presumably included in all the rest.

Alexos finds this unendurable. He wonders, not for the first time, if his father would allow him to be taught in his chambers by tutors from now on.

The master, who has been standing at the back of the crowd, sees that the welcome is going badly; the boys aren't up to the challenge and the prince is distressed. He makes his way to the front.

"My lord Alexos," he says with an unaccustomed low bow, "you have been in our thoughts every day since you fell ill. We sacrificed to Zeus and Athene and Apollo to bring you safely through your ordeal." The boys all nod energetically at this: *Yes, it's true, we did!* "We were most relieved when we heard that you had survived. Most relieved.

"But even then," the master goes on, "your ordeal was not over. You were left with paralysis in your legs. The royal physician has told me of your struggle to build up your strength again, so that you could walk with a cane. It was painful and difficult, he said, but you fought like a lion." The boys let out sighs almost in unison.

Alexos is transfixed by the master's performance. *Get it all out there*, he thinks, *that must be the plan: speak the unspeakable.* He feels a twitch at the corners of his mouth, as if a smile was trying to form.

"And then—forgive me for mentioning this if it's too painful to hear—but just as you had grown strong again and were ready to return to life, an even greater tragedy struck."

Oh, thank you for that, Alexos thinks. *Thank you for knowing that that was the worst.*

"The loss of our dear prince Matteo, so beloved by everyone who knew him, was devastating for us all.

We sacrificed again to the gods for the speedy progress of his soul into that happy place where the good live for all eternity. But, Alexos, our sorrow was nothing, *nothing* compared with what you must have felt. I know you were ill with grief. I would guess it was the worst thing that has ever happened in your life."

"Yes!" Alexos says. He is so grateful that this man, the quietest master in the school, always so strict, dull, and precise, has the wisdom and the daring to say these very hard things out loud.

"I wish you to know that we were with you through the whole journey. You are one of us, Alexos. Your princely status may set you apart, but these boys are your friends and they care about you. They have mourned your every sorrow. And now they want to welcome you back with the full understanding of everything you have endured and the courage you have shown in the face of it."

The master bows again as a sign that he's finished speaking. Then he steps back and all decorum is abandoned. The boys are all around Alexos now, squeezing his arm and patting his back, laughing and talking. The sympathy and affection, which they had not known how to express till now, is released in a flood of boyish exuberance. Alexos knows he doesn't deserve it, but he accepts it willingly as another of Athene's merciful gifts.

He stays for the rest of the classes, but returns to his rooms after the midday meal, when the afternoon training begins. He is shocked to discover how tired he is. The bitter days of winter will have arrived in earnest before he's strong enough to train again.

During that time, Suliman has worked with the master of arms to equip an exercise room for the prince's special use. Benches have been constructed and wrapped with padding, iron bars of varying sizes brought in, oversized pallets laid on the floor, and ropes hung from the rafters, to which rings and wooden rods are attached.

The boys have been following this activity with intense interest. When Alexos is finally ready to use this equipment, they are eager to know what everything is for and how it works. The master of arms looks to Alexos for permission to answer. It is, after all, his private regimen, and not really any of their business.

"Go ahead," Alexos says.

"Very well. The prince will use these various devices to strengthen his upper body, both because it will help his mobility, compensating for his legs, and because he can't maintain his overall strength in the usual ways."

"What about the rings?" Leander asks.

"They're for pulling up, like so." The master

demonstrates. "It's harder than it looks. Try it; you'll see."

"Yes, Leander," Alexos says. "Please give it a try."

"All right. Watch and learn." Leander poses briefly, flexing his muscles, then slaps his hands together as if wiping them of dust. Finally he takes hold of the rings. "Agggghhhhhhh!" he grunts as he pulls himself up, the rings spreading apart and making it harder. "Grrraaagh!"

"Elegantly done," Alexos says, when Leander drops to the ground. "Beautiful."

"I know. Wasn't it? Master, may we train with them too?"

"That's entirely up to the prince."

Titus is trying the rings now and finding it just as hard.

"Please?" Leander begs.

They seem to have forgotten—or if not exactly forgotten, then thoroughly accepted—Alexos' damaged legs. They understand what he hopes to accomplish and enthusiastically support it. There's something about this that makes it possible for him to accept it too.

"Please, please, please?"

"Oh, for heaven's sake, Leander—yes. But it's my equipment, all right? I can't use yours, so I'm not standing in line to take my turn."

"Oh, thank you, thank you, thank you! Yes, yes, yes!"

"Don't be tiresome, Leander," the master says, though he can't resist a smile. "Now Alexos has work ahead of him—as do you all. Scoot."

"But can't we just watch for today so we can learn what to do? I ask most respectfully, Master. I think this is a really good way to get stronger—in addition to the other things, of course."

"I don't mind," Alexos says.

So they stay.

Really, he's more than glad. He's never felt so included, so thoroughly a part of the group. And their interest touches him, the way they gather to watch, discussing the finer points of his technique and offering to help.

Alexos lies on the bench and raises an iron bar straight up, then lowers it over his chest: up and down, up and down. As he does this, Markos hold his legs so Alexos won't strain his back. Felix and Titus stand on either side of him, holding the bar till he's ready, then taking it away when he's done. His classmates vie for the honor of assisting him.

Alexos has smaller weights, too—short, thick bars he can move independently. He raises them at shoulder level, or extends them to the side. Sometimes his body itself is the weight. He lies facedown on a pallet and pushes his torso up or hangs from the suspended swing and hauls himself off the ground.

All of it is harder than it looks, harder than he expected. But true to his nature, Alexos pushes himself, and after months of systematic exercise he can see that his body is changing. His shoulders look broader, his arms and chest have grown. Weights he struggled to lift before are easier now. His endurance has also improved. He now spends as much time training as his classmates do.

Suliman, pleased with the results, adds new exercises to the prince's routine, to develop balance and flexibility as well as strength. They are more complex and therefore more interesting to Alexos. He's missed working with the sword: the quick decisions that have to be made, the heightened awareness, the speed of the action, the way subtle movements are joined with powerful strokes. The new routines aren't as engaging as that, but they do require him to think, to use a variety of muscles at the same time. And they allow him to move in a graceful, rhythmic way. He's missed that too—being graceful.

Alexos supports himself by holding on to one fixed, suspended ring while grasping a movable ring with the other hand. The far end of the movable rope is controlled by a willing volunteer who keeps it at just the right amount of tension. Alexos pulls it hard, down and to the side, as if throwing the discus. Or he pulls the ring back, also against tension, as if preparing to hurl a spear.

While someone holds his legs, he sits up with his arms crossed over his chest and twists to the left and then the right.

He feels aches in different muscles now: his belly and back, his hips and buttocks. And he finds their growing strength makes a difference. He walks with more confidence now. Sitting and rising are easier, too.

The worst of a very hard winter is over and they're well into a cold, wet, dreary spring when it occurs to Alexos that with a specially constructed harness (and perhaps some adjustments to his brace) he might be able to ride a horse again. But he keeps this precious dream to himself, half afraid to give it voice. Meanwhile he works on designing it in his head.

It will be a sort of chair that sits on the horse's back. The chair will have to be strapped onto the horse and Alexos strapped into the chair. He'll need something to hold his legs in place so they don't flop around. But none of this seems impossible. A wooden structure covered with leather and fitted with straps—how hard could that be?

At last he gathers his courage and mentions it to Suliman, who laughs.

"I wondered how long it would take you to arrive at that conclusion."

"You think it would work?"

"Of course. It was always one of my goals for you. In my country, saddles are common. We put them on horses, on camels—I have even heard of people putting them on elephants. But I warn you that it will be painful. We can build you a comfortable seat, but we can't change the anatomy of the beast you ride, and your legs will be forced into an unnatural position. Here, let me show you.

"This is your accustomed way of sitting. Now, imagine that the great barrel chest of a horse is between your legs. Your thigh must rotate out from the hip, like so, and your calf must turn at an angle, thus, to embrace it. After a time, muscle and bone will cry out in protest. And that's not even considering the brace, which will press against your leg. We can make adjustments to the brace and add some protective padding, but it's still going to be painful. And it will hurt even more when you get down."

"Good."

Suliman frowns. "And why is that good, Alexos? You *want* to feel pain?"

"Yes. It will help me remember."

Dark brows shoot up. "Are you really in any danger of forgetting?"

It's hard for Alexos to answer that, mostly because of the way Suliman has framed the question. "In a way. I keep getting drawn back into life. There are moments when I actually feel happy. The world is starting to seem normal again."

"I would say that is both desirable and healthy— being drawn back to life and feeling happy. It's natural to turn from darkness and seek the light."

"Nothing about me is natural or normal. I'm not like other people."

"Oh, Alexos!" Suliman draws back in his chair, as if recoiling from something appalling. "Do you truly think you're the first person ever to suffer, the first ever to do something horribly wrong?"

"I'm sorry."

Suliman shakes his head. "I did not expect such self-importance from you. I thought you were wiser than that."

Alexos doesn't understand why Suliman is so shocked by what he said—because he really *isn't* like other people. He could list the reasons why, but he hasn't the stomach for it. So he looks sheepishly down at his hands and waits for whatever comes next.

"You accepted Athene's forgiveness, and mine. You chose life over death. You committed yourself to serving the kingdom, as you were born to do, and serving the goddess, who chose you. But you won't commit. You stand in the doorway, as if you can't decide whether to come or go. Make up your mind, Alexos. If you wish to cower in the darkness and make a fetish of your pain—that will be a terrible waste, but it's your life. Go ahead."

Though the rest is left unspoken, Alexos hears it loud and clear: *But if that's your choice, I will have no more to do with you.*

"It's hard," he says. "And confusing."

"Of course it is." His expression is still grim but he's edging away from the anger. "One of the reasons I want you to be able to ride a horse again is that it will enable you to travel, to see your kingdom and learn how the people live."

"That's what I want, too."

"I'm glad, because you really need to see it for yourself, Alexos. And once you have grasped the enormity of the misery that's out there in the world—how brutal the lives of the poor can be, how truly helpless they are—then maybe you can well and truly step through that door and shut it firmly behind you, put your own problems aside, and make yourself useful. You have enormous power, you know. Why not use it to help someone else?"

"Yes," Alexos says. He understands now. "I will."

"That's my brave boy."

"I wish I could leave right now."

"It's sleeting outside, Alexos."

They can't help but laugh, and the tension breaks.

"Suliman, do you know where Attaros is?"

"The village where young Peles lives—the boy who won the laurel crown?"

"Yes."

"It's far to the south, I believe. Probably three or four days' ride."

"That's where I want to go first."

15

THE ROADS! BY ALL the gods on Olympus, why had no one warned them about the roads?

It's full summer; the sun is high and the days are long. You'd think it would be an excellent time for travel. And so it would be *if the snow weren't still melting*! And judging by the great, filthy piles of slush that linger all over the countryside, it's likely to *go on* melting till winter comes again. As a consequence, the roads, which were not good to begin with, have become streaming rivers of sucking mud. And there's no avoiding them by cutting across the fields, because they are even worse. There are two abandoned carts stranded hub-deep in muck to prove it.

Travel is hard in other ways, too. The inns, when they are to be found, are dreadful, the stinking straw mattresses crawling with vermin. The food is disgusting. And the horses tire so easily from slogging through the mire that they must be rested every few hours. To make it to Attaros in eight days, let alone four, would be a positive miracle.

Yet for all their complaining, there's not one of them who would dream of turning back. For the truth is, they rather enjoy the mess and the excitement of their many small disasters. Except for the prince's personal guard, who ride with them to assure his safety, they're all of an age, these ten boys, fourteen years or soon to be. And as the country folk would say, their sap is rising. One minute they're loud and boisterous, pelting one another with clods; the next they're straight-backed, dignified young gentlemen, nodding and flirting with the peasant girls they pass along the way.

A few of them have seen more of the world than Alexos has, but not by much, and they are genuinely eager to learn. Like the prince, they will one day have important roles to play in the management of the kingdom. It's good for them to get a sense of its geography and the character of the land (not to mention the state of the roads), as well as the condition of the people, their livestock, and their fields. They absorb this vast amount of new information with the earnestness of youth.

"How can they grow crops in a slough like that?" Markos asks, gazing in horror at the wasteland that surrounds them.

"Obviously they can't," says Felix. "If they could, there'd be green shoots up by now."

"What do they eat, then?"

"All you ever think about is eating, Markos!"

"Shut up, Titus. Leave him alone. And besides, Markos isn't nearly as fat as he used to be."

"Oh, spare me your kindness, Leander. I was thinking about the people, not myself. They have to eat, so there must be crops growing somewhere. Certainly we never lack in the royal city."

They fall silent at this. They've seen too much poverty already: the tumbledown houses, the barren fields, the haggard faces of dirty children. Is it like this all over the kingdom, they wonder: thousands and thousands of people living on the ragged edge of starvation while they, the sons of rich men, have more than enough to eat?

It's a sobering thought. It makes them cringe.

"Have you noticed how few able-bodied men there are?" Gaius says. "Mostly we just see boys and old men, women, and children."

"The men have all gone to the borderlands, you slow-wit. Soon as they turn eighteen, they have to serve. Isn't that so, Alexos?"

Alexos is ashamed that he's never thought about this before. "Yes, Timon, I believe you're right."

"Then what about Peles? How old is he? It'd be a right bad job if we went all this way only to find out that he's gone."

"He was sixteen when he won the crown," Alexos says. "He'll be seventeen now."

"Gaw! That's close. When's his birthday?"

"I don't know, Titus! For heaven's sake! I'm a prince, not an oracle."

Finding Peles of Attaros, the improbable hero of the festival race, has become their primary goal. It's what Alexos had planned all along, though he'd suggested it to his classmates with some trepidation. He'd been afraid they'd think it a foolish thing to do. But Leander had jumped at the idea; and wherever Leander jumped, the others followed.

"Oh, yes!" he'd cried, clapping his hands with excitement. "We must do it, Alexos! I don't know how much you remember about the race, since you were more or less verging on death at the time, but he was quite the most amazing creature I've ever seen. Greasy and ugly as sin he might be, but *by the gods* he was a beautiful runner!"

"Yes, he was. I remember that much."

"Shall we bring him home with us? He could teach the master of arms a thing or two."

"Take care, Leander. He may be poor and humble, but he isn't our plaything. He's the champion of the festival race and—"

"Alexos! I never meant it like that."

"All the same, we must watch what we say and do. Be respectful."

"I wouldn't offend him for the world."

As they continue south, the roads begin to improve. The country folk here have bothered to pitch some stones into the mud. It's not handsomely done by any means, but it helps. Then gradually, mile after mile, the number of stones seems to increase and they've been more carefully placed. It occurs to Alexos that *this is a very good idea.* An enlightened ruler would build such roads all over his kingdom—bridges, too—making travel and the transport of goods much easier and more efficient.

The farther they go, the better the surface they ride upon. Now the rocks are large and flat, neatly arranged with very little space in between. Someone has even taken the trouble to wedge small stones into the gaps. There is real craftsmanship here, the kind you see in a well-built wall.

"What do you suppose?" Gaius asks.

"We're getting closer to the borderlands," Leander says. "The army must have built these roads."

"No," Alexos says.

"Who, then?"

"I think the people did—the stonework is different from village to village. And I think they were paid to do it."

"Paid?"

"The prize money—remember?"

"Merciful heavens! You think Peles is responsible for this?"

"I believe he had the vision and then he made it happen. It's just a guess. We'll see if I'm right."

"Gaw!"

16

ATTAROS IS MUCH LIKE every other village they've passed along the way. The mud-daub walls of the cottages have crumbled away in places, leaving fist-sized gaps where the wind and rain can pass through. The thatched roofs are sagging and black with mold. And while there are a fair number of hens roaming about and they've seen the occasional pig, there are hardly any sheep or goats. Certainly there are no oxen to pull the village plows.

Naturally, the sudden appearance of ten richly dressed boys, accompanied by officers of the Royal Guard, all of them mounted on horses, causes a sensation in the village. The people leave their work and run to the road and stare as the gentlemen pass by. They could not have looked more astonished if Zeus himself had arrived in a golden chariot, holding his thunderbolt aloft.

When they arrive at the home of Peles, a woman is waiting in the doorway. Someone must have run ahead to warn her they were coming. Her cottage, Alexos notes, is no larger or grander than her neighbors', but it's in much better repair. The roof has been newly thatched and the walls freshly plastered.

"If you've come for my son, you're too late," she says before anyone can speak.

"We have come to see Peles of Attaros," Alexos says, in case there is some mistake, "who was the champion of the festival race."

"I know. But I said you're too late. He's not here."

"I am Prince Alexos, son of King Ektor, and these are my companions."

"Yes," she says, as if it was obvious.

Alexos knows he ought to reproach her for her rudeness; he will seem weak if he does not. But he can't bring himself to do it. Either the woman is mad or she's so sick with grief she no longer cares what harm might come to her. So he keeps trying. "We've ridden many days to pay our respects to your son, so—"

"You're *too late*!"

"Is he dead, lady?"

"He may be, for all I know. If not, then he'll die soon enough. The king's men have taken him for the auxiliary. So if you wish to *pay your respects*, you will have to go to the borderlands."

"She's out of hand," Delius mutters. "She can't talk to you like that."

Timon grumbles in assent.

"Leave her be," Alexos says, keeping his voice very low. "I will handle it." Then he returns his attention to the mother of Peles, who is already stepping back into her cottage. Next thing, she's likely to shut the door in their faces.

"Madam," Alexos says, "I would speak with you in private." He tries for authority, but she's not impressed.

"Your horse will not fit through my door."

There are actual gasps now, not only from the boys but from the soldiers, too.

"No," Alexos says coolly. "Nor shall I ask him to. I shall get down and walk inside. I would be grateful for a chair to sit on, if you have one."

"I have a stool."

"That will do."

Leander and Titus dismount and get to work unbuckling the straps. This has become a familiar routine for them, performed many times a day. They unfasten the bands that bind his legs, then the ones that hold him in the saddle, and finally they ease him down—a sort of sliding and catching sequence—till he stands on solid ground. Still they support him while his brace is locked and his cane fetched.

As Suliman had warned, there's always a terrible stab of pain when Alexos tries to stand or walk after hours in the saddle. He has learned to conceal it, but there's no way he can hide how unsteady he is till he gets his land legs back. So he practically has to be carried into the cottage and settled on the promised stool.

"Will you sit also?" he asks the mother of Peles when the others have left and the door is shut. Wordlessly, she fetches a second stool for herself.

Alexos glances around the single well-swept, tidy room, with a cold fire pit in the middle and a faded laurel wreath hanging on the wall, and notes that there is only one pallet rolled up in the corner. Peles would have taken his with him, of course. The men of the auxiliary must provide their own gear: bedding, weapons, and whatever body protection they can devise. No wonder they die in droves.

"When did they take him?"

"Last month. He wasn't yet eighteen, but they said he was close enough."

"I shall tell my father."

Her smile is bitter. "And he will care?"

"He might. May I ask what your son had with him in the way of weaponry?"

"He made a spear. He has a knife."

"Well, the gods willing, he won't need them. For I shall, as you suggested, go to the borderlands to pay my respects. Then I will bring him home to you."

"No. You can't do that. He is already sworn to the king; to leave the army would be desertion. I'd rather he died honorably in battle than at the end of a noose. And even if that were not so, he'd be ashamed to come back when every other mother's son is down there fighting."

"Then I will have him transferred to the Royal Guard."

"Huh!" she says with a mirthless laugh. "Like those men out there, you mean? The ones with the shiny armor and the fancy helmets?"

"Yes."

"You don't know much, do you?"

"Apparently not."

"Peles is not like them. All he knows is farming."

"And running."

"Yes, running too."

"And patching roofs and plastering walls."

"He can do practical things. He knows how to work with his hands. But he's humble and unschooled, while they're all gentle born and educated fellows who've never touched a plow in their lives. He would be laughed out of your Royal Guard."

"You are correct that they are different. My men inherited their high station, and life has been easy for them, whereas your son is a champion who earned his greatness through merit. To my mind, that makes him infinitely more deserving."

"You're not proud—for a prince."

"I have a lot to be humble about."

"If I'd spoken to the soldiers who took my Peles the way I've talked to you this day, they'd have had my head in a moment."

"Then it's well you did not."

"And your father—is he proud?"

"He's a king, madam. He has spent his life fighting for Arcos and has many scars to show for it. He has every reason to be proud."

She looks pointedly at his legs. "They say you were chosen by Athene to rid us of our misery."

"Do they?"

"Yes. It is widely believed. I wonder, though."

Now it's his turn to laugh. "So do I, madam. So do I."

"I didn't think you'd answer straight."

"And you were correct. He's your only son, then—Peles?"

"Yes."

"And your husband?"

"Dead."

"That's very cruel."

"It's very common." She softens a bit. "I admire you for coming here, Prince Alexos—to see how we suffer. And if you are indeed what people say, then I beg you to have your conference with the gods sooner rather than later. Else there will be nothing left of Arcos to save."

"That rests in the hands of Athene. But I promise to rescue your son if he still lives. Then I'll set him some useful tasks that will make a difference in the lives of the people—as he already has with the roads."

"Who told you?"

"You just did. I only guessed and you confirmed it. Have you a message for me to give your son when I see him?"

She loses her composure. Blinking back tears, she stammers, "Say . . . say he is the best boy that ever was. And . . . I am proud of him."

Alexos feels tears rising in his eyes, too. "I will, madam. I will say it exactly as you did just now, for those are the words every son longs to hear, and Peles well deserves them."

He rises from the stool now. She marvels at his maneuvers with the brace and the cane. When he gestures with his free hand that he needs her support for a moment, she rushes to hold him steady till he has his balance.

"Riding a horse takes its toll," he says, "my legs being as they are."

"Does it hurt?"

"Of course it does."

"Oh."

She opens the door. Titus and Leander are waiting to hoist him back up into the saddle. But before they can get started, the mother of Peles calls him back.

"Prince Alexos," she says. "One more word?"

He hobbles back to the doorway. Now that Alexos is standing, not sitting face-to-face with her on little stools, he is struck by how small she is—small, help-less, poor, and alone, yet incredibly ferocious and brave. He senses there is something important to know about this, something he ought to remember in the future, about the people he will someday rule, and about the smallness of mortals in the eyes of the gods. He isn't sure he has it all, or understands it properly, but it kneads at his heart.

"What is it?" he says.

"I just wanted to say"—she is whispering now; her words are only for Alexos and she doesn't want the others to hear—"that you *also* have reason to be proud, same as your father. You are a good boy and I know you'll make a fine king one day."

"Thank you, lady," he says. "I hope you are right. But for now, at the very least, I will find your son."

They are well away, riding in silence, before Leander finally speaks. "That was inappropriate, you know, the way she behaved. Your father would never tolerate such rudeness and familiarity."

"No. I hate to think what he would have done."

"Yet you didn't even raise your voice. Was that wise?"

Alexos swings his head around, suddenly angry. "Don't presume to tell me how to be a prince," he snaps. "You have no idea."

Leander is stunned. Alexos has never pulled rank on him like that before. And it's all the more wounding to Leander because that peasant woman had been allowed to say any old thing she liked, whereas *he* was brought up short for merely asking if that was wise.

Suddenly, on the impulse of a moment, Leander makes a face. It's one he perfected in his younger days, when the boys used to mock Alexos, usually as soon as he had left the room. They'd all done it, but Leander's imitation was by far the best: chin up, lips slightly parted, lids drooping lazily, brows raised.

Leander knows in an instant that he's made a terrible mistake. It was childish and cruel, making that face. Worse, it wasn't even a good likeness. Alexos isn't *proud*; he doesn't *look down his nose*. He is just deeply, painfully private.

"That woman back there," Alexos says, drilling Leander with his eyes, "has lost what little she ever had. She is desperate, sad, and alone. She knows nothing of kings and princes except what they take from her. Why should I be cruel to her?"

"I'm so sorry, Alexos."

"And she is perhaps the first truly honest person I have ever met."

They don't say anything more; they just ride together, staring straight ahead. Both of them are thinking hard about what was said and done, feeling heartsick about it. But it's Leander who finally breaks the silence.

"That was extraordinary, what you said: the first truly honest person."

"Was it?"

"Yes. Did you mean that she was honest because she was rude, even to you?"

"Don't make it complicated, Leander. She showed her true feelings and said exactly what was in her heart. No one ever does that, especially people like her when speaking to someone like me. It was a terrible risk. But it was also a gift. I learned a lot from our little exchange, things that will help me be a better king. Had she bowed and scraped and treated me like some descending god, I would have learned nothing at all."

Leander is mulling this over when Alexos turns and gives him a probing look. "And that impression you did of me back there, I learned a lot from that, too."

"Oh, gods, Alexos. I was just really hurt and angry."

"I know that. But you've done it before, I would guess many times—behind my back, to entertain the others. You might have waited, you know, till I had time to be well away, so I couldn't hear the laughter."

"Oh, Alexos, I'm so sorry. That was a long time ago. We were cruel, stupid little boys."

"Yes, and I shouldn't have mentioned it. I know you're not like that anymore." He looks down at his hands holding the reins. He's making a decision. Then his eyes rise to meet Leander's with an almost beseeching look.

"The mother of Peles has inspired me to be honest, too. So forgive me, Leander, if this sounds strange. I value our friendship very much—not because you are the greatest star in the firmament, which you are, always the best of the best, the prize, the one everyone adores, but because you are kind to me. You make me laugh and are at ease in my company. You treat me like a *person*, Leander. So I'm sorry I spoke as I did. I don't like the way it sounded. And it would break my heart if I were ever to lose you as a friend."

"Gods, Alexos!" Leander laughs out loud, his face alight with pleasure. "You can certainly rest easy on that account! I would follow you into a gorgon's den. You have only to ask."

"I shall tell my father that," he says with a wicked grin.

"Your *father*? Why?"

"His men worship him, you see. They would walk on burning coals for him. He assures me this is true."

"Oh?"

"Yes. But he feels I fall rather short in that department—inspiring devotion, having friends, being liked, that sort of thing. So it struck me when you said that, how close it was to my father's words, and it made me smile. I much prefer the gorgon's den to the burning coals, by the way."

"Oh, I agree, if I do say so myself."

"A far richer metaphor. I can just see you running into the cave, wildly slashing the air with your sword while covering your eyes with the other hand, lest the sight of the gorgon's hideous face and snakelike hair strike you instantly blind."

"I think it's turned to stone, not blinded. But listen, Alexos. While we're speaking our hearts like the mother of Peles, I have a confession to make. I overheard what she said to you as we were about to leave. I wasn't trying to listen in, I promise."

"That's all right."

"Well, I bring it up now because, while it was nice what she said, and it was close to the mark, she didn't do you half credit. You are not a good boy, Alexos; you are an astonishing human being. And you will make a *remarkable* king one day."

17

THEY'VE BEEN RIDING SINCE daybreak through a treeless landscape, monotonous and empty. Now, at midafternoon, there isn't a cloud in the sky. The boys are wearing wide-brimmed hats against the punishing sun, but nothing can really protect them. It beats relentlessly down on their backs and arms; the hard-packed clay reflects its rays up into their faces. The road shimmers dizzily in the terrible heat. It's like being inside an oven. The horses are near their limit and the boys are exhausted. Their one universal thought is, *How much farther?*

So they are beyond grateful when Nestor, the captain of the prince's guard, halts on the crest of a ridge. "Behold the famous borderlands," he says. "Gentlemen, come have a look."

They ride forward and gaze eagerly down at the encampment below. Titus speaks for all of them when he says, "Huh?"

"Not what you expected?" Nestor says with a grin.

"No," Alexos says. "I thought it would just be a lot of tents."

"Really, my lord? Why?"

"Because that's how an army camp is always described, at least in the stories of the ancient wars. Tents and huts, unless there's a ship nearby to sleep on."

"True, my lord. But remember, our war is very different from theirs. Tents are useful when you're on the move, advancing or retreating. But our border hasn't changed since the Punishment began. So doesn't it seem natural and wise to build a permanent headquarters with everything an army needs?"

"It does indeed, Nestor. It makes perfect sense."

But it's more than a little disappointing. The elements of hardship and danger were essential parts of his boyish fantasies about life on the borderlands. He'd pictured his father in his tent at night, lying on a camp cot wrapped only in his cloak, shivering with cold while the winter blasts shook the fragile canvas walls.

There were many variations on this same theme,

involving blood and wounds, sleeplessness and dirt, cold food, and every other form of harsh discomfort that his adolescent brain could devise. And the self-less life of misery his father supposedly endured had always made it easier to forgive Ektor's taunts and jibes, his coldness, and his cruelty. Now Alexos almost wants to laugh.

"We do have some tents, however," Nestor is saying, "as you can plainly see. The auxiliary sleeps under canvas. They don't mind. They're not used to comfort anyway."

Alexos thinks they probably *do* mind, especially on stormy nights in winter. But he doesn't say this to Nestor. He just adds it to his growing list of things he hopes to change when he becomes king.

"Look!" Leander says excitedly, pointing in the distance.

"What?"

"The defenses! Remember?" And he starts quoting the passage they'd all had to learn in school, the famous command of Olympian Zeus: *"Thy ramparts shall be of earth and wood, but never of stone."*

The others join in and they recite the rest in unison. *"Nor mayest thou shield thy sight from the face of thine enemy; for it is meet that thou shouldst see the hatred in their red-rimmed eyes by day, and the flames of their torches by night, these thy sworn enemies, whom once thou loved as brothers."*

But memorizing those lines in class has not prepared them for the actual defenses, which are almost comical: flimsy wooden barricades running along both sides of a patchy strip of trampled grass where the battles presumably take place. The posts are set well apart from one another, leaving an opening wide enough for the soldiers to gaze upon the famous red-rimmed eyes of their enemy, wide enough even for a slender man to squeeze through and walk over into the enemy camp. Just inside these pitiful blockades are two facing ditches set with angled pikes. The whole thing looks positively ancient, like something from a thousand years ago—long before Troy, before civilization even. And it is all the more ridiculous when set beside the sprawling, modern military town it is supposedly there to protect.

"That was most impressive, gentlemen," Nestor says with a smile. "I see you have been well taught. Now, unless you have any other questions, I propose we ride on down there and get out of this unspeakable heat."

Everyone in the stable yard looks up as they ride in— the grooms and the blacksmiths shoeing horses, the fellow with the handcart taking horse droppings out to the dung pile, the three others pitching hay from a wagon, the half-dozen soldiers waiting for their horses to be brought out, and a few men who are leaning on the fence because they apparently have nothing better to do. They watch with something akin to horror as Alexos is unstrapped from his saddle and hauled down from his horse. They continue to stare as he stands, supported by Titus, while his brace is set and his cane fetched and put into his hand.

They think they're being subtle, but they're not. Leander, annoyed, picks out the worst offender and goes on the attack.

"You!" he shouts at a ginger-haired lad with a face covered with freckles. "Carrot-head!"

The boy recoils. "Sire?" he says.

"Keep your eyes to yourself."

"I will, sire."

"Good. Now go get us some water. And when you've done that, I want you to clean my friend's boots." The boy disappears, and all over the stable yard, the staring stops and men go back to their business.

"Thank you," Alexos says, dropping onto a bench with a groan of relief, grateful for an excuse to sit down and rest before walking across the compound to see his father.

"Bunch of oafs," Leander grumbles.

"You were pretty hard on that boy, you know. Everyone was staring; he wasn't the only one."

"Yes, but he was the worst. And I understand that you don't want people bowing and scraping and all that—but his *jaw* was actually hanging open"—Leander demonstrates—"like he'd just seen a two-headed pig!"

"Well, I do put on quite a show. Ah, Nestor—what news?"

Nestor squats in front of Alexos, his elbows on his knees, so the prince won't have to rise or look up at him as they speak.

"We've been given a guest room in the officers' compound. They'll bring in cots. I'm told the room is rather small for so many. It'll be crowded."

"That's all right. It's only for one night."

"That's what I told them. There's still some question as to where you'll be housed, however."

"I'll stay with everyone else."

"I'm afraid that's up to the king."

Alexos shuts his eyes and sighs quietly. "I see. Thank you, Nestor."

"I'll have the baggage sent over. Shall we stay while your boots are cleaned?" They exchange a knowing smile. Nestor has not been fooled by Leander's little ruse.

"No. The rest of you can go ahead."

"Very well, my lord. I'll leave Pitheus behind to accompany you."

Alexos nods, though it seems ridiculous that he should need personal protection when he's surrounded by his father's army. Still, rules are rules. At least Pitheus knows to shadow him from behind, and to do it subtly.

Carrot-head is back now, quite impressively managing to carry a heavy pail of water, a net bag filled with wooden cups, and the rag and polish he'll need to clean Alexos' special riding boots. After serving out the water none of the boys really wants—they all carry waterskins when they travel, so they aren't particularly thirsty—Carrot-head kneels at the prince's feet and goes to work with a will.

"I never thought I'd actually get to meet the famous prince Alexos," he says with an ingratiating smile, apparently hoping to make up with flattery what he's lost through rudeness.

"Famous?" Alexos says. "For my beautiful hand at the lute, you mean? Or is it my prowess for mathematics that goes before me?"

Blood rushes to the boy's face. Leander comes in for the kill.

"Just to be clear, Carrot-head: you *still* have not

'met' the aforementioned famous prince. You are cleaning his boots. They are not the same thing."

"No, my lord. Of course, you are right. It's just that we are all so delighted and honored to have the prince here, that in my excitement I was presumptuous." Then, having apologized, he is more presumptuous still. "May I humbly ask, Your Majesty, if you will grace our presence for long?"

"Oh, for heaven's sake," Leander snaps, quite beside himself now. "What's wrong with you? No, you *humbly* may not! It's none of your business!"

"I am terribly sorry, my lord. I only asked because we are looking after your horses, and we'll need to arrange things according to your plans. If you're off again this afternoon, we'll just wipe them down and feed and water them, but not—"

"We leave tomorrow, early," Alexos says, tired of this conversation.

"Very good, Your Grace. We'll have them all bridled and ready to go first thing in the morning."

"You do that," Leander says. "And if you say another word I may have to cut out your tongue."

The groom ducks his head and doesn't speak again, just attends to his work. And he does a good job of it, too. By the time Alexos' boots are gleaming and the groom has slunk away, he has his strength back, more or less.

"Well, I'm off," he says without much enthusiasm.

"Shall I come with you?"

"No, I have Pitheus. And to be honest, I need some time alone to prepare myself."

"I understand."

"But I'd like you to stay with me tonight—wherever my father decides to put me."

"Of course."

"I'll send for you when it's over."

Leander nods agreement and gives Alexos a sympathetic smile. "At least you're all buffed and shiny for your conference with the king."

"Oh, I assure you, Leander, my father will not notice my boots."

18

EKTOR IS STANDING WHEN Alexos comes in—always a dangerous sign. The way he leans forward, his large hands gripping the corners of his worktable, he looks like a wild beast ready to pounce.

"What in the name of Zeus are you doing here?" he says. His voice is so abrasive it would have felt like an assault even without the stinging words. And for a moment Alexos is powerless to speak. Then suddenly rage is rising in his belly.

"Why, thank you, Father," he says. "I'm delighted to see *you* as well. And how nice to find you so pleasantly housed, even here on the borderlands—every comfort, stylish decorations, my goodness!" He looks pointedly at the fresco on the wall opposite the entry door, his head cocked with feigned amazement. "And what exactly *are* those frolicsome maidens meant to be—*wood nymphs*?"

Ektor is stunned. This sort of thing has never happened before. "I have no idea," he says, almost defensive. "That's been there since my great-grandfather's time. It's nothing to do with me."

"Charming, though—all that ivory skin, soft eyes, flowing hair . . ."

"Alexos!"

"And the whole day off from fighting to enjoy it all. How very nice for you."

There is a long, cold silence while the king recovers from this unthinkable exchange. "Well, if you've come to see blood, my boy, then you ought to have been here yesterday. *By the gods*, I should have had you strangled at birth! Now sit down and tell me why you're here."

"No need. I won't be long."

"I said *sit*!"

Chastened and more or less returned to sanity, Alexos pulls up a chair. His father sits too, folding his hands on the table and waiting with exaggerated impatience while Alexos does his thing with the brace and leans his cane against the table.

"By ancient tradition," Ektor says in his lecturing voice, "just as we declare a truce every night, we don't fight on the feast days of the gods. Today, as it happens, is dedicated to Hephaestus, which now that I think of it is rather fitting—that you should arrive on *his* particular day." This is a jibe and a cruel one. Ektor delivers it with a smile.

"Because Hephaestus is a cripple, you mean? Like me?"

"Indeed. And yet he is also immensely powerful."

Alexos can't think of a response. Nor does he know what his father intended by that business about Hephaestus, except obviously to wound him. He speeds on to his business, the sooner to be gone.

"I've come with a simple request," he begins. "And as I believe it's the only favor I've ever asked of you, I hope you'll do me the kindness of granting it."

"I'll decide when I know what the favor is."

"All right. I want one of your men transferred to the Royal Guard on special assignment to me. I assure you, Father, you won't miss him."

"I'll be the judge of that. Who is it?"

"One of the warm bodies in your pitchfork brigade."

"The *auxiliary*?"

"Yes. Though I'm told this particular warm body has both a homemade lance and a knife. I don't suppose that makes a difference."

"Alexos, I can't transfer a *peasant* to the Royal Guard!"

"I would think, as king of Arcos, you could do anything you like. And since I ask you as a personal favor, the only one I have ever—"

"Oh, you are so tedious!"

"Just transfer the man and I'll go. He's nothing at all to you."

"Does he have a name, this peasant with a lance?"

"He does. Peles of Attaros."

The king gapes. "That fellow? The runner?"

"Yes."

"He's in my auxiliary?"

"He is, though he's not yet eighteen. Apparently your recruiters dismissed that as a technicality. He'll be eighteen eventually—if he lives that long."

"Bloody hell!"

"My thoughts exactly. And seeing as he was the champion of the festival races, you might make an exception in his case—bend the rules, give him some sort of promotion."

"Ha!" The king is half amused, half amazed. "Peles of Attaros, in my auxiliary!"

"If you'll just write out the order, I'll see to the rest. I know you're a busy man."

The king takes a tablet and stylus and hastily begins to write.

"What will you do with him when you get him home?"

"I want him to help me with my running style."

Ektor stares at his son, appalled.

"That was a joke, Father."

"It wasn't funny."

"No, I suppose not."

"That should do it," Ektor says, handing the finished order to Alexos. "Give this to one of the officers downstairs; they'll send someone to find your man. Do you suppose he knows how to ride?"

"I doubt he's had the chance to learn. But he's a natural athlete. He'll pick it up quickly."

"I expect so. Gods, what a beautiful runner he was!"

"Yes. I remember. Thank you, Father." Alexos rises, eager to go.

"I hope you don't plan to leave this afternoon. The nearest shelter is six hours away."

"We'll go first thing in the morning."

"Good. There's a room for guests just down the hall. I'll have it set up for you."

"That's all right. I can stay with my men."

"Your *men*?"

"My companions, my friends."

"Your *friends*?"

"Yes, I have friends now. Isn't that a wonder?"

Things had been going so well, with that easy talk

about Peles the beautiful runner, and now his unaccountable temper has popped up again and ruined everything.

"Are they the ones who taught you to be so rude and disrespectful?"

"No, I'm afraid I learned that all by myself."

"I wouldn't be proud of it."

"I'm not." Alexos feels sick; he desperately wants to leave, but apparently his father isn't finished with him yet.

"As it happens, Alexos, you cannot refuse the king's invitation." He states this as if it were a matter of law. Maybe it is. "You may ask one of your friends to join you if you like, in addition to your personal guard, of course. The accommodations will suffice."

"Thank you, Father. I'll bring Leander."

"Excellent choice. I've had my eye on that boy for a while. A little high-spirited, but he'll settle down. He's by far the best of your class, I think."

Another jibe. Alexos consciously ignores it.

"And I would like Peles to stay with me, too. He'll be a bit confused by his sudden change of fortune. There are things I'll need to explain before we leave in the morning. And if he is to serve me, we might as well start right away."

"That's reasonable. Anything else?"

"No. Thank you, Father. I've been insufferably rude."

"Yes, you have."

"I don't know what came over me."

To his surprise, Ektor leans back in his chair and laughs.

"I do," he says. "You're finally growing up, learning to stand on your own two feet—if you'll pardon the allusion—and speak your mind. And I must say, Alexos, *it's really about time!*"

19

PELES IS WAITING IN the guest room when Alexos returns from supper. He's standing, stiff and straight, like a sentry on duty. Apparently he thought it improper to sit in the bedchamber of a prince. And his hands are clasped behind his back, as if to say that though he's been here alone for a good long while, he hasn't touched anything at all.

Now, seeing Alexos, he sinks to one knee, hand on heart, head bowed. "Your Highness," he says.

"Welcome, Peles," Alexos replies. "You remember Leander?"

"I do, Your Highness." Peles, still kneeling, bows to Leander.

"And these three gentlemen constitute my personal guard: Nestor, Pitheus, and Silanos. Gentlemen, this is Peles, champion of the festival race."

More bowing. Subtle glances exchanged among the guards.

"Now, Peles, please sit and we will talk."

But Peles doesn't sit. He is still kneeling. "I wish to thank you for your kindness, Your Highness," he says. "It is quite beyond imagining."

"You are welcome, Peles. It was my pleasure to help you. Now, since we are making a beginning and will be together much of the time from now on, I would like to make a couple of requests."

"Of course, Your Highness."

"First, please get up. And once you've done that, please sit down. Take that stool over there. It's perfectly proper, I assure you."

When Peles is reluctantly seated, perched on the very edge of the seat, as if not wanting to take too much of it, Alexos continues. "Second, if you wouldn't mind terribly, you can dispense with the Your Highnesses— except on public occasions, of course. Do as Leander does. Follow his lead."

"Please excuse me, my prince, but what is appropriate for a great nobleman's son would surely not apply to the likes of me."

"The *likes of you*?" Leander says, all cheerful amazement. "The champion of the festival race, you mean? Come now, Peles! I'll grant that you are greatly my inferior in birth. But we ran a fair race, did we not? I did my very best, yet you were the winner. So why don't we just say that the two balance each other out?"

Peles is unable to say anything to this. He looks terrified and confused.

"Excellent," Alexos says, moving on. "Now I have asked that you be assigned to my particular service. I will need you to assist me in personal ways, just as my friends do. I will also want your advice and guidance on certain matters."

"You want advice from *me*?"

"Yes. You know far more about the land and the people of Arcos than I do—more than any of us, really. You've seen for yourself how we live at court. Well, that has been more or less our sole experience of the world. Our travel through the countryside has been quite a revelation, but it's only a beginning. We saw what you did with the roads in your region and were very impressed. I imagine you have other ideas about ways we could make the kingdom work more efficiently for the betterment of all."

Peles' jaw hangs open and he's blinking wildly. "Well, yes," he stammers. "I will gladly tell you what I know . . . would you mind if I called you 'my lord'?"

"Only once out of every—let's say, ten sentences. How would that be?"

"I'm sorry. I don't know what a sentence is, my lord."

"Well, you just spoke one. And then I spoke one. This is another. When you say something and it comes to an end, that's a sentence."

"I understand, Your Majesty. I will try to count them."

"Please don't, Peles. Just treat me like a normal person most of the time. How would that be? It's what I would prefer."

"Yes, my— Yes."

"Good. Now before I forget, we met your mother while we were in Attaros. She told us you were here. She asked me to tell you that you are the best boy that ever was and that she is proud of you."

There is a long silence. Then, "She is a fond mother."

"So she is. You're lucky to have her."

"I am, sire." He purses his lips, as if there was something more he'd like to say, but isn't sure whether it would be proper. Alexos raises his brows and holds out a hand, inviting him to speak.

"I just wanted to tell you, my lord, how very sorry I am about what happened at the race. I saw how flushed you were, feverish-like, and I noticed that your legs were trembling. I knew there was something amiss, that you were probably very sick. I ought to have stopped and helped you instead of finishing the race. It has gnawed at my conscience ever since, especially after I heard that it was the summer sickness you had. My brother died of it, you see, and so I knew what a terrible illness it is. That you kept on running and finished the race is past imagining."

"Well, your conscience may be clear. Nothing you could have done would have made the slightest difference. Even my physician, who is quite the best in the world, could not cure me, only help me to recover. Whereas your winning the race—no offense, Leander—was the only good thing to come out of that very bad day. And, Peles, I'm sorry about your brother. I didn't know. Your mother said you were her only son."

"I am now, my lord."

"A terrible loss." Alexos cringes at his own trite, inadequate words.

"It was. He was the sweetest boy. But then, you lost a brother, too, so you will understand."

Alexos sucks in breath and turns his head away. Peles sees immediately that he's made a mistake. Leander quickly changes the subject. "You'll be glad to hear," he says to Peles, "that we'll be passing through Attaros on our return to the capital. We thought we might break our journey there if the village folk will put us up."

"Of course they will," Peles says, impressed by the subtlety and tact with which Leander had given Alexos time to compose himself. It's not the sort of thing he's come to expect from highborn folk, who are generally impatient and rude.

"Well, it's decided then," Leander says. "I don't suppose you've ever ridden a horse before?"

"No, my lord. We have no horses at all."

"Not even one to pull a plow?"

"We had an ox till recently. Two are better, but we just had the one. He was shared by everyone in the village. Then he died and we have not been able to replace him. I had planned to save up my wages and send them home to Mother so she could buy a new one."

"Well," Alexos says, "with your new promotion, your wages will be substantially higher than they are at present. I'll give you an advance on your earnings so you can give it to your mother when we pass through Attaros. How much to buy an ox?"

"Three silver *stater*, I would guess. But that is a vast amount, my—"

"It will not be a problem, I assure you."

"You are most astonishingly kind."

"It's your money; you will earn it through honest work. And it seems so much more practical to do it now, so the villagers can get the ox in time to do some planting before it's too late in the season."

"Yes, Your Majesty, that is true."

"Good. Now, we leave tomorrow, first thing. If there are any belongings you want to fetch, you'd best run get them now."

"I have nothing, sire, except my pallet and a knife. I gave my lance to a friend in the auxiliary. I hope that was all right. I thought it a shabby thing to carry in such fine company. And my friend had nothing at all."

"You did right, Peles. He needs it and you do not. The king's guard will provide you with a proper sword and lance and teach you how to use them, though I doubt you'll ever need to. I have trained swordsmen already. *You* I want for your good mind and excellent heart."

Peles purses his lips again, his brow furrowed.

"What is it?" Alexos asks.

"It's nothing, my lord. It's just that I am overcome, you see. For I never expected to meet with such goodness in the world—certainly not among the highest of the high. And when you said, just now, that I had an excellent heart, it near brought tears to my eyes. For you have one of your own, my prince, and I wondered if perhaps you didn't quite know that about yourself, being so earnestly set upon doing everything perfectly and setting your goals so high."

Alexos and Leander both gape at him, open-mouthed.

"By the gods, Alexos," Leander says when he is

finally able to speak, "how have we managed without this fellow all this time?"

Alexos lies on his cot, eyes open in the darkness, listening to the soft, even breaths of four sleeping souls in a single room, with the occasional cough, snuffle, snort, or rustle as one of them turns over. Outside the door, Pitheus keeps watch.

Whatever night sounds there are on the borderlands, Alexos can't hear them. The king's headquarters building is not in the traditional style: wrapped around a courtyard with the doors and windows opening onto an inner garden. It's more like a very large, two-story box. And though there are air vents high on the walls, the room has no windows at all, only a single door. Alexos assumes this is for security.

The principal rooms for living and sleeping, including the king's apartments and the guest room where Alexos now lies, are all upstairs. The offices are below, where the business of war is conducted. It's an efficient design, he supposes, but it would be wearing after a while, living in a windowless box. He wonders if, when his time comes, he might not prefer to sleep in a tent. It would be cold in the winter, but at least he could hear the wind.

He sets all this aside, closes his eyes, and

consciously clears his mind, sweeping away the day's accumulation of random thoughts. It's like the ritual washing before a visit to the temple. This is how Alexos prepares himself to think of Teo.

He begins as he always does, with his brother's face. He recalls every detail—the large eyes and dark lashes, the round cheeks, the sweet chin, the odd little nose. He remembers the varied expressions it wore: excitement, boredom, joy, disappointment, drowsiness. Teo never hid his feelings, as Alexos always has. He was a trusting child. But then, why shouldn't he have been? He'd been loved and petted all his life. Until the end.

But Alexos is getting off track. This is supposed to be about Teo, not about him.

He thinks of Teo's voice, high-pitched and sometimes grating. The smallness of his hands. The soft perfection of his skin. He remembers the foods his brother liked best, the games he liked to play, the stories he asked to hear over and over.

When Alexos has finished his litany of Teo in life, he turns to Teo in death. And, *oh, gods*, how this hurts him every time! But he must do it, and he always feels better for it, having emptied out all that bitter pain, the guilt along with the sorrow.

I loved you, Teo, he whispers in his mind. *I loved you*

more than you ever knew. I love you still, just as much. If I could give you my life and take your death, I would do it without hesitation. But I can't. Nor can I go back and undo the terrible thing I did. I can only say I'm sorry. And though it isn't enough—nothing could ever be enough—it's all I have. So, I'm sorry, Teo. I'm sorry. I'm so very sorry!

Alexos knows his brother lives a blessed life in the Underworld. Athene takes him there in his dreams to show him how happy Teo is. It's a great consolation, those dreams, but they never last. Always, Alexos has to leave. Not even in death will he be permitted to stay with his brother. For when that time comes, Lord Hades will send him someplace else.

Enough! He's ready now. He thanks Athene, a long and heartfelt prayer, putting himself as ever in her hands. Then he is done. His muscles begin to relax; his breathing grows easy and regular. He listens to the hypnotic sound of it: *in, out, in, out, in, out.* At last he slides over the edge of wakefulness and into the darkness of sleep and the dream that follows.

Hand in hand, Teo and Aria walk through a pristine woodland. Watching them, Alexos remembers how sad he'd been to think that his brother had never seen a forest that wasn't brown and dying. Well, now he has. The trees here are green-beyond-green, lush, healthy, and glistening with dew.

The children are approaching a clearing. Aria stops and, with the second finger of her free hand, touches her lips: *we must be quiet now.* Then she points to her feet and shows Teo how to walk without making noise: toes first, then heels. He follows her example in an exaggerated fashion. She bites her lips to keep from grinning, but her eyes are alive with merriment. He can see how much she loves him. Alexos loves her for it.

Teo has grown since the last dream. This comes as a surprise. Alexos has always assumed that once a spirit crossed into Lord Hades' realm, it would stay exactly as it was. But clearly that is not true. Teo's tunic—the same one he was wearing on that terrible day—must have become too small for him. Someone has taken it apart and added panels of a different fabric at the shoulders, sides, and hem. Who was it, he wonders—the father? Aria?

They have tiptoed into the clearing now. Aria guides Teo to a log, where they sit and wait. Like everything else in this enchanted place, the log is clean and beautiful. It doesn't look like the remains of a tree that has died, fallen, and broken apart. It looks like something the gods made for them to sit upon.

It strikes Alexos for the first time that Aria isn't just a feature of the world beyond the River. She, too, is dead. He wonders how she died, how old she was when it happened. Is the man her real father? Did they die together? He doesn't suppose he'll ever know the answer, but he's glad they have each other.

Aria is pointing now. Teo looks up at her but she gestures with her hand: *don't look at me; look there!*

And into the clearing the creature comes: sniffing the grass with its long, delicate snout, its fur russet with white at the breast, its tail a soft, silky brush. Teo has never seen a fox before. Now his mouth forms an O of amazement. Aria's face is aglow with pride, seeing his delight as the fox comes closer and closer till it reaches the very center of the clearing. Then it sits, its tail wrapped neatly around its dainty feet, and looks directly at them.

Slowly Aria rises.

From far away, Alexos hears screams and shouts, the pounding of feet. That's odd! There are no other souls in this part of the Underworld, only the three of them. . . .

He's awake and sitting up when the door swings open. Pitheus leans in. "Rise and make ready!" he says. "We're under attack."

20

NESTOR AND SILANOS ARE up and frantically dressing. They had not even slept in their tunics, trusting in
the king's army and the nightly truce to guarantee the
prince's safety. Now there's no time to put on breast-
plates and greaves. Swords, shields, and helmets will
have to do. Silanos dashes outside to stand guard with
Pitheus while Nestor stays to manage the boys.

As it happens, they are managing perfectly well on
their own. Peles has already lit the lamp and Leander is
hurriedly wrapping the prince's leg with the protective
bands that go under the brace. It's a complicated business, usually done with meticulous care. But there's no
time for that either. The task is made harder by Alexos
himself, who is pulling his tunic over his head, strap-
ping on his sword belt, and generally not staying still.

Peles fetches the brace and waits till Leander is finished. Then Leander, Peles, and Alexos work together, fastening the leather straps that hold it on.

Pitheus opens the door again. "I just got word they've set fire to the barracks."

"That's a diversion," Nestor says. "Their real business is here."

"I understand," Pitheus says. "They're not in the building yet, but it won't be long. There's heavy fighting in the street by the main door."

Nestor quickly assesses the situation. Peles and Leander have finished with the brace. But all three of them are barefoot and Leander's weapon is on the floor beside his cot.

"You two, put your sandals on; I'll help the prince. Leander, get your sword. Do it now." He kneels at Alexos' feet, slips on his boots, and hastily ties the laces.

"What about my father?"

"He has his own men to protect him. You are our only concern—and I'm sorry but we really have to hurry!"

Pitheus comes in. "Now!" he says urgently.

From below they hear the tearing of wood as the raiders break down the door, then shouts as men scramble through the breach and into the building, rapid footsteps on the stairs.

Roughly, Peles takes Alexos under the arms and Leander grabs his legs. Then they haul him out the door like a piece of furniture. There's no time to stop and rearrange themselves to carry him more efficiently. They just run as they are— stumbling and bumping against the walls, with Nestor in the lead, Pitheus and Silanos protecting the rear—through the darkness to the far end of the corridor.

"Where are we going?" Alexos shouts.

"Out the side door," Nestor says. He says it in a hoarse whisper, a warning to Alexos to keep his voice down. They don't want to call attention to themselves.

At the end of the corridor, they turn to the left and head down a flight of stairs. There are no torches in the sconces here, no lamps; they have to feel their way in the darkness, step by step. Alexos is tilted at an angle now, his head higher than his feet. This is more comfortable for him but it's harder for Leander, who now has to bear most of his weight.

They stop when they reach the landing. Nestor had been sure there'd be a door here, matching the one on the east wing of the building. But there is none, just another flight of stairs leading down to a basement storeroom. Nestor curses. "Keep going," he says.

Halfway down, Leander loses his footing and Peles

is pulled off balance. They hit the stairs hard, a shocking blow, followed by a bruising slide over sharp-edged stone. For a moment they just lie there, sprawled and gasping.

"Alexos?" Leander whispers. "Are you hurt?"

"No."

"Dead?"

"No."

It's amazing how Leander always finds the perfect thing to say—often, as on this occasion, the very opposite of what would seem appropriate.

"Good," Peles says, catching the spirit, "so now, if my lord Leander will please pick up the prince's legs, perhaps we can find a less painful way to carry him down the stairs."

The storeroom is large and cool and the darkest place of all. Alexos doesn't like it. If the building is set ablaze, as it almost certainly will be, the whole structure will collapse on top of them, and the thought of being buried in an avalanche of burning timbers makes him want to scream. They have to get out of this death trap—*now!* If they run into raiders, so be it. Better to fight their way out. Better to die by the sword, if it comes to that.

"We have to go back," Alexos says. "This was a

mistake." He doesn't even try to hide the panic in his voice.

"No, my lord," Nestor says, "I think we'll be all right. It's a storeroom, so it must have a door. It'll be on the north wall, opening onto the alley in back. Since we're below grade, I expect there'll be a ramp. I'm sure I can find it."

"But won't it be locked?"

"Probably bolted from the inside."

"I hope you're right."

"Yes, my lord. So do I."

They wait while Nestor feels his way along the north wall. They hear the soft scuffing of his sandals in the darkness, the thump or clang as he knocks against amphorae filled with olives or wine, barrels of salted fish, boxes of linens.

Upstairs, the chaos continues; but here in the basement the sounds of fighting are muffled by layers of wood and stone, reduced to background noise, like the wind on a stormy night. Alexos sets that aside and listens instead to the sounds of the room—Nestor searching, the others shifting nervously, their quiet breathing. And beyond that, faint but unmistakable, footsteps on the stairs.

"Shhh," he hisses in warning, and for a moment they all freeze. Then Nestor continues his search, but more quietly now, while Leander and the other guards creep toward the stairway door, their swords out and ready.

And suddenly Alexos understands what this is all about, why the raiders are here on this particular night when they've never broken the truce before. This is no ordinary attack. It's a limited strike with a specific target, planned at the last minute when, quite unexpectedly, *Alexos arrived*.

How King Pyratos came to hear of it is anybody's guess. Maybe the odious Carrot-head was actually a spy ("May I humbly ask, Your Majesty, if you will grace our presence for long?"). Or maybe the Ferran sentries simply saw the boys ride in. It wouldn't be that hard; all they had to do was peer through the pitiful barricades that divide the two armies.

But however he found out, Pyratos wouldn't hesitate to break a sacred truce if he saw an advantage in it. And the chance to kill both father and son with a single blow, thus putting an end to the royal line of Arcos, was an opportunity not to be missed.

Upstairs, the battle to kill the king continues: shouts and screams, heavy thumps as bodies are slammed against walls, the metallic ring of sword on sword, the crashing as chests and tables are overturned. But Ektor is only half the prize. The other half is sitting on a storeroom floor, feeling particularly helpless and exposed, while outside on the landing, men with swords wait in silence, hoping they haven't given themselves away, getting ready to spring out and catch them unawares.

No one moves. Though Alexos can't see them in the gloom, he knows that Pitheus, Silanos, and Leander are somewhere near the door, frozen in a defensive position, every muscle taut, waiting. Alexos, too, is primed for action, his sword out and angled for a sideways sweep. He reminds himself to swing high enough to strike at the knee, above the protective greaves.

It's better than nothing, a way to fight back, but he'd far rather be standing. He'd also like to have something to hold on to—his cane, for instance, which is still upstairs leaning against a wall.

Now he hears the slightest intake of breath. Nestor has found the door. Then the silky swish of hands on wood and iron, exploring the bolt apparatus, trying to imagine what it looks like and exactly how it works. When the moment comes, Nestor will have to shoot the bolt free and open the door in a single, rapid motion. There must be no delay, no unexpected complications. Because once he starts, it's going to make a lot of noise.

Still, nothing. The wait seems endless. They strain

to hear the slightest sound—the creak of a board, the whisper of metal sliding against leather as a sword is slowly drawn. Alexos isn't sure whether he's actually hearing a soft tread, mostly drowned out by the noise from above, or if he's just *feeling* the ominous presence on the other side of that door.

No, he's hearing it, and it's inside the room, coming closer, practically beside him now. But Alexos doesn't swing. It's probably Leander, who always seems to know what Alexos needs, often before Alexos does. And sure enough, there comes a gentle touch on the shoulder. Then, squatting behind him, Leander grips Alexos firmly under the arms and heaves him up.

Alexos does what he can to make this easier. He leans forward, planting his left foot to keep his legs from sliding. Once he's upright and balanced, Leander leads him slowly away from the center of the room. They find a large cask for him to lean on for support. Then, with a last consoling touch, he melts back into the darkness.

There's no way the raiders could have failed to hear them. Leander had grunted softly with the exertion of lifting him up, Alexos' brace had creaked, and he'd dragged his right foot as they walked. But it probably doesn't matter. The soldiers already know they're in here. Any moment now.

There is only the briefest warning as the latch is raised. Then the door from the stairway flies wide and slams against the wall. At the same moment, on the other side of the room, Nestor opens the storeroom door. Dim orange light pours into the room, followed by clouds of acrid smoke. It startles the attackers and blinds them for a moment, giving Nestor time to join the others.

There are four against four and they're evenly matched—or they would be if the prince's guards were wearing all their armor and Leander had anything besides a sword. They've paired off, two by two, all of them trained swordsmen, so natural and assured that for a moment it feels more like a demonstration of swordsmanship than men actually trying to kill one another.

And they might have gone on like that for a long time—striking and trapping, dancing and ducking—had Peles not crept unnoticed out of the shadows, a crate held high over his head, and brought it down with a sickening thud on the back of Leander's opponent. For a moment they stand in stunned amazement looking down in wonderment at the inert figure. Then Leander dives back into the fray and Peles runs across the room to Alexos.

"We need to go," he whispers.

Alexos hesitates. He is watching the fighting, his heart in his throat.

"Please forgive me, Your Highness, but I know what you're thinking. And I feel bound to remind you that it isn't your duty to stay here and fight. Your duty, if you'll pardon me for mentioning it, is to survive this attack. For if you and the king should both die here tonight, then Arcos is truly lost."

Peles is right on both counts. That *was* what Alexos was thinking. And it *is* his duty to run away, just as it was his duty to go on living when he'd rather have died. So, step by awkward step, they make their way toward the door.

"If you could move a little faster, my lord, that would be good," Peles adds.

"Doing my best," Alexos mutters, then tries harder. They are locked so tightly together, Alexos can smell the man's sweat, feel his breath, warm against his cheek.

It does not occur to either of them how visible they've become, two dark shapes against the glowing light from the fires. And one of the raiders, having a clear view of the figures in the doorway—a tall youth in a long tunic who swings his right leg stiffly with every step, and another man who is holding him, helping him walk—knows this must be Alexos, the lame prince of Arcos.

In a single, fluid movement, he lunges at Silanos, driving him back for a moment, then whirls around and runs across the room. Instantly, Peles swings Alexos to the proper angle for using his sword, then ducks down and wraps his other arm around the prince, steadying him in a protective embrace, becoming a human shield.

It happens so fast that Alexos has no time to think. He can only do what he's done so many times before, first in the practice yard, then in his exercise room. Using the muscles in his back and hips for added power, he swings with all the might of his strong right arm. The motion is smooth and familiar till the sword strikes bone; then the recoil throws him sharply back. He and Peles come close to falling, but it's the soldier from Ferra who drops like a stone.

Then Peles all but drags him into the night.

21

THE FLAMES AND SMOKE are more apparent here. Figures dart along the streets, shadows in the glowing air, like patrons pouring out of a theater after the play is over. That's how it feels to Alexos, like the end of something.

Peles leads him through a warren of winding streets and back lanes, always tending in a northerly direction, away from the central compound. They don't talk; they save their breath, because this isn't easy for either of them. Finally they come to a blind alley that looks to be a builder's staging area. Boards are stacked neatly against one wall. Near it are a pile of gravel, a heap of stones, and all manner of boxes and barrels. Several handcarts lean against the walls. Peles stops and looks at them.

"No," says Alexos. "Don't even think it."

"But, Your Highness, we could move so much faster—"

"No, Peles. I mean it. But you *can* find me a staff. Then I'll be able to walk on my own, and faster too."

"You're sure, my lord?"

"Oh, for heaven's sake, Peles, just find me a staff! Look in that pile over there."

Alexos leans against the wall, breathing hard, exhausted.

"Nothing too heavy," he calls to Peles' back. "And not too big around to grip with ease."

"I will try, Your Highness."

The sky is pulsing with orange light; the fires must be spreading. And though Alexos can't tell for sure from where he stands, he's afraid the headquarters is burning too. Great clouds of smoke are building in that direction.

He thinks of his father and wonders if the guards have managed to protect him, if they've gotten him away to safety. He thinks of Leander fighting experienced soldiers twice his age without benefit of armor or a shield. And he tries not to imagine their deaths—his father, his friend. But it's hard. Alexos is afraid he's going to be sick.

"My lord?" Peles is back with a handful of sticks.

He notes the grim expression on the prince's face but doesn't remark upon it. "If any of these are acceptable, I will smooth the hand grip for you."

Alexos tries them one by one—it's a good, simple task; it takes his mind off death for a moment—and picks the best of a bad lot. Peles finds a rock and goes to work, rounding off the sharp edges and filing away splinters. Then they're off again, still moving north toward the edge of the compound. It grows darker as they move away from the firelight, dark and eerily still. No one's here at all. Every man has gone to fight or put out the fires.

Earlier, when they were riding into camp, Alexos had mentally measured the distance from the stables to the central buildings, knowing he would have to walk it. But he hadn't noted how far the town extended to the north. Now, even though they're moving faster and more efficiently than before, it seems they'll never reach the edge of the town, and Alexos is nearing his limit. The staff Peles found for him, though better than nothing, is heavy and too short. The hastily applied protective wrapping under his brace is chafing badly.

"I have to sit down," he says. "At least for a little while."

Peles stops, but glances around, still uneasy. "Of

course, my lord. This is a good enough place to rest, I suppose."

"Or to hide till daylight. There are probably cots in those buildings. We could lie down."

Peles gets that look again, like he's summoning the courage to tell the prince, with profuse and polite apologies, that he's absolutely wrong. "I'm sorry, Your Highness," he says, "but we ought to go on as soon as you are able. When we reach the tall grass, then you can lie down and sleep."

"But there's nobody *here*, Peles!"

"I know. And there probably aren't many raiders left, if any at all. And even if there were, they wouldn't likely stray this far from the central compound. But it *only takes one*, my lord. And as I mentioned before, everything depends on your survival."

"Are you saying that you think my father is dead?"

"Oh no, Your Highness! I'm not saying that at all. But seeing as we aren't absolutely sure, one way or the other—"

"You have made your point, Peles, and you are right."

"Thank you, Your Highness."

"Let's go."

They plod on, more slowly now. The streets in this district are badly kept, potholes everywhere, and it's impossible to tell in the dim light whether they are shallow or deep. Peles, who can apparently see in the dark like a cat, guides him carefully around them.

The tumbledown buildings on the edge of the town have now given way to derelict tents, sagging and mildewed, dreadful. This is where the auxiliary lives, where Peles slept till now. Alexos knows it's the natural way of the world: the rich live better than the poor. But it still makes him feel ashamed. Someday he will try to make things just a little fairer, at least in the kingdom of Arcos.

At last they leave the northernmost boundary of the headquarters encampment. The ground here is cleared but rough, a wasteland of stones, weeds, and garbage. But still Peles urges him forward, into the wild stubble and on to the long grass.

It's harder to walk here; the ground is spongy and uneven. Alexos' staff keeps getting caught in the underbrush. But Peles has a particular place in mind, a slow rise that drops sharply into a dry gully, and he seems unwilling to stop until they get there. So, on they go, stumbling and plodding. In the distance, the sounds of fighting have grown fainter. Now and then there are moments of complete silence. It must be nearly over.

At last they reach the rise. Peles helps Alexos to

sit on the edge of the bank, then supports him as he slides down. "You can sleep now if you want, my lord; you'll be safe here. Then, with your permission, I'll go for help."

"Yes," Alexos says. He slumps against the rough bank, not bothering to pick out the small stones that press into his back. "Please find out what you can," he adds. "About my father, and Leander, and the others. Come back and tell me."

"I will, my lord."

"Be off, then, Peles. And may the gods protect you."

22

ALEXOS WAKES TO PELES leaning over him, gently shaking his shoulder. It's still dark and Alexos aches in a thousand places.

"The horses are here," Peles says. "I'm instructed to say we need to hurry."

"But what did you find out? Is my father all right?"

"Nobody seems to know, my lord. It's all disorder and confusion. I'm sorry."

"What about Leander?"

"Leander is here," Leander says, sliding down from the top of the bank. There's a makeshift bandage on his right arm, just above the wrist.

"You're wounded."

"I am." Leander says this brightly, as if he'd just been awarded a prize. Alexos supposes that in a way, he has: his wound is a badge of honor. "Come on, Peles. Give us a hand. I can't haul him up by myself."

Despite the chaos back in the camp, the soldiers have managed to identify Alexos' particular horse, find the saddle, and put it on correctly. With Leander's guidance they get him mounted and strapped in. Then they are off: Alexos and about twenty men he doesn't know, plus Leander, who rides just behind him, Peles, who is off in the back somewhere, and Nestor, who takes the sweep position.

The waning moon gives precious little light, so they trudge through the darkness at a crawling pace, Alexos in the middle of a tight-packed group, like the yolk in an egg. Now and then a horse or rider will accidentally press against one of his legs. The third time this happens, Alexos mentions it; after that, they're careful not to do it again.

Alexos is desperate for information, and though he doesn't doubt what Peles told him earlier, he knows that sometimes finding things out depends on who you ask—and who does the asking. He turns to the soldier on his left.

"Will you tell me your name?" he asks.

"Kyros, Your Highness."

"Can you give me any news of my father, Kyros?"

"I'm sorry, my lord. I've heard nothing at all. I was just told to escort you back to the city. They'll send news by messenger once the situation is clear."

The situation. That's one way to put it. "But the fighting is over?"

"I believe so, Your Highness."

"Surely, then, it would have been safe for me to stay—at least long enough to gather my companions and find out whether the king survived. Why leave in such a hurry?"

"We can't be sure we've killed all the raiders till we've made a thorough search of the camp. And there's no assurance that King Pyratos won't launch a second attack. Getting you quickly away was deemed the prudent thing to do."

"By whom?"

"By my lord Theodorus, who, as I'm sure you are aware, is second in command after your father."

Alexos nods, though in truth he has never heard of Theodorus, or any of the king's other generals. He is growing daily more conscious of how little he knows.

Twenty-odd men on horseback make a good amount of noise—the clopping of hooves on clay, the creaking of leather, the dull metallic sound of armed men in motion, and here and there a soft conversation. So they don't hear the approaching rider until he is close upon them.

Instantly, the men on the outside peel off and turn back. Those nearest the prince become the spokes of a wheel, of which Alexos is the hub. The rear guard lines up in battle formation.

But the early morning light soon reveals a familiar face, one of Ektor's officers, and the escort stands down. The messenger is coming in with reckless speed, mud flying, his horse heaving with the effort. He reins in his mount so quickly that she dances sideways on her hind legs to keep from plowing into the others.

"I have a message for the prince," the officer says, breathing hard.

Already Alexos is riding back to speak with him. To do this, he is forced to leave the road, which is blocked, and slog through the sticky muck and melting snow along the verge. His guards ride beside him, a very inelegant business, with more jostling and bumping against his legs.

"I am here," Alexos says, conscious of his voice, trying not to sound like the terrified boy he is. "What news?"

The officer bows from the waist. "Your Highness," he says, and then he pauses, very briefly, as if summoning his courage. "It is my unfortunate duty to inform you that your noble father is dead."

Alexos gets stuck halfway through a breath; he can neither draw it in nor let it out. "Are you sure?" he finally says.

"Yes, Your Highness. I am sorry."

"Have you seen him yourself?" He can't bring himself to say "the body."

"I have, Your Highness."

"How did he die?"

"At the hands of the assassins sent by Pyratos, the criminal king of Ferra, breaker of oaths, blasphemer of the gods."

"I know that. But where?"

"*Where*, Your Highness?"

"Yes. Where was he killed?"

"In his headquarters, my lord."

"But which room? Where *exactly*?"

The messenger looks at Alexos with an odd expression. "In the hallway."

Not the room with the frescoes, then, the room where Alexos had been so rude to his father. He's not sure why that matters, but somehow it does.

"Was there a sword in his hand?"

The messenger relaxes. He understands now what the boy wants to know.

"Yes," he says, "and he did not cross the River alone. He took the souls of three of his attackers with him. He died most nobly, like a king."

Alexos can't imagine a world without Ektor striding through it. His father had always seemed unstoppable, a force of nature like thunder or wind. Yet someone *has* stopped him, and now Alexos will never see his father again.

But Ektor's voice still echoes in his mind, as gruff and cold as ever. *Don't be such a child! Be a boy, for heaven's sake, not a dreary old man. You are so tiresome! I have spent too much time with you already.* And now there *is* no more time; it is all spent. Only memories remain, and they are hard.

Suddenly, to his great mortification, Alexos finds that he is weeping. He struggles to get control of himself, but if anything, it gets worse.

"Take a deep breath and hold it." It's Nestor's voice. Alexos hadn't even noticed he was there. He tries to take a deep breath, as advised, but he chokes in the effort and goes into a spasm of coughing. It's hideous and shameful; but once he has the coughing under control, he seems to be over the crying too. The others wait in stony silence, their faces expressionless. When Alexos seems fully recovered, the messenger continues.

"You are the king of Arcos now, Your Majesty," he says. And when Alexos doesn't respond, just blinks and does something odd with his mouth, the messenger continues with what he's been sent to say. "More men will be following. They should catch up with you soon and will escort you the rest of the way. I don't think you are in any danger, but we can't take chances. You understand."

Alexos knows there are questions he should ask, but he can't think what they might be. He tries hard. The army, he decides. He should ask about that.

"Who is in command?"

"My lord Theodorus, Your Majesty. You need not concern yourself on that account. There was considerable damage to the buildings, but the army is sound and in good hands for now. Once you return to the city, you may decide whether he or someone else should take charge—until such time as you are ready to do it yourself."

This is more than Alexos can comprehend: leading an army, guiding a kingdom. How is it even possible?

"Your Majesty," the officer says, more softly than before, "this is a moment of crisis. You must return to the *polis* of Arcos, meet with your advisers, and prepare yourself to rule."

Alexos nods, but makes no move to go. "Now?" he says, still dazed.

"As soon as you are ready, my lord."

Alexos doubts he will ever be ready.

"All right," he says.

Part Two
The Island

Seven Years Later

23

OUT IN THE WINE-DARK sea, far from any shore, there is an island. It is small, with a mountain in the middle, and it's shrouded by fog in every season of the year—hidden from passing ships, invisible to the gods, invisible even to the great lord Poseidon, whose realm this is. Only Athene knows it exists, because she put it there, and has carefully protected it these seventeen years.

Now she is preparing to destroy it. If everything goes as planned, if the many threads of her intricate web come together as she intends, this blessed island— with its meadows and forests, soft grass, and perfect trees whose leaves gleam as if they had been polished, the delicate waterfalls that drop into clear pools far below, the birds and foxes and fireflies, and the wind that sings in harmony—all will sink back into the sea from whence it came and disappear forever.

The three good souls who live here—Claudio, Aria, and Teo—don't know this is about to happen. They go about their days unaware. They sleep peacefully in their little cave dwelling, fitted by the goddess with smooth stone floors, rectangular rooms, arched doorways, and natural stone benches of varying shapes and sizes, all exactly as required to serve as tables, beds, and stools. They eat from the trees that reach down to offer them fruit and nuts. They drink from clear springs that appear whenever they are thirsty.

But while they can't see into the mind of Athene or envision the complex string of events she has already set in motion, they can feel the change in the air. They've grown restless of late, perhaps even a little bit bored with their effortless life in this remote and beautiful place, which, despite its divine perfection, seems to get smaller every year.

The children don't really understand what's troubling them. Maybe it's just that there's nothing to do. They've read every scroll in their possession many times. Their father has told them all his stories. Teo, now twelve, still has his lessons every day, but they're only going through the motions. He picked up most of what Aria learned back when she was learning it, and whatever he didn't quite grasp at the time, she later explained.

So he and Aria have taken to inventing projects to fill their time. Most recently, they measured and mapped the island, naming and cataloging all its inhabitants, plants and animals both. But once that was finished, they came to a halt. It's strange—there used to be a thousand things they wanted to do. Now they can't think of one.

There aren't even any chores to do. Clothing is the only thing the island doesn't provide, and in the past they spent many hours mending and remaking their garments as they threatened to fall apart or didn't fit anymore. But they have no cloth that's fit to use; mostly it's just scraps and rags. And their thread, made from unraveled bits of fabric, is so old it snaps under pressure. Then Teo lost their only needle, and that was the end of it.

Not that it really matters that Claudio's robe, formerly a coverlet, is ripped halfway up the side, or that Teo's tunic is bursting at the seams, or that Aria has been reduced to wearing one of her father's old tunics, soiled and much too big for her, belted with a frayed and dirty cord. They don't care. Who is there to see them? They are alone on an island.

What troubles them is this restlessness they can't

seem to shake, the growing presentiment that something's about to happen. They're like the host who's prepared a feast and now everything is ready—the table is set, the food prepared, the lamps all blazing—and there's nothing left to do but wait for the guests to arrive. That's how it feels: *finished, waiting.*

Of late, Claudio has given up all pretense of going about his normal routine. He sits at the edge of the garden staring down at the harbor all day. But the view never changes. It's still just the beach, the sea, and the fog.

Teo and Aria wait with him. At times they get fidgety and wander off to bathe under the waterfall or go in search of foxes; but always they come back. They sit at his feet making grass whistles or flower crowns. Without being quite aware of it, they have moved from feeling expectant to actually *longing* for something to happen.

One afternoon, it finally does.

"Look there!" Teo cries, pointing out to sea. "See, the fog is lifting!"

And so it is. Though the sky is still overcast, the mist is rising from the water. And far in the distance, dark and discrete, great ballooning clouds with sharp, defined edges are beginning to form. Bright webs of lightning flash out of their shadows. Even here on the island, they can feel the roll of thunder.

"Oh!" Aria cries. She has never seen a storm before. And no one, anywhere, has seen a storm like this.

"Don't be afraid," Claudio says. "It's just a tempest at sea." Yet despite his easy words, he leans forward anxiously and studies the storm through squinted eyes. "It is odd, though—the clouds. See how luminous they are? All the many colors?"

"They're beautiful," Aria agrees, "in a terrible sort of way. But why is the storm only in one place? See, all around it on every side, the water is calm and bright. Is that how tempests usually are?"

"No."

"Papa," Teo says, "are those *ships*? See, there: in the very darkest part of the clouds, a little to the edge on the left."

Claudio squints still harder. His eyes aren't what they used to be. "Yes," he finally says. "Yes, you're right."

The children have never seen a ship before either, at least not that they can remember. They've read about them, though, and they understand that wherever there are ships there will also be people. Other people—something else they've never seen before. Or at least not that they can remember.

"Isn't it dangerous, being on a ship in a storm like that?"

"Very dangerous."

"But wait!" Teo cries. "See—they're sailing out of it now. The people will be all right!"

And Teo is mostly correct. At the far side of the cloud cluster a favorable wind is driving the little fleet away from the storm and out into the calm seas. But one ship remains in the tempest's powerful grip, tossing wildly in the heavy swells. It looks as if, any moment now, it will pitch over and sink.

And yet it doesn't; it continues to move forward. Caught by an altogether different wind than the one that propels its fellows, it is heading directly south toward the island's rocky shore.

"May the gods protect them," Claudio whispers. "Hurry, we must go down there. Maybe we can be of some help."

They are up and running in an instant, down the winding path that hugs the cliff and leads to the beach far below. In places along the way, their view is obscured by bushes and trees. Here they run even faster, anxious to reach the next open spot to see how the orphaned ship is faring. It's flying in now at tremendous speed, just skimming the tops of the waves as seabirds do, still pursued by those ominous clouds.

"Is that normal?" Aria asks.

"Not in the least," Claudio says. "Go!"

They continue down the slope, one sharp turn followed by another. After a long wooded section where they can see nothing at all, they come again to an open place. Here they stop and stare, openmouthed, as the ship comes racing toward them: past the ring of jagged rocks, into the harbor and onto the beach, the bow carving a deep cleft in the sand. And there it comes to a shuddering stop.

Teo and Aria are off again, sprinting down the path, breathless with excitement. But Claudio doesn't move. He's staring, dumbfounded, at the pennant the ship flies. He blinks, then blinks again.

"Wait! Stop!" he calls in an urgent whisper, just loud enough for them to hear. "Turn around. Come back. Hurry!"

"But, Papa—" Teo pleads.

"*Now!*"

"But *why*?"

Neither he nor Aria moves an inch.

"There's a man on that ship who is a danger to us. I want you to come back *right now*!"

Reluctantly, they return.

"What man?" Aria asks. "And how can you know

he's dangerous? You've never even seen—"

"Yes I have, daughter. I have seen that man. I know all about him. And for now I want you to trust me and go back up the trail as quickly and quietly as you can. Stoop low as you pass the open spaces. They must not know we are here."

24

AS THEY RUN, THE island follows closely in their wake, erasing every trace of their existence. Eager vines creep out to cover the path; grasses sprout from hard-packed earth; stones rise up, aged and speckled with lichen, as if they'd been there a thousand years. When they reach the top, they find their garden choked with weeds and woody brush, shoulder high in places. And by the time they have gathered up their few belongings and carried them away to the temple of Athene, the entrance to their cave home has been buried under a mass of thorny vines.

The island is hiding them from the enemy, Claudio says. Or maybe Athene is doing it. Or perhaps, in some unfathomable way, they are one and the same.

Only the temple remains. It's a humble place with

no columns, no portico, and no altar, just a shallow cave at the base of a cliff enclosed by a stone facade. Inside, the walls, floor, and ceiling are the natural black rock of the cliff itself, arching overhead, smooth to the touch. And standing against the far wall, as pale as the little room is dark, is an image of Athene about the height of a full-grown man, which Claudio carved himself.

A small votive lamp at the feet of the goddess fills the temple with soft, flickering light. It has done so without ceasing for seventeen years, a miracle of sorts, due entirely to the sweet-smelling, long-burning oil made from the cluster-nut, which grows nowhere else in the world but here.

This small, shadowy room, formerly so bare and austere, looks almost cheerful now. The family has piled their belongings against the front wall and spread out their pallets on the floor. Claudio has lit a second, brighter lamp.

"Now," Teo says when they are all seated. "Tell us."

"I will," Claudio replies. "But understand: this is not easy for me. Just as the island is protecting us by covering our traces with brambles and weeds, so I have tried to protect you with my silence all these years. I see I must break that silence now, because unless you know my history, you cannot fully appreciate the danger we face. And since telling that story forces me to tell another, I'll have to give you both—but out of order, for I believe that is the kindest way to do it."

Claudio reaches over and takes Teo's hand. Teo looks up at him, puzzled, wondering why he's been singled out for this solemn attention.

"One night, eight years ago, I woke from a dream in which I heard a child calling for help. That dream was sent by Athene; and having gotten my attention, she then guided me down the path to the beach, the same one we walked today."

"Oh," Aria says. She knows which story this will be.

"Aria woke and followed me. So we were both there to see a little skiff come floating out of the fog and into the harbor. We saw the waters grow still and the sand rise up so the child in the boat could step safely out onto dry land. It was a little boy, about four years old. And at first he was so frightened that he wouldn't speak. He only managed a single word. I asked him his name, and he said, 'Teo.'"

"I don't understand."

"*You* were that little boy, son. This is the story of how you came to be here."

"But I thought—"

"I know. Listen now; there's more.

"We never knew how you came to be alone in that

little boat, adrift on the dangerous sea. But whatever happened, I felt sure it would be painful for you to remember. Also the life you left behind: your home, your parents and friends, and everything familiar, now lost. And since you were so very young, we—Aria and I—hoped that with time you would forget it entirely and come to believe you'd always been here with us. You might say we conspired to make that happen. I don't think we ever actually lied. We just left things unsaid. I know it must be disturbing for you to hear it now."

Teo is blinking back tears. "You're not my father, then?" he says. "Aria's not my sister?" Claudio grips Teo's hand a little tighter.

"Not blood-born, but in every way that matters. I love you as my son; Aria loves you as her brother." Aria scoots over and wraps an arm around Teo's waist and leans her head on his shoulder.

"Teo, I must also tell you that your miraculous salvation was neither good fortune nor an act of nature. The goddess brought you here so you would be safe—and so you could be with us. There was purpose in it."

Teo nods.

Claudio takes his daughter's hand. They are linked now, all three.

"This next story happened earlier, seventeen years

ago. As you will see, Teo is absent from it. That's why I had to explain first how he came to us."

He pauses, gathering his thoughts.

"The man I saw on the deck of that ship, the man who frightened me, is my nephew, Pyratos, king of Ferra. He's my late brother's only son."

"Your brother was a *king*?" Aria's eyes are bright with astonishment.

"Yes. And when he died, his son was just fourteen, too young to rule on his own. So my brother asked me—as a favor, on his deathbed—to safeguard the kingdom and guide young Pyratos until he came of age. Of course I was glad to do it."

"You ruled a kingdom?"

"Yes, Aria, and I did my best. I gave the boy the respect he was due. He was king after all, however young he might be. I was careful to include him in all the decisions I made, teaching him as we went along. But we were ill matched. He thought I was overly cautious, ploddingly slow, worse than the world's dullest schoolmaster. And I thought him headstrong, reckless, and impulsive. I was the wrong man for the task, I'm afraid; that's the heart of it. Pyratos needed a heavy hand, not reason and kindness."

"I'll bet he wouldn't have liked a heavy hand either," Teo says.

"No, but he wouldn't have been so bold if he'd been afraid of me."

Claudio sighs and gazes up at the ceiling, the slick stone shimmering with the light of both lamps. He seems reluctant to go on. But he does.

"By the time Pyratos was seventeen, he was well versed in general statecraft and all things military, thanks to my careful training. But he'd also formed some very definite notions of his own on the direction that Ferra should take. I felt his ideas were dangerous, radical even. If he followed that path he was sure to further stir the anger of the gods. I tried many times to warn him.

"One day when we were alone in the council chamber, we argued about it. He lost his temper and struck me hard with the back of his hand. I fell off my stool and onto the floor. Then he stood over me and shouted curses.

"After that, of course, there was no going back—for me or for him. I sent Pyratos a respectful message offering to resign my position so he could choose someone more to his liking to advise him. He wrote back accepting my resignation, then put me under house arrest, seized all my lands and worldly goods, and refused to take any more advice from anyone.

"Guards were posted outside my door. Except for

the servants who did the marketing, no one was permitted to leave or enter the house. Lydia, my wife, was ill at the time, yet neither a physician nor an apothecary was allowed inside the walls. I'm sorry, Aria; that's how it was your mother died."

Aria looks down at her hands, her cheeks flushed. All of this has been upsetting, but it seems especially cruel that, not only had her mother died so young, but Aria had never known her at all, had never even wondered who her mother was. Everything she knew about mothers came from books. She looks up at her father, blinking back tears.

"I'm not finished yet; I'm sorry. Do you think you can bear it?"

"I must. I need to know."

"All right. So Pyratos, having already taken my beloved wife, my freedom, and my fortune, he now determined to have my life as well.

"Late one night he came to my house with a troop of armed men. He sent a servant upstairs to wake me. When I came down, he was surprisingly polite. He said he wished to discuss some urgent business in private. So we withdrew into my study and shut the door. I thought he'd had a change of heart, and I was glad. But his courtesy was only for show.

"'Uncle,' he said, when there was no one around to

hear, 'you have become an impediment to me, so I am sending you away. Out of respect for the memory of my late father, I'll spare your reputation. I'll come up with some sort of story to explain your disappearance. No one needs to know that you've been banished. Now you'd better get packing. You sail at first light.'

"And that was it. I never saw him again until today."

"Yet you knew him by sight?"

"He hasn't changed that much. He looks, I'm sorry to say, very like my brother.

"So. I collected a few things in haste and at dawn the following morning, Aria and I—you were hardly six months old at the time—went on board the ship. It was a fat, broad merchantman with a single mast, old and good for nothing but scrap. And no one would tell me where we were bound. I should have been suspicious; I'm embarrassed now to think how trusting I still was.

"We sailed into the deep waters off the southern coast. When we were two days out, a smaller vessel joined us, at which point our entire crew deserted the merchantman, leaving us alone on board. Understand, one man cannot possibly manage such a ship alone; it would take a crew of eight at least. But that was the point, you see; we were meant to die, to drift helplessly with the currents till we were capsized in a storm or perished from hunger and thirst. And—I'm only guessing here—I expect Pyratos claimed the ship was lost at sea: *an unfortunate accident, nobody's fault, such a tragedy!*"

"But we didn't die," Aria says.

"No. And you will notice a striking similarity between Teo's story and the one I am about to tell you: for we were saved, just as he was, by the goddess Athene.

"While Aria slept in the cabin below, I went back up on deck. A storm was brewing, black clouds building on the horizon, and already the wind was up and gusting hard."

"Like the storm we saw today?"

"Very much the same. The ship tossed wildly. Waves crashed over the railing. I was terrified, as you can imagine. But I turned to Athene, who had always favored me and guided me with her great wisdom. I knelt on that rolling deck and raised my arms to the skies and sang out every song of praise I knew.

"As I did so, I saw a great, dense bank of fog rising up out of the sea. But it wasn't formless, as fog usually is. It had a distinct shape. And the longer I stared, the more the fogbank took the appearance of land. I saw the green of trees, the edge of a single mountain—unquestionably, an island.

"And then the ship turned very neatly, quite of its own accord, and headed directly for the only safe harbor. We ran right up onto the beach, as Pyratos' ship did today. I carried Aria down a rope ladder to safety. Then I went back to unload the things I'd assembled for the voyage. When I had finished and had found a place of shelter—our cunning little cave house, ready and waiting—I stood where we were today, looking down at the beach. A colossal wave came rolling in and devoured the ship entire.

"Now let me tell you this, my dearest children. Since you have never known—or in Teo's case, can't remember—any other home but this, you can't truly appreciate what a blessed place it is. In the world beyond, I assure you, trees don't lean down and offer their fruit to you; nor do springs rise up when you are thirsty; the grass is not so lush and green; the wind doesn't sing pleasant harmonies. Our little place of refuge is perfect because the goddess made it so; and she made it especially for us."

He pauses and looks first at one and then the other, with such intensity that he seems to expect them to respond in some particular way. It's as though there's a piece missing out of his story, an error or contradiction, and he's waiting for them to find it.

They do not disappoint him.

"So Pyratos thinks you're dead," Aria begins, eyes half closed, brows furrowed in deep concentration. "And he probably lied about what happened—well, he would, wouldn't he? So if he finds out that you're still alive and right here on the island, he'll be afraid you'll tell about the terrible thing he did. Are kings allowed to do murder?"

"No. Ferra has laws."

"Then since he tried to kill you once, he might try again, if only to keep his secret safe."

"That's correct."

"And the goddess is hiding us so that won't happen."

"Wait," Teo says. "That doesn't make sense."

Claudio nods. Teo has found the flaw.

"We saw that ship come in. It was exactly the same as what you just described, except that it hasn't been washed away. And it's like my little boat, too. All three were brought here safely, with no lives lost, and in a way that is contrary to nature."

"And?"

"The goddess brought you and Aria here because she is merciful, because you were innocent and someone had put you in danger; she even created this island for you."

"And then," Aria picks up the thread, "when Teo was in danger, she brought him here too, so we could all be safe and happy together. So why would she do the same for Pyratos? He isn't innocent. He doesn't deserve her mercy. And in bringing him here, she is working against her original kind intentions, putting us in danger all over again."

"That is indeed the question. You have stated it perfectly."

"But what's the answer?"

"Only the goddess knows. We must trust she has her reasons."

25

~~

THERE ARE TWO CAMPS, one large and one small.

The main encampment is on the high ground just above the beach. Pyratos has ordered a stand of saplings cut down to make room for his men and all their equipment: tents, trunks, casks, boxes, a table and benches, cooking equipment, and several amphorae of wine. What was once a charming little meadow, surrounded by trees and dotted with tiny bell-shaped flowers, is now a flattened plain of matted grass, littered with a jumble of gear.

Some distance away from the main camp is a natural clearing in a grove of ancient broad-leafed trees. Here Pyratos has placed his prison camp. It's a simple, uncluttered affair: just six guards with minimal equipment, a man chained to the trunk of a tree, and the man's three attendants, who stay near him.

The tree to which the prisoner is tethered stands at the edge of the clearing, a great old oak, probably six feet in diameter. Its girth offers a bit of privacy, since he and his men have settled themselves on the side that looks away from the camp and into the forest. But unfortunately, it also robs the prisoner of freedom to roam, because the chain to which the manacles are attached is only so long, and most of that length is taken up in encircling the tree.

The guards, a remarkably good-natured bunch, agreed that this was a problem. But it was the only chain they had, meant for use in a ship's cabin, not wrapped around a big tree. They offered to remove one of the iron cuffs if that would help.

The prisoner's physician said this would be a marked improvement. A blanket would also be welcome. The guards were happy to comply.

It's dark now, their first night on the island. The guards have gathered around a little brush fire. They talk in low voices while the prisoner and his men, out of sight behind the tree, listen intently to their conversation.

"We're stuck here, that's the gist of it."

"Nay, I think not. Soon as the fleet reaches port, they'll send out a ship."

"And how will they find us?"

"They'll remember where we parted in the storm; they'll know where to look."

"In this fog?"

"It'll lift. They'll send a ship, and they will find us."

"Would *you*?" This from another man, who hasn't spoken before.

"Would I what?"

The speaker's voice drops, almost to a whisper. "Send a ship to find Pyratos and bring him back to Ferra?"

This comment is greeted with gasps of surprise and soft, dark laughter.

"Well, you've got a point there. If I were *himself*"—he leans on the word for emphasis, as if to say, *you all know who I mean, but I won't speak his name*—"I wouldn't sleep so easy at night. Especially now that we're off here in the wilderness, where if something were to happen, no one would be the wiser."

"Truly—you think there are those among us who would go that far?"

"I do. I've heard their grumbling and their secret—"

"Shhh! What was that?"

"I didn't hear anything."

"A twig snapped, something like that."

"Ooooooh—perhaps there be *monsters* here."

The others laugh.

"Or a spy, maybe."

They fall silent at that. They've been dangerously indiscreet, trusting in the distance between the two camps.

One of the prisoner's men now emerges from the darkness and approaches the campfire and the guards. "Ho, Peles," one of the men says. "We thought you were asleep, so quiet you were over there."

"Near enough," Peles says. "Soon."

"So where might you be going this time of night?"

"To relieve myself."

"There's plenty of trees need watering over where you came from."

"Excuse me, gentlemen, but that's where we sleep."

"I didn't know the peasants of Arcos were so particular."

"Would you rather I do it here, then, beside your campfire?"

"Oh, for heaven's sake, let the fellow go do his business."

As there is no further discussion on the matter, Peles steps into the privacy of the forest and the men return to their talk. But now they are more careful what they say.

"They'll be searching the island tomorrow, that's what I heard."

"Do you suppose they'll find any villages here? It seems such a strange little out-of-the-way place. It's not on any map, the captain said."

"I doubt anyone lives here at all. If they did, it wouldn't seem so empty. There'd be cottages and fields, boats in the harbor, that sort of thing."

"Makes sense. Who's first watch tonight?"

"Janos," says the officer, "then Stefano."

The men are exhausted, as anyone would be who'd departed early from the borderlands, sailed for hours, looked death in the eye through a terrible storm, been cast ashore on an island, then spent still more hours unloading the ship, setting up a prison camp, and making a fire—all before having their first bite to eat since breaking their fast that morning. They shuffle over to the neat pile at the edge of the clearing and gather up blankets and roll their cloaks to rest their heads upon. Then they return to the warmth and cheer of the fire and arrange themselves to sleep on the grass.

Janos sits nearby, leaning against a tree. He knows it isn't a good place for keeping a proper watch. It's too far from the prisoner, and the light from the fire makes it hard to see into the darkness beyond. But he doesn't like to sit alone in this strange place in the gloom of night; he prefers to stay close to the others.

And besides, this prisoner isn't likely to run away,

even if he weren't chained to a tree; and his attendants are too loyal to leave him. So keeping watch is really just a formality. And should Janos doze off—which of course he'll try very hard not to do—no harm done.

Peles saunters out of the forest, calm and cheerful as always.

"Sleep well," he says to the guards.

"You, too."

He crosses the clearing and returns to his place beside the king of Arcos. He lies on his side, his head propped up with one hand, and speaks softly into his master's ear.

"It was a lad, sixteen or seventeen, I'd say."

"And?"

"He may be inclined to rescue you."

"Does he speak our language?"

"Aye—and that's strange, now that you mention it."

"How many others are there?"

"'Not many.' That's all he would say."

"Anything else?"

"He wants to meet with you in person. I hope you'll forgive me, Alexos—I said he might, but he should wait an hour or two until the guards are well asleep. I told him to come around to this side of the clearing. Was that a mistake?"

"No, you did right. I take it you trusted this fellow, then?"

"Trusted, yes. Absolutely. As to whether he has the cunning and the skill to pull off a rescue, that's another matter altogether. He seemed—how can I say it?—very young, very innocent. Soft, like—"

"Shhh. Lie down, Peles. Feign sleep."

In the silence that follows they hear the voices of men approaching from the other camp. The guards hear them too, and they have picked out one familiar voice from all the others. They jump to their feet and do their best to look alert and respectful.

"I thought you were going to build a cage," Pyratos says.

"Well, Your Majesty," says the officer, "we did consider that, but there weren't materials for building one and we felt the prisoner ought to be constrained right away. So we've chained him to that tree over there."

"Let's have a look. Bring the lamp, will you?"

Pyratos and his men cross the clearing. Peles, Leander, and Suliman rise as he approaches; Alexos, having no choice in the matter, stays where he is. Wordlessly Pyratos studies the chain. He jerks at the free end, hard; Alexos' wrist comes with it. Pyratos studies the iron cuff, as dispassionately as if it weren't attached to a body at all.

"Only one manacle?" he shouts to the guards. "You've released this other one? Or did he manage to get it off himself?"

The officer, who has been standing back, now joins the group. "Oh, no, Your Majesty. He could not possibly have opened it. We released it because he is quite secure with the single cuff, and it enabled him to lie down and attend to personal matters—eating, you know, that sort of thing."

Pyratos stares at the officer for a while, just to make him squirm, then, "Leave us," he says, to everyone in general.

When they are gone, Pyratos sits on the ground in a regal sort of way and sets the lamp between them. It's the first time Alexos has seen his enemy up close like this. He was kept belowdecks throughout the voyage; then when they came onto the island, the king was busy elsewhere. Now, as he looks into the face of the man who murdered his father, Alexos is caught completely off guard. Pyratos might be a statue of Apollo brought magically to life. His form is manly, his face strikingly handsome, and his pale hair is as beautiful as that of a god.

"Well, well," he says. "So this is the famous champion of Athene." He glances down at the legs covered with a blanket. He is looking for the equally famous deformity, of course, and disappointed that it's not on view. "But surely you don't need *this* on such a warm night. Here, let me help you." Dry wit, so terribly clever, loving every moment.

Pyratos pulls the blanket away, tossing it on the ground. Then he leans forward, chin out, and stares pointedly at Alexos' legs. "Oh, what a pity," he says. The lamplight, shining on his face from below, leaves ghoulish puddles of darkness around his eyes.

Alexos, full of helpless rage, says nothing.

"But I don't suppose it really matters." He reaches over to touch the iron brace, drums on it playfully with his fingers. "Athene would have to find herself a new champion anyway. You won't be much use to her without your head."

Alexos recoils, as from a snake. "Isn't there supposed to be a trial first?"

"Oh, yes. First the trial, then the execution. And never fear, Alexos, it will be a thorough spectacle, befitting your kingly status. All of Ferra will turn out to enjoy it. Perhaps I should give a feast."

"And here I thought the point of a trial was to determine the guilt or innocence of the accused."

"And so it is. As it happens, you will be judged guilty."

"Of what crime?"

"Has no one told you? Really? Conspiracy to murder, my dear boy."

Alexos licks his lips, which are suddenly dry. "And who am I supposed to have killed?"

"My uncle, of course, the duke of Ferra. I'm amazed

you could forget such a masterful bit of trickery. You and old Ektor urged me to send an envoy to Arcos to discuss terms for a peace accord—remember? So I sent the duke and you sunk his ship, though it was flying the flag of truce. Your father has already paid for that crime. Now it's your turn."

"You know that's ridiculous. A complete fabrication!"

"Do I?"

"I heard about your uncle's death years ago, when I was just a boy. Even then it was old news. I would have been two or three years old at the time he died, hardly capable of conspiracy. As for my father, he would rather have disemboweled himself than do such an ignoble thing. Nor would he have sued for peace, as that is contrary to the express commands of Olympian Zeus. Everything about your pitiful tale is wrong. The judge won't believe it; no one will."

"Don't worry. I'll make sure they do. Then, *chop!*— off with your head."

"You are a dreadful man, Pyratos."

The king of Ferra rises without comment and takes up the lamp. "Enjoy your reprieve, you sad little king, for it will be brief." With a merry chuckle he saunters away.

Alexos shivers as a chill runs down his shoulders, into his arms, his belly. He hunches over, shuts his eyes, and concentrates on breathing.

"Alexos?" Suliman is beside him now. "Are you all right?"

"No. But I can't talk about it right now." His eyes are still closed. He is still shaking.

And then they are all around him, his companions, in a conspiracy of touching. Suliman is stroking Alexos' hair, like a father consoling his little son who has lost his best toy. Leander straightens the disordered tunic, then lays the blanket back over the prince's legs, gently tucking it in all around. And Peles has slipped in on his other side. He lays a gentle hand on Alexos' shoulder and whispers in his ear.

"My lord?"

They are treating him like a child, Alexos thinks. He doesn't mind at all.

"What is it, Peles?"

"Before we were interrupted, I was telling you about the boy who so earnestly wants to help you. Do you want to hear the rest? I think you will like it."

Alexos nods. He's still breathing heavily, but the trembling has stopped.

"The lad said, 'This island belongs to the goddess Athene. I am under her protection, and I believe your master is, too. He is not meant to die here, I am sure of that.'"

He opens his eyes and looks at Peles. "How remarkable!"

"Yes, my lord. I thought so, too, and I was quite inclined to trust him. But you will judge for yourself when you meet him."

"Soon, you say?"

"Later, when the guards are all asleep."

"Yes, I remember now. You told me that before."

He listens to the silence. It is absolute. And for a moment he wonders if that is a beautiful thing, or a premonition of death.

26

THE NIGHT IS UNCOMMONLY dark, lit only by a cres-
cent moon shining weakly through the fog. Around
the dying campfire the guards are dead asleep, seduced
by the softness of the silky grass and the fresh island
mist on their sunburned cheeks. Janos has slumped
against his tree, eyes closed, snoring softly.

Aria waits in a thicket at the far side of the clearing. She has hidden her hair under a brown woolen
cap, left on that long-ago ship by one of the desert-
ing sailors. Claudio had picked it up, thinking it might
prove useful one day. And now it has. Dressed in her
father's tunic and wearing the sailor's cap, Aria has
transformed herself into a creditable boy.

It's been a while since she last heard any sound
from either camp, except for the snoring guard. Surely

it must be safe to make her move.

Softly she makes the call of a small, croaking frog—once, twice, three times. Moments later, a cricket responds, their agreed-upon signal. Aria creeps out into the open, taking care to keep the tree between herself and the sleeping guards.

Peles, seeing her approach, touches the king's shoulder to wake him, while one of the other attendants, an older man, rolls over as if in his sleep, opening a space for her to sit beside him.

It ought to be dark here, as it is everywhere else. The moon is just an eyelash of light shining dimly through the fog, and the fireflies left the island when Pyratos arrived. Yet it seems a few of them still remain. They hover around his face now, as if inviting her to look.

Aria has read about the great heroes of yore, and often they are described as *handsome*. This she has long understood to mean that they are pleasant to look at, as flowers and foxes are. But her personal experience with men and their faces has been severely limited. So *handsome* remained an abstract notion, not something she could picture in her mind.

Earlier that night, as she sat in her spying place above the prison camp watching and listening to the guards, she had realized that humans came in many different forms. Faces could be long or round; noses small or large, long, broad, upturned, or drooping. Hair might be curly, straight, or sparse. But not one of the guards, and certainly not the man called Peles, had struck her as especially beautiful. So it must be that the writers of stories described a man as *handsome* to distinguish him from the rest.

Now as she studies the prisoner-king by the light of a few dozen fireflies, she sees that *handsome* means more than merely pleasant. It is something that makes you catch your breath. It stirs secret yearnings you never even knew were there. But even more than that, *handsome* is the capacity in a face to express who a person really is.

And while the king of Arcos is unquestionably a lovely thing to gaze upon, he is deeply marked by tragedy, worn by unrelenting struggle. There is such fierce intensity in those glittering eyes, desperation almost, and at the same time a deep fragility, that Aria longs to comfort him. She wants to take him in her arms and stroke his hair as she used to do when Teo was sad.

Now that she thinks of Teo, she can see how very alike they are, her brother and this man. That would explain the sudden rush of affection she is feeling.

She leans down and whispers in his ear, so close that his hair brushes her cheek. "Your man Peles tells me that you are the king of Arcos," she says.

"That's true. I am." His voice, even as he whispers, is deep. The sound of it sends a peculiar thrill running through her.

"You seem very young to be a king."

"I was younger still when I became one."

"Well," Aria says, "I would like to help you. But there are only a few of us and we have no weapons. The best we could do is set you free and hide you where you won't be found."

"And how would you set me free?"

"Your man said he could lift the keys from the officer's belt."

"Really?" The king smiles and his face is suddenly transformed. It's softer now, affectionate, amused. "Then I trust he can do it. Peles is a man of many talents."

The king is staring searchingly at her and she begins to fear that her deception hasn't fooled him. She puts a hand to her cap, making sure it's pulled down low enough to cover all her hair. "I will have to consult with the others first, before I commit to anything. They will want to know more."

"All right."

"I heard what King Pyratos said, so I know a lot already."

"But how is that possible? Where were you?"

"Right over there." She points.

"*Gods*, that was risky!"

She shrugs. "I know how to be stealthy. So is there anything else you feel you should tell me—how you came to be Pyratos' prisoner, why he wants to kill you?"

He's silent for a time, forming his thoughts. "I met him for the first time this evening, but he has long been my enemy—not only because our kingdoms are at war with each other, but because he murdered my father. He would have done the same to me if Peles hadn't helped me escape. That's how I came to be king at such a tender age. I was not yet fourteen."

"How did he kill your father?"

"He didn't do it himself, if that's what you're asking. He sent a small force of assassins into our camp, in strict violation of a long-standing truce between sunset and dawn."

"I see."

"After that, we never trusted his word again; we increased the security all along the border, building more watchtowers and doubling the number of sentries. But I made a mistake, left one place unprotected, and Pyratos noticed."

"What was it?"

"A swamp. It's on the coast, about ten miles north of the border, where a river runs into the sea. It's completely impassible, miles and miles of sucking sand, choked with reeds and grasses. I didn't think we needed to put a watchtower there, or post any sentries. That's how they came in.

"I was asleep in my tent at army headquarters. I'd only just arrived. Unlike Pyratos and my late father, I don't live and rule my kingdom from the borderlands. I leave the war to my generals, who are far more competent than I, and concentrate on finding ways to help my people. But I am obligated to go down there once in a while, and this happened to be one of those visits.

"Pyratos had been planning and preparing for a long time. His men were ready to go at a moment's notice. They had devised all sorts of special equipment: belts ringed with bladders inflated with air that allowed them to float, breathing tubes, special shoes shaped like frog's feet to propel them through the water, poles with flat disks on the bottom so they wouldn't sink in the mire. They were very clever, I'll grant them that, but it was still a difficult assignment, even with the special gear. Yet they made it through those miles of swamp and onto dry land.

"Then, under cover of darkness, they entered our camp from the rear, silently killing as they went. They slaughtered my personal guards, men who have served me since I was a child, then came into my tent. I woke as they were forcing a gag into my mouth. Then they bound me with ropes and made my attendants carry me away, threatening to slit my throat if they made the smallest sound. Pyratos insisted they bring along my physician, too, so he could keep me in good health."

"Why would he care about your health? He wants to chop off your head."

"He wants a public trial first, *then* the execution. But you heard all that already."

She nods.

"When we reached the swamp they put me into a slender little knife of a boat, light and buoyant and pointed at both ends. They'd towed it behind them when they came in; now they towed it out with me inside. It was rather like being in a very narrow coffin. Peles and Leander floated, paddled, and poled along with Pyratos' men. Suliman, my physician, who was not able to swim, clung to the stern of the boat. It was horrible for them all, far worse than it was for me.

"A skiff was waiting at the edge of the reeds to carry us to Ferra. They have a large military port just south of the borderlands, full of transport ships. We were transferred to one of them, put in a cabin belowdecks. Then Pyratos came on board and we headed south along the coast, bound for the *polis* of Ferra. But a violent tempest rose up, as you know, and blew us out to sea. There's no need to tell you the rest.

"As for your other questions, I don't know why Pyratos would feel such personal hatred for me and my late father. We did nothing to harm him; we just pursued the war as we were commanded to do. He may want to put an end to the royal line of Arcos so he can claim the kingdom. But that doesn't explain the grand public trial. He could have had me assassinated right there in Arcos, as he did with my father. And if it was personal satisfaction he wanted, he could have put a knife between my ribs this very night. Yet he didn't. I honestly don't understand it."

"Oh," Aria says. "I think I do."

"Tell me, then."

"Pyratos is the guilty party."

"You mean he killed his own uncle?"

"I am sure of it. And there must have been gossip about it over the years—the people know, or at least they suspect. From what I heard the guards say, he's not well liked in Ferra. Actually it's worse than that: there are rumblings of murder and rebellion. So Pyratos hopes to put all that to rest and secure his throne by giving the people someone else to blame."

Alexos thinks it over. "Yes," he says. "That sounds

right. I must say that for a gentle country lad, you have a very subtle grasp of court intrigue."

"Nonsense. I know nothing at all about 'court intrigue.' I never even heard that phrase before. I've lived here all my life and everything I know about the world comes from reading stories."

Impulsively, she grabs his hand and squeezes it hard. "I'm sorry I can't free you tonight," she says. "I hate to make you wait another day. But I have to consult with the others. I promise to come back tomorrow, though, whatever we decide. About this same time. Be ready to leave, just in case."

"Please be careful."

"I will." She hates to go. Part of her wants to stay here forever, reclining on the soft grass, whispering in the darkness to this handsome young king, who . . .

"What shall I call you?" she asks. "I know you are king of Arcos, but you haven't told me your name."

He smiles. "It is Alexos."

"Oh. I like that very much. May I call you Alexos, or would it be improper?"

"Of course you may. But now you must tell me yours."

"Oh," she says. "Um." Would Heracles sound silly? Yes, definitely. Achilles? Hector? "You can call me Hector."

"That isn't your name, though, is it?"

"I have to go." She squeezes his hand again. Then wordlessly she rises and vanishes stealthily into the night.

27

CLAUDIO SLIPS INTO THE temple and quietly closes the door behind him. "They're searching the island," he says. "But don't be alarmed. I'm sure they're just looking for resources, food and water. And they'll want to know if there are people living here, warlike or otherwise. It's what anyone would do under the circumstances."

Aria, who was dead asleep when her father came in, sits up and gazes at him blearily through half-closed eyes. She wonders why, if they're not to be alarmed, he's creeping around and speaking in whispers.

"But the important thing to remember is that they're *not* looking for us. They have no reason to suspect that anybody's here. The path leading up from the beach is well hidden. I doubt they'll ever find it.

And even if they do, they'll see nothing at the top but weeds. If we stay hidden till they've finished their search, I think we should be all right."

"But what if they never leave?" Teo says. "Will we have to stay hidden forever?"

"I trust the goddess to arrange things so that doesn't happen."

Aria urgently needs to speak with her father, but she's bone weary after a few brief hours of fitful sleep. She rubs the back of her neck, makes a circle with her head, rolls her shoulders, takes deep breaths.

"Hard night?" Claudio asks.

"I hardly slept at all."

"Bless you, child, you mustn't worry so. Athene will protect us."

"No," she says, "that's not it. There's something I have to tell you and you're going to be angry. Please try to understand if you can."

"I will try." But he looks wary.

"Last night you put out the lamp very early. You and Teo went right to sleep. But I could not; I just lay here thinking and wondering about—well, everything, really. And I had the strongest desire to go and see it for myself—the camp, Pyratos, all that you described."

"You *went out*?"

"I did. But, Papa, listen. I know every corner of this

island. We mapped it, remember—Teo and I? And I'm light on my feet. I can sneak up on wild creatures and not scare them away. So I believed in myself, you see. I felt sure I could go out there and have a look and no one would be the wiser."

"And?"

"I was right. No harm was done—and I learned a lot."

Claudio nods and waits. He is still reserving judgment.

"I was crouching in the garden weeds looking down at the men and the tents and whatnot, when I noticed another light some distance away. It was coming from that clearing—you remember, Teo, where we saw the fox that first time? Papa, it's another camp. Pyratos is keeping a prisoner there."

"I know that, Aria. I saw it when I went to look yesterday afternoon."

"Well, I went to investigate. I found a good hiding spot between a boulder and a bush where I could look down on the camp unobserved. I was so close to the guards—they were sitting around their little campfire—I could hear every word they said.

"They were talking about whether the people of Ferra might send a boat to rescue them. And one of them asked, 'Would *you*? Would you send a ship to bring Pyratos back?' And the others laughed. Then someone else said he wonders that Pyratos can even sleep at night, for fear that his own soldiers might do him harm."

"His men don't support him, then. Good to know."

"It certainly sounded that way. But they were nervous. They dropped their voices when they talked about Pyratos. So it's not open rebellion or anything."

Claudio nods.

"Now this is the really important part. You said you knew about the other camp. But do you know who the prisoner is?"

"I expect you're about to tell me."

"Alexos, the king of Arcos."

In the dead silence that follows she hears Teo make a little noise, a quick intake of breath, then another, deeper one.

"What?" Aria asks, turning to her brother. "Do you know something about him?"

"No. The name just struck me of a sudden. *Alexos.* It feels familiar, but also sharp, like stepping on a thorn. That doesn't make any sense, does it?"

"I wouldn't discount anything, son. There must be some meaning in it."

"Well, there's nothing sharp about *this* Alexos, I

assure you, Teo. He's very young, thoughtful, good of heart."

She hesitates now, worrying about what comes next. So far her father has been remarkably calm. But that's likely to change once Pyratos comes into the story.

"I had gone around to the other side of the clearing—being very quiet, Papa, very careful. I had made arrangements to speak with the king, but only after the guards were asleep—"

"Wait! You *made arrangements*? How could you possibly—?"

"The king has a manservant, Peles. He told the guards he was going into the forest to make water, but really he went there to talk to me."

"How did he know you were there if you were so quiet and careful?"

"I wondered that too. But Peles said he heard silence where there should have been crickets and frogs."

"This gets worse and worse!"

"It does, Papa, but not because of Peles. He told me who the prisoner was and that he was in mortal danger. I said I would like to help, but first I wanted to meet him. I also said I couldn't promise anything, that I'd have to consult with the others first. That's how I put it: *the others*. He doesn't know we are only three."

"Please don't drag this out, Aria. I am sick with dread waiting for the part where it gets worse."

"Well, as I said before, I had worked my way around to the other side so we could have our meeting. And I was sitting very still, waiting. Then Pyratos came into the camp. Papa, don't look at me like that! It was dark as pitch and I was well hidden behind a grove of trees. I couldn't see them, so they couldn't see me."

"Then how do you know it was Pyratos?"

"I could tell the moment he came into camp, by the way he talked. But also the guards called him 'Your Majesty.' And Alexos said, 'You are a dreadful man, Pyratos.'"

"I believe you."

"But it's what Pyratos *said* that's most important. And when you hear it, I'm sure you'll agree that we must rescue the king of Arcos."

"I have aged ten years just listening to this."

"All right. If Pyratos is able to leave this island and return to Ferra—which he fully expects to do—he will put the king of Arcos on trial for conspiring in the murder of a certain great nobleman of Ferra. And though Alexos is innocent, he'll be found guilty all the same and executed on the spot. I heard Pyratos tell him so. He made a joke of it."

"Aria—"

"Wait, listen! This nobleman was lost at sea. He was a duke. He was Pyratos' uncle."

Claudio's eyes grow wide, and for once, he is speechless.

"Papa, he is charged with *your* murder! And he will die for it, too, if we don't save him. Please, please, give me your permission to go to him again tonight, as I told him I would do, and say that we will give him safe hiding. Peles claims he can steal the key to the manacle. It's possible. It can be done."

"Yes, I agree we must help him. But this is my affair, Aria, not yours, *my* moral obligation. I will bear the risk."

Aria shakes her head. "You don't know the island as I do, and you're not nearly as stealthy. You'll make a noise or go the wrong way. Besides, they're expecting me."

He just sits staring into the middle distance, looking sad, shaking his head.

"I'm not a child, Papa. I'm seventeen and fully capable of doing important things, same as you."

Claudio notices the brown cap lying on Aria's pallet. He picks it up, turns it over in his hands, picks out a golden hair, and drops it on the floor. "Daughter," he says, as if to the cap, "is the king of Arcos aware that you are a girl?"

"He is not. I covered my hair. I spoke in a low voice."

"Well, thank the gods for that much anyway."

"May I go then, with your blessing?"

He opens his hands in a gesture of surrender. "May Athene protect you in your errand of mercy," he says. "But oh, my dearest child, *do be careful.*"

28

IT'S BEEN DARK FOR many hours and the guards are all asleep, but still there is no sign of the boy. They understand that he never committed to the rescue, but he did promise to come. Has he had second thoughts? Did the others convince him that it was too great a risk?

They're ready to go, just in case. Cloaks and boots are on. Alexos is wearing his brace, and his cane is close at hand. Now, being so far committed to action, it's especially hard to wait.

"I don't suppose," Suliman says softly, "that the young man is aware of your limitations—that you won't be able to creep away quietly and in haste, as he probably expects?"

"No, I don't suppose he is."

"I see."

"I'm afraid I shall have to travel in the same humiliating manner as I was dragged out of Arcos."

"Not dragged," Leander says. "Gently carried."

"I stand corrected."

"And I'm guessing," Leander continues, "that it'll be up a mountain this time, not through a fetid swamp—which I find infinitely preferable. But we're up for anything, eh, Peles?"

"We are indeed, Leander."

"All the same," Suliman says, "it's only fair to tell him how matters stand before there's any stealing of keys and unlocking of manacles. Much harm could be done if things go awry. He may not be willing to chance it once he learns of the complications."

"I know that, Suliman. I will tell him."

Alexos lies back and closes his eyes. He has no control over anything, so he might as well rest while he can. But he doesn't sleep, or not exactly. He slides into a state of half dreams; strange thoughts drift, lazy and unbidden, through his consciousness.

Most especially he thinks about the island. He's seen very little of it—just the beach and this clearing. Yet the perfectly formed trees, the remarkable softness of the grass, the ever-present fog—they are exactly like the Underworld as seen in his dreams. Is it possible, he wonders, that he is dead and simply doesn't know it? Was that the Stygian river they crossed during that terrible tempest? Was Charon at the helm?

He doesn't feel dead. His body aches, every inch of it, even the parts that don't move. But who can say if the dead feel pain? Probably they do, at least the wicked ones.

"You all right?" Leander whispers in his ear.

"Why do you ask?"

"You sounded rather nightmarish just now—gasping and moaning."

"I dreamed we were all dead and this was the Underworld."

"*That's* unpleasant."

"Oddly not. It was almost peaceful. Leander, was there anything particular you noticed about that boy?"

"Such as?"

"I don't know. Anything. Did he seem familiar to you in some way?"

"No. But he was awfully pretty for a lad dressed in rags. Not coarse and ugly as peasants usually are—eh, Peles?"

This is a tiresome old joke that the two of them seem to enjoy, but Alexos isn't in the mood for it now. "Pretty?" he says, keeping to the subject.

"Yes. Like a girl."

And suddenly Alexos cannot breathe. He's

feverishly working it out in his mind and his body is alive with the implications. His heart is racing, his gut is clenched, and he can't settle himself as he swings between wild joy and absolute terror. He thought he was long past such feelings.

Not really caring whether he lives or dies (except that his death would be a disaster for Arcos and contrary to Athene's inscrutable plans) has brought him a strange kind of peace. He accepts all pain and humiliation as his well-deserved penance, and that has been liberating too. He thought nothing could touch him anymore. But he never anticipated this!

A frog croaks in the forest, then croaks twice more—and it's the worst possible time. Alexos isn't ready. He doesn't know what to do. But Peles is already giving the signal that all is safe. And then come the soft, careful steps of someone approaching, quiet but just barely audible if you're listening hard, which he is.

Suliman rolls over, as he did the night before, opening up a space beside the king. The boy sits as noiselessly as he crept into camp.

"It's all right," he whispers. "The others have agreed. If you're ready, we can go tonight."

"Wait. First I have some questions."

"Then make it quick. We'll have to circle around to avoid the guards and Pyratos' camp. It'll take a lot longer that way and I want to get you hidden before first light."

"I understand. But there are things I need to know. It's important."

"Go ahead, then."

"Are there trees on this island that reach down their branches and offer their fruit? And winds that sing like a choir of heavenly voices?"

"How did you know about that? The wind has fallen silent since you came; and there are no fruit trees in this clearing."

"I dreamed it, a long time ago. I thought it was the Underworld. Perhaps it is and I'm already dead." He lays a warm hand—the one that isn't shackled—on Aria's arm. "You don't feel like a ghost," he says.

"That's because I'm not."

"Tell me, then: among your people, is there a family, a brother and a sister? He is dark, like me; she is older, with hair that shines like gold."

"Why do you ask?"

"Because I dreamed them, too. There is also a kindly father—a bearded man, quite devoted to his children. Do you know such a family?"

"I might."

"You said there were only a few people here. Surely you must know them all."

"I'm not free to discuss them."

"But they are well?—you can tell me that much. Is the boy grown, healthy and happy? And the girl, she must be a woman now."

"They're both very well indeed. You will meet them soon. But we'd best go now while we can."

"And the boy," he says. "Has he also lived on this island all his life?"

"No," she says slowly, plainly growing uneasy. "He was four years old or thereabouts when he came to us."

Alexos catches his breath. "How? How did he come?"

"In a boat. Athene brought him here to safety."

"And he's been happy ever since? Content?"

"I told you before: yes."

Alexos swallows hard, tries desperately to control his voice. "And what is he called, the boy? Do you know his name?"

"We'd better go," she says.

"Just tell me his name. That's all I ask. Please."

Their heads are already close together as they speak in whispers. Now she leans closer still, her lips almost touching his ear. Her breath smells like clover. "His name is Teo," she says.

There's no hiding his feelings now. He pulls away

and covers his face with his free hand. He's weeping, making too much noise. Peles and Leander lean in, anxious. Suliman sits up. Aria doesn't know what to do.

"I lost a brother," Alexos finally says when he has recovered himself. "He was only four, and he looked very like the boy in the dream. That's all. It upset me."

"I'm sorry."

"I'm sorry too, because I cannot come with you."

"But why? Last night you said—"

He tears off the blanket. His tunic rides up in the process and, by the light of a few dancing fireflies, his leg in its metal brace is revealed. "This is why. I can't walk without a cane, nor move with any speed. I would give you away with the noise I made."

"But, Alexos," Peles whispers, "we can—"

"Hush," the king snaps, determined to make this his excuse—and as humiliating as possible, too, because the scab is off and it's a fresh, new wound again.

"I'll come back tomorrow when you're more yourself," Aria says, making to rise.

"Wait. One more thing, please."

"What is it?"

"Come closer."

She does, and in an instant his hand is touching her cap, pulling it off. Her hair comes tumbling down.

It's hard to say which of them gasps—all of them, probably. And the sound of it, coming as it does after all Alexos' weeping and the rising of their whispers, has woken the guard. But they are so caught up in this revelation that they don't see Vasos coming till he has Aria by the arm.

29

PYRATOS EMERGES FROM HIS tent, thoroughly annoyed: his men have disturbed his sleep with their loud conversation, and there's no excuse for such stupidity! They know which tent is the king's, yet they stand right outside it, practically shouting. What in Hades were the blasted fools thinking, anyway?

The answer to his question is simple: they were thinking that Pyratos would be furious if they waited till morning to tell him about this interesting new development. On the other hand, he would also be furious if they woke him up. So this had been their ruse, and it had worked.

Now the king of Ferra looks around the camp with fire in his eyes. He takes in the assembled soldiers, the prisoner's guard, the sentries. Then he sees the girl and his expression suddenly changes. "Well, what have we here?" he says with a predatory smile. The men move aside to let him pass.

"I found her in the prison camp, Your Majesty," Vasos says. He has a firm hold on Aria's arm, more out of nervousness than any ill intent. All the same, she'll have a bruise there by morning.

Pyratos looks her up and down, studying her in a dispassionate way, as if she were for sale in the agora and he's deciding whether or not he wants to buy. He registers approval of her face and hair, disgust at her shabby clothes and bare feet. Then he makes a little snuffling sound, as if laughing through his nose.

At the same time Aria is staring back at Pyratos, and is shocked to see the unmistakable family resemblance. His hair is pale gold, as hers is, as her father's was before it turned white. He has the same noble brow, the same long face. Even the eyes are the same color, pale green.

"You are certainly familiar!" Pyratos snaps. And at first, Aria thinks he means she looks like family. But then the sentry grabs the back of her head and tilts her face down to a more seemly angle. Apparently she is not permitted to look directly at the king, though he is free to look at her all he likes.

"She claims to live alone on the island," Vasos says.

"No villages, no other people. She eats fruits and nuts and lives in a cave."

"She's lying, of course."

Aria sighs, rather too loudly. Vasos grips her tighter in warning.

Pyratos cocks his head, as if to see her better. "Now I wonder: What *shall* I do with you?" He's apparently decided to buy.

"You could let me go. I am perfectly harmless."

"I could do that, yes. But I think I'd rather clean you up and let you amuse me with stories about your adventures on the island. I don't suppose you dance? Play the lyre?"

She blinks, a little confused. "No thank you," she says.

The men laugh.

"You'd rather live alone in a cave than enjoy my company? Really, my dear, there are many who would leap at the chance."

It just slips out: "I'd rather die."

"*Excuse* me?"

"I'd rather die."

"And why is that?" He's leaning in too close. She feels his hot breath on her face.

"Because you are a monster with blood on your hands. You killed both my parents. And were it not for the merciful Athene you would have killed me t—"

He slaps her hard across the face. Then he slaps her again. But she's past fear now and well into righteous anger. She can't stop herself.

"Do you really not recognize me, *cousin*? I am your uncle Claudio's child. Surely you remember him. You took his fortune, put him under arrest, allowed his wife to die untended, then sent him off in a ship, believing he was banished—"

Before she can finish, his arm is around her neck. He presses hard against her throat until she gags. She flails wildly with her arms till he pins one of them down, but she goes on punching him with the other. With her heel she kicks his shin. She knows she's not really hurting him, only making things worse. Probably he'll kill her in his rage. She doesn't care.

Instead, he freezes in surprise as the glade is suddenly filled with music—rich, majestic, and uncommonly loud: horns blasting over the sound of strings and flutes. The wind has never made that kind of music before. This has the quality of a fanfare.

"What is that?" Pyratos says.

Everyone looks around, alarmed.

Now the fog thickens and shimmers with light, and within that light a vision slowly forms. At first it's just ambiguous shapes and random flashes of color. But soon they begin to fuse and meld into a recognizable scene. They see a room, a throne, a king sitting on the throne—Pyratos, in fact, as he'd been when he was younger. Standing before him, cap in hand, is a disreputable-looking creature. The sort of person you might expect to pick your pocket.

Pyratos has released his grip in his astonishment. Aria darts away and returns to Vasos, who takes her arm again, but more gently now. The figures in the air begin to speak.

"I believe I've got it, Yer Majesty," the disreputable fellow says. "Clear as clear. The duke goes off on his voyage, lugging all his books and whatnot along with him, 'cause he thinks he's being banished. Then when we're well out to sea, another boat will meet us and we'll all go over to that one and row away."

There are gasps from the men. Pyratos waves his arms. "Stop that thing!" he bellows to no one in particular.

But it doesn't stop.

"And?" the young Pyratos says in the vision.

"We never, ever, *ever* speaks of it to no one."

"And?"

"We never, ever, *ever* comes back neither, 'cause we're supposed to of drownded along with the duke. And some other fella, that enemy king, is supposed to of done it."

"Good. We understand each other. Now, I am

paying you all handsomely to do this, more money than you could ever hope to see in your lives. So if any one of you so much as breathes a word, or decides to come back to visit his mother, then I promise that man a long and very painful death. Do you understand?"

"I do, Yer Majesty. I do indeed."

"Then you sail tomorrow. And may I never look upon your poxy face again."

"That you will not, Yer Majesty. I guarantees it."

The vision fades, the last few words having been drowned out by a rumble of angry voices. The men move away from Pyratos, as they would from a leper.

The second vision comes up more quickly. Now they see two ships at sea, a large one and a smaller one. The duke, a younger Claudio, holding the infant Aria in one of his arms, is pulling at the sleeve of a sailor with the other.

"Surely you cannot mean to leave us here to die."

"Surely we can. For we've been hired to do it, y'see, and by someone very important—very, *very* important, if you catch my meaning, such as you don't say *no* to lest you wants to lose your head. 'Tis a pity, though. He never said there'd be a child."

The men leave the ship and row away. The storm rises. Claudio shields his baby daughter with the hem of his cloak. The sound of wailing winds and hammering rain fills the island camp.

King Pyratos, who is not an unintelligent man, senses the rising fury of his men and he is wise enough to be afraid. "Stop that thing!" he cries again. And this time the scene pauses. But it doesn't go away. Claudio still stands on the deck of that empty ship holding his innocent child to his breast as heavy clouds loom overhead and raindrops, frozen in motion, wait to strike them.

"For shame!" comes a voice from behind him. Pyratos spins around, as if fearing a knife at his back.

"Is it true?" comes another.

"No!" Pyratos cries. "I don't know what that is, but it's a brazen lie. No one in Ferra mourned my uncle's death more than I did. He withdrew from his responsibilities at court after his wife died, and I respected that. But he returned to my service and agreed to go on a secret diplomatic mission. We hoped to reach an agreement with the king of Arcos to lessen the carnage on the borderlands. Claudio was on his way to discuss the terms when that swine King Ektor, in collusion with his swinish son Alexos, sent warships to attack our peaceful party, though the duke's vessel plainly flew the flag of truce."

"Liar!"

"Any man who touches me dies a traitor's death."

"And who would arrest us?"

Pyratos looks to his captain of the guard, who stands behind him.

"Dimitrios!" he says. "Do something."

"I regret, Your Majesty, that I no longer choose to serve you."

"Nor I," cries a voice from the crowd.

"Nor I!"

"Nor I!"

Pyratos takes a deep breath and clenches his hands into fists. He is rallying now, fully aware that if he doesn't seize this moment, soon it will be too late. He climbs onto one of the benches so everyone can see him and thrusts his right hand into the air. The bright image behind him remains unchanged, the duke and his child still in peril. The men fall silent.

"I know I haven't always been a good king. My uncle gave me wise advice and I didn't heed it. Like any young man thrust into power before he's ready, I made mistakes. But I would have grown under my uncle's tutelage had his life not been so cruelly cut short. Instead, I became wild with rage over his murder. I pursued the war against Arcos with a passion that consumed me."

There is more grumbling from the men.

"Hear me out," Pyratos cries, "and then you shall judge."

They fall quiet again.

"I would never have harmed my uncle. He was like a second father to me. And looking back, remembering his soft and careful words, I am astonished at the subtlety of his mind, the greatness of his understanding, and the goodness of his heart. Indeed, if he could be brought back to life this night, I would gladly give over my throne to him, abdicate, and let him rule in my stead—"

"Would that it were so!"

"Sadly, that is not possible. He is lost to us forever. But his wise counsel is not. And though in my grief I followed the poisonous path of revenge, this night I have been recalled to my better self. I swear to you"—and here he literally beats his breast—"that the trial of King Alexos shall be my last act of retribution. Once my uncle's death has been fully and truly avenged, I will put away all thoughts of war and rule as Claudio would have had me do. I shall devote the rest of my life to honoring his memory. And you will find in me a friend to the poor, a supporter of all that is honest and fair. What say you, my good men? Will you pardon me for the sins of my past and give me another chance, so that I may become everything I ought, for which I was anointed by the immortal gods—your true and righteous king?"

It's a good speech, spoken with passion, the pauses in all the right places. His men aren't inclined to trust him, but they're moved by his words. They are searching their hearts and consciences, wondering what to do, when Claudio steps out of the fog and into camp, dressed in his dingy robe, formerly a coverlet, yet strangely godlike with the noble features of his face set off by his snowy beard and long, wild hair. As he appears, the vision fades and he is bathed in a circle of golden light.

A hundred men gasp as one. Many sink to their knees. The king tumbles off the bench, onto the ground. It is the kind of entrance every actor dreams of.

"Nephew," he says, addressing Pyratos, who is even then scrambling to his feet. "I am glad to know you remember me so fondly."

For a moment the king is speechless. Then: *"Claudio?"*

It's not that Pyratos doesn't recognize his uncle—the man hasn't aged that much. He simply can't believe his eyes.

"As you see," Claudio says.

"But I thought—"

"—that I was dead. I know. And indeed, it was a very close thing. But Athene was kind to us and brought us here to this island. And so I stand before you now, very much alive."

Aria pulls away from Vasos, who doesn't try to stop her, and runs into her father's arms.

"I rejoice that it is so," says the king, trying his best to sound sincere.

"And I also rejoice, nephew, that you've had such a sudden and dramatic change of heart, that you see the error of your ways and regret the evil you have done. That *was* genuine, was it not—all those things you said?"

Pyratos chokes, clears his throat, and tries again. "Yes," he says. "I was sincere in confessing my failings. I shall be a better king heretofore."

Nikomedes, one of the chief noblemen of Ferra, steps forward now, bows low to the duke, then turns to the king. "If that is so, my lord Pyratos, if you spoke honestly—"

"I did. I meant every word from the depth of my heart."

"Then I am glad. For it was such a stirring speech, it very nearly brought me to tears. I warrant I could give it back to you word for word even now, especially the part where you said—what was it exactly?—'If only my uncle could be brought back to life, I would give over my throne to him this very night. I would abdicate, and let him rule in my place.' Something like that; close enough. So tell us, did you mean that, too? Or was it just another lie?"

"I . . . I meant it at the *time*, but you see—"

But his words are lost in a roar of derisive laughter. It is so full of scorn that even Pyratos can see that he is finished. Not one man among them would support him. He's made a pledge and they are holding him to it.

"And I mean it still," he says.

The laughter stops.

"Then, if you will," Nikomedes says, "say the words properly here and now so that there shall be no mistake. I will help you if you like."

"No, thank you, Lord Nikomedes, I am quite capable of abdicating with no assistance from you." Pyratos stares down at his feet, takes a couple of deep breaths, then looks up into the expectant faces of his men.

"As the gods have wrought a miracle and brought my dear uncle Claudio back from the dead, and as he was ever highly esteemed for his wisdom, his temperance, and his judgment, I hereby renounce my throne and my title of king, though it came to me by rights as the only son of—"

"Get on with it!" shouts a voice from the crowd.

"My title, as rightfully mine, is rightfully mine to refuse, abdicate, and resign. And this I now do, formally and absolutely. I choose as my successor the honorable duke, my uncle Claudio."

He removes the diadem from his head and makes

to hand it to his uncle, but Lord Nikomedes steps in.

"That was handsomely done, Pyratos," he whispers. "But it wouldn't be proper for Claudio to crown himself. So if you haven't the stomach to set it on his head, which I certainly understand, then I will gladly do it for you."

"No," Pyratos says, shooting Lord Nikomedes a venomous look, "I am quite capable of doing that as well. Uncle, will you kneel?"

Claudio does and Pyratos lays the diadem on his head. Then, giddy with relief now that he is safely on the other side of the most dangerous crisis of his life, he adds (and who can say whether he means it or not), "May the gods forgive me for my many sins. Long live King Claudio!"

30

CLAUDIO SITS AT THE table with Pyratos and Lord Nikomedes. They discuss, phrase by phrase, the exact wording of the document that will officially transfer the throne of Ferra from Pyratos to his uncle. As each section is agreed upon, Nikomedes writes it down.

Pyratos leans pointedly away from the other two, as if none of this really has anything to do with him. When asked a question he nods and occasionally he speaks, but never once does he look at them.

Aria watches, impatient. She knows what they're doing is important, but it's taking so long! Meanwhile, the king of Arcos is still chained to a tree. Why couldn't they free him first and work on the document later?

Teo appears at her side and slips an arm around her waist. She responds in kind, hugging him close and leaning her head on his shoulder. "I didn't see you," she says. "When did you get here?"

"Right after Papa. I came in from the side."

"You were supposed to wait in the temple. Why did you come here at all?"

"Papa had a strong foreboding that you were in danger. He told me to stay behind, but I followed him. I was worried too. What happened to your cap?"

"Oh," she says. "The king of Arcos pulled it off."

"Why?"

"He didn't say. I think he knew me for a fraud."

"And then there was trouble?"

"Yes. Did you see?"

"Some of it. More than enough—I saw it as I was coming down."

"What do you suppose they'll do with Pyratos? Is it possible they'll let him go free?"

"I guess that's up to Papa."

Nikomedes has finished the document. Claudio signs it, then hands it to Nikomedes, who turns it around to face Pyratos, giving him the pen. For a moment, Pyratos stares at the instrument, as if he can't remember what it's for. Then, in a single rapid movement, he scrawls his name and angrily tosses the pen aside.

One last step remains and then they will be done. Nikomedes holds a stick of sealing wax over the lamp's flame. When it begins to melt, he holds it over the scroll. Thick gobbets of molten wax drop onto the parchment, dark red against ivory, like dried blood. He reaches out to Pyratos as if asking for something. But Pyratos just scowls at the lord's open hand.

Finally Claudio leans in and whispers to his nephew and, as if in physical pain, Pyratos slides the gold signet ring from the little finger of his right hand. He looks at it for one last, bitter moment, then throws it as he had the pen. The ring bounces and is about to go flying off the table, but Claudio catches it neatly and hands it to Nikomedes, who presses the bezel into the hardening puddle of wax, imprinting the document with the royal seal of Ferra.

Pyratos doesn't watch; he's turned away again. So he's spared the sight of his uncle slipping the ring onto his own finger: the ultimate symbol of kingship, more important even than the crown.

The men rise and Pyratos turns to go, but Claudio calls him back. Then he walks around the table and, to everyone's surprise, offers both hands to his nephew in an unmistakable gesture of forgiveness. With amazement and relief, Pyratos takes them. However false his apology may have been, Claudio has accepted it.

The official business now over and Aria's patience having come to an end, she releases Teo and goes to stand beside her father. He is in conversation with Nikomedes and a few of the other nobles, so she makes herself obvious and waits. The result is pretty near immediate; the men fall silent and turn toward her.

"The king of Arcos is still imprisoned," she says. "Shouldn't we go free him now?"

"Yes, daughter, we should."

It's decided that Dimitrios and Lord Nikomedes should be the first to approach the prison guards. As men of the highest rank, well-known and highly respected, they are the most likely to be believed. They also bring Vasos, who is one of them, to vouch for the truth of everything they say.

But the guards are already prepared for astonishing news. There's been enough going on this past hour, between the fanfare, and the glowing lights, and the shouts of angry men, to make them conclude that something momentous has occurred.

Nikomedes takes the lead, explaining in a simple way what happened. Then as proof of Pyratos' abdication, he unrolls the document and presents it to the guards for their inspection. They lean in and study it with interest, though none but the officer can read (and even he can't make out the writing in the darkness of early morning). But it certainly looks official. One of them touches the seal with his finger and nods, satisfied.

Then their new king is brought forward. This turns out to be a lovely moment, for one of the guards remembers Claudio from the old days. He exclaims and falls to his knees, then laughs aloud. If there were any remaining doubts, they have been dispelled.

The guards are glad to set their prisoner free. But the key to the manacles is on a ring which is on the officer's belt, so first he must undo the buckle and take off the belt. Aria can't wait another second. She worms her way through the knot of jabbering men and streaks across the clearing to the tree.

"You will not believe—" she gasps breathlessly.

"We heard," Leander says with a dazzling smile.

"Oh, but they are so very *slow*! I cannot bear it."

The officer finally arrives and shoos everyone aside so he can get down beside the king to unlock the iron cuff. When it's done and the officer has stepped back again, Aria takes his place beside Alexos. Gently, she touches the raw place on his wrist where the manacle has worried the skin. But he doesn't look down to examine the damage. He only looks at her.

"Aria," he says—oh so solemnly. His voice is whispery, shaking.

"How did you know my name?"

"I dreamed it. But listen, please." He seems absolutely terrified; she can't imagine why. "Before I get up from here, before we go anywhere and things are said and done, I want you to know how grateful I am for what you tried to do. You put yourself in terrible danger; I was frantic with fear when they took you."

"It was nothing worse than a slap and some ugly words. And now you are free, Pyratos has gotten what he deserved, and everything's right with the world. Please, let me help you rise."

"I'm too heavy for you to manage. My friends are well accustomed to doing it."

She sees that this is true. Peles and Leander slide in, one on either side of the king, each gripping him under the arm and lifting him with ease. Now the physician hands him the cane and for a moment they remain as they are, making sure Alexos is steady.

"You've been immobile for a long time," the physician says quietly. "You'll be stiff and the pain will be worse than usual. Take care you don't fall."

Alexos doesn't look at him. He just gazes down at the grass, his thoughts somewhere else. He is breathing hard and there are tears welling in his eyes. But he nods to say that he's all right, he can manage on his own. Then, as grave as a prisoner going to his execution, Alexos advances haltingly toward Claudio and the other officials.

Aria watches him with a strange mixture of pity and awe: the roll of his shoulder as he leans on the cane, the way he swings the imprisoned leg forward and carefully settles his weight upon it. And somehow he is all the more beautiful to her because part of him is damaged and because he has accepted it with such ease and grace.

Halfway across the clearing, Alexos stops. Teo has just emerged from behind the tall brush that grows along the path. Both stand frozen, staring at each other in silence, and everyone feels the charge of tension in the air. The moment expands unbearably until finally Alexos speaks, his voice clouded with emotion.

"Teo?"

And Teo says, *"You!"*

"Leander, help me," the king whispers, harsh and urgent. "Peles, slide the latch so I can kneel."

But Leander doesn't move. He just stares, open-mouthed, at Teo. Beside him, the physician sways slightly, as if knocked off balance. Only Peles does as he is bid.

"Oh, Teo!" Alexos cries, his voice rough with pain.

Aria looks from her brother to the king of Arcos,

then back again. Something momentous is happening here, something she doesn't understand. (She ought to; she's been given plenty of clues: all that talk of dreams and a lost brother, the questions about Teo and whether he was happy, and how very alike they are.) But she hasn't made the connection yet. All she knows is that Alexos is distraught, kneeling in the grass, and her brother is angry.

"*You!*" Teo says again, moving toward the king now, his cheeks burning. "You were my *brother*!"

Alexos rocks back as if struck by the word: *were.* "Yes," he says.

"And I was in a little boat on the edge of a river. There was no fog in that place—"

"Arcos."

"I climbed into the boat because I wanted to please you. I thought we would—"

"—go fishing."

"Because you were sad and I wanted to make you happy again. You'd been away for a long time and I missed you. I was so glad we were together again. I was also frightened because you seemed so changed. But I never expected . . ."

Alexos hangs his head. Teo comes nearer. He is standing directly in front of his brother now, staring down at the dark, curling hair, so very like his own.

"You untied the line from the post and flung it over the bow; but you didn't get into the boat. You *pushed* it away, looking at me the whole time with this face I didn't recognize. You *pushed* me out into the current that carried me down the river and out to sea. And I was *just a little boy*; I was scared and I was alone—and so very wounded that *you*, of all people, would do that to me!"

There is stunned silence. Alexos has raised his head and looks directly into his brother's face. "Yes," he says, as if the words were being ripped out of him. *"All of that is true!"*

Teo comes closer. He is heaving with emotion and there aren't any words to express it, only the movement of his hands, pushing his brother away, as Alexos had once pushed him. Alexos sways to the side but regains his balance, so Teo shoves him again. This time he falls hard. His head strikes the ground with a loud *thunk*, like a gourd that has dropped and split.

The sound is horrible, but it only stokes the fire of Teo's rage. Screaming and sobbing, he kicks at his brother—two, three, four times, aiming most especially at his legs. And there's no telling what else he might have done had Claudio not grasped him from behind and pulled him away.

"Stop," Claudio says, gripping his son with all his

strength. But the boy continues to struggle. "Stop! I mean it, Teo. You've done enough."

"I hate you!" Teo shouts to his brother, who lies unmoving now. "Papa, let me go! *Let me go!* I can't be here anymore!"

"Will you go directly back to the temple?"

"Yes." Teo is heaving great, wrenching sobs now, pulling hard to get away. "Please, Papa, *please*!"

Claudio turns his son away from the damage he has done, points him toward the path, and releases him. "Quickly, then," he says. "I'll come as soon as I can."

Aria watches Teo as he runs away, sobbing, watches her father watching him, then turns back to the king of Arcos and takes in the scene, the consequence of what has just been revealed. The physician is kneeling beside Alexos, examining his scalp for wounds. Leander has stepped back, as if recoiling from something loathsome, his handsome face contorted with horror and disgust. Peles just looks stunned.

And all this while Aria's rage has been building. What she felt before was nothing to this. Pyratos was just a worm. But *this* is evil beyond all imagining. Now she advances on the sad little scene, her eyes wild with anger.

"It was *you*?" she demands, standing over Alexos.

"*You* were the one we've been wondering about all these years, the one who sent Teo off alone in that little boat, knowing he would almost surely die? *His brother?*"

"Yes!" Alexos shouts.

"Then you are *vile*! Worse even than Pyratos! How can you bear to live with yourself?"

"I can't."

"Good. I hope you die. And I hope it's painful and terrifying, because—"

Once again Claudio intercedes. "Daughter, don't. There's enough hurt here already. Go comfort your brother. I will follow."

She looks defiantly up at him, then turns back to Alexos and spits at his face. It isn't well aimed and lands on his knee instead, but she sees how it wounds him and is glad. She jerks away from her father then and, without another word, dashes away.

She is running flat out, desperate to catch up with Teo. She can hear the pounding of her feet on the grass, the rhythmic rush of blood in her ears. She is weeping and sick with anger and disgust—all the more because she'd half convinced herself she loved that man. She'd admired him, pitied him, and had been so eager to set him free—when all the while, beneath that beautiful guise, there lurked a vile, ugly, foul, disgusting, monstrous beast!

She is so sick she stops to vomit. And it's as though more than bile comes out: something slick, dark, and bitter. For a moment her head is spinning and she's afraid she will fall, so she drops onto the path and sits until she's recovered herself.

Then she's up and running again—through the main camp, past a knot of astonished, silent men, then up the overgrown trail toward the temple. There are rocks here now, and creeping vines; she trips over them in her haste and falls. But always she rises and goes on, pushing herself to the very edge of her endurance, her legs aching from the rapid climb.

At last, completely out of breath, she stops, leans over, and heaves to pull air into her lungs. And from far below, she hears her father's voice as she's never heard it before. It rises like a whirlwind in the air: a cry of rage, horror, lamentation.

"By all the gods in heaven—*no! He did not have to die!*"

31

THE SOFT GRAY OF dawn has given way to the cool light of early morning, but inside the temple it is dark, lit only by the small, flickering lamp at the feet of Athene. Teo is just a shape tucked in close to the wall. He looks strangely small and childlike curled up that way, his long legs drawn against his chest, his long arms wrapped around them, his head bent over to complete the circle.

Aria is sick with disappointment. Teo was supposed to wait for her. They'd talk, and comfort each other, and then decide together what to do next, how to recapture the perfect life they'd had before all those wretched people came and ruined everything.

Instead, he's turned his back on her and gone to sleep.

She crawls over and lies beside him, curled up too, her back against his. She feels the warmth of his body, feels the slight movement as he breathes. It almost helps, but it's not nearly enough. She wants him to wake and talk to her. She wants her father to come back and make everything all right. She wants things to be as they were. She wants, and wants, and wants. But Teo doesn't move, Claudio doesn't come, and she is left alone with her grief and her anger—and maybe also a touch of shame. After a while she crawls back to her own pallet and pulls the blanket over her head.

How long it is before Claudio returns, Aria doesn't know. She's asleep when he comes in. He brushes against her knee as he sits down, waking her. She peers out from behind the blanket.

He has lit the other lamp. Now he leans against the wall, drags in a deep breath, and lets it out in a rush. It's the sound of total exhaustion. He looks at Aria with sober eyes, his head tipped down, his expression unreadable.

"You smell of smoke," she says.

"I know. Is Teo asleep?"

"It's hard to tell."

He shoots her an odd look. "How long has he been like that?"

"The whole time."

Claudio leans over and gives Teo's shoulder a gentle shake. "Son? I need you to sit up now and talk to me."

Teo curls up tighter.

"Teo!" Claudio's manner strikes Aria as uncommonly lacking in tenderness. But then, she's had no experience with firmness. "That's enough. Sit up now."

Teo also hears the edge in his father's voice. Slowly he unwraps himself and settles into a sitting position. He looks awful. He looks like an old person inhabiting the body of a child. In the lamplight his eyes are enormous and sad.

"I can only imagine how hard that was for you," Claudio begins. "It was painful just to watch it. But there is more to this matter than you could possibly know. And now we must discuss it."

"I already know," he says, covering his mouth with his hand, his eyes wide with terror.

"I don't think you do."

"I heard. Oh, Papa, I didn't mean to do it. I was just . . ."

"Teo, child—*stop*! What did you hear? What do you think you have done?"

"I killed him!"

"No."

"Yes. I heard you say it, that he was dead."

"Then you misunderstood. It had nothing to do with you at all."

"Who was it then?" Aria asks. "Who died, if not Alexos?" She had reached the same conclusion.

"While we were in the prison camp, the men held a hasty trial and found Pyratos guilty. They killed him on the spot . . . all of them, together, a wound from every man. It was a dreadful thing to behold." He shudders, lets out a ragged breath. "We burned his body this morning. That's the smoke you smelled."

"But why were you so angry? I never heard you like that before. You were *screaming*!"

"He was a man, Aria, not much over thirty years of age. And now he is nothing but ashes, and bone, and blood on the grass. Don't you find that disturbing?"

"He tried to kill you."

"Yes. And tonight he was exposed and publicly humiliated, ridiculed by his men, and his crown was taken from him. I thought that was sufficient. I'm not a tyrant. I didn't want his blood on my hands. So I forgave him. You and everyone else who was there saw me do it. My intention was perfectly clear. I hoped to make a new beginning."

"Pyratos was a monster, Papa!"

"Yes. But think, daughter: he tries to kill me, then

his men kill him. Am I now to kill those men for killing him? Where will it end?"

Aria looks down and studies her fingernails.

"What about Alexos?" Teo asks.

"He is bruised and battered, but very much alive."

Teo droops with relief. "I'm glad," he says.

Claudio sits in silence for a long while, thinking. He seems very far away. "Do you remember the story of Arcoferra, how it fell from grace and was punished by the gods?"

Aria can't imagine why he's bringing that up now. The children always found it a particularly unpleasant story: Zeus tormenting generation after generation of innocent people for a crime committed so long ago that nobody even remembers what it was. They did like the part about Athene, though, and how she promised to send a champion to deliver them someday.

"Well, that story is true. You will recall that Zeus split the country into two warring states. Alexos is the king of Arcos. I am now the king of Ferra. Technically, that makes us enemies."

Ah, she thinks. *I see where he's going.*

"I would not relish going home to pursue a war against Teo's brother. But I don't think I shall have to; because I finally understand why Athene put us in danger after so many years of tender care, why she brought Pyratos and Alexos here. *This* is the long-awaited moment. The goddess has fulfilled her promise and chosen her champion. Actually, it seems she has chosen three."

"Do you know who they are?"

"I do. Alexos was the first."

Teo sucks in breath.

"That shocks you, I know, considering what he did. But Athene is subtle in her ways. We must accept that she is wiser than any mortal and always has her reasons."

"What about the other two?"

"I am getting to that. Aria, on the day you were born I took you to the great temple of Athene in Ferra and did your augury myself. It was a strange thing to do; the tradition has always been that the champion would be a prince—and not just any prince, but the heir to one of the two thrones. You were neither prince nor heir, and a girl besides. But I had such a strong compulsion to do it, I thought it must be the will of Athene. And I was right: you were revealed to be the chosen one."

Aria cannot speak. She tries, but nothing comes out.

"I didn't know about Alexos then. I only heard this morning."

"Heard how?"

"Suliman told me, the physician. And now I see the pattern. The goddess didn't bring us to this beautiful island only to save our lives. This sweet place, this paradise, is where she wanted her champion to grow and learn. But there's more.

"Then you came, Teo. And that night, after Aria had gone back to bed, I carried you here to the temple. I laid you, sleeping, on the floor—right there, at the feet of Athene—and performed your augury. I didn't have any proper amulets, so I used common stones. I did this, as with Aria before you, because I felt compelled to do it.

"Teo—you, too, grasped the amulet for greatness. You are both her champions, on which she rests her hopes for the future of the poor, suffering mortals over whom she has watched these many years."

They look at each other, then turn as one to stare at their father.

"By choosing her champions, she has committed herself. It means that Zeus and the whole pantheon of gods have consented to hear our plea. Now you must play your parts."

"What are we supposed to do?"

"I don't know, but Athene does, and she will leave nothing to chance. Assume from now on that everything that happens is part of her plan. And on that note, the court physician of Arcos is waiting outside to speak with Teo."

"He's been waiting all this time?"

"He's a very patient man. And as I said, assuming that nothing happens by chance, there must be a reason he is here. Shall we let him in?"

Suliman ducks under the low doorway as he comes into the temple. He's a striking figure—exotic, regal, dark.

"May I sit?" He addresses Teo, who nods.

"Thank you." Suliman arranges himself on the floor, making sure that the hem of his long robe covers his feet. He takes particular care with this, as if it was something learned in childhood, an important matter of courtesy. In his hand he holds a wreath of spring-green vines, but he sets it in his lap for now and makes no reference to it.

"Prince Matteo," he begins, "I want to assure you that your brother did not send me here to ask your forgiveness. He knows that is not possible. But there is something he wants me to tell you, because he thinks it might ease your mind. Equally important, he wishes to right a grievous wrong. That is why I've come. Will you hear me?"

"I've seen you before," Teo says, squinting at the

physician as he tries to remember. "Before you came to the island, I mean. Back in my old life."

"Yes, we've met before."

"You went in and out of a room. Someone inside was very ill."

"Alexos had the summer sickness, a very dread disease. I was taking care of him. You waited outside his room every afternoon for weeks. You hid behind a chest."

"And a beautiful lady talked to me. She seemed to think I was a mouse."

Suliman almost smiles. "Yes. We pretended not to see you. But it raised our spirits that you came every day. You were such a sweet child—I expect you still are. There was no one in the palace who did not love you."

Teo resists the obvious reply.

Suliman notes this and says it again. "*No one*, Teo, from the sweepers to the chancellor himself. But none loved you half so much as your brother did. And he wants you to know that never for a moment did he stop loving you. What he did was unspeakable; it was an act of madness, born of despair. And when he came to himself and understood that he'd sent you to your death, he wanted to join you there. Indeed, he tried very hard to die."

"Why didn't he, then?"

"Athene wouldn't allow it. He belongs to her, you see."

"Her champion."

"Yes. And since living was more painful than a merciful death, he embraced it as a penance. But I have not come here to plead your brother's case. I will say no more about it. I will only relay his message: that you did not deserve what he did to you. You didn't provoke it or cause it in any way. And even in his moment of madness, Alexos never stopped loving you; he never wished you harm. He believes you to be the finest creature the gods ever made."

Teo stares at Suliman as if feeding off his words. Aria finds it terribly unnerving; she reaches out to touch him, but Claudio stops her.

"I remember," Teo says.

"Now, here is the second thing. At the time this all happened, Alexos had just recovered from his illness. As you saw this morning, it resulted in the paralysis of his legs. He would never again be the boy he was, the runner with wings on his heels. It was only after great effort that he regained the strength to walk as he does now—haltingly, with the help of a brace and a cane. And your father, King Ektor, already displeased with him for having failed to win an important race, though

Alexos was severely ill at the time—"

"I remember that too," Teo says, as if in a trance, the memories flowing back one after the other. "The race for the laurel crown. It was horrible. I thought for a moment he was going to die; everyone did."

"Just so. And Ektor, stung by his son's conspicuous and public failure, and holding certain opinions on the subject of what a king should be—that is to say, a warrior—decided that Alexos was no longer fit to rule. So he changed the terms of succession in your favor. *You* were meant to inherit the throne upon his death."

Now he picks up the wreath but doesn't yet hand it to Teo.

"Your brother has worn a kingly crown only once in his life, on the day of his coronation. Since then it has been kept in the treasury. As he doesn't have it with him, he can't give it to you now. So Peles made this for him; it's a symbol of that which is yet to come. In this way Alexos formally acknowledges that you are the king of Arcos."

Teo takes the wreath and studies it with a faraway expression.

"Alexos will affirm this publicly, in the presence of everyone on the island, and upon your return to Arcos, to all who need to hear it. Then he will leave the royal city and live in seclusion elsewhere. You will never have to see him again.

"I'm sure it is overwhelming for you, becoming king at such a tender age. But there are wise counselors in Arcos, the same ones who helped Alexos after Ektor died. They are good men, Teo. They will be at your side to advise you for as long as you need them. If I can be of any help, you have only to ask."

He is finished now. He folds his hands and waits.

Teo fiddles with the wreath, tugging at a leaf, accidentally pulling it off. "But how could he do what he did if he loved me?"

"He was broken. That's the best answer I can give."

"What broke him?"

"A lifetime of impossible expectations, rejection by his father, loneliness, failure, humiliation, sickness, the ruin of his body, the loss of his life's purpose—all by the time he was twelve." He pauses, considering whether to say more, then goes ahead. "On that same terrible day, Alexos heard his father speaking with his chancellor. Ektor said that it would have been better if Alexos had died than to be as he is now."

Teo shivers, feeling it.

"He's cobbled himself back together because duty demanded it—though I'm not sure he could have done it if Athene hadn't sent him dreams of you, of Claudio and Aria, here on this beautiful island. He took it for a blessed afterlife and it comforted him enough that he was able to go on. But he is still broken."

There is silence now.

"Tell me again," Teo says to Suliman after a while.

"Which part?"

"About the breaking."

"Well, there is an old saying in my country, about camels. You will not have seen one, but they are remarkable creatures, taller than a horse with great humps on their backs. They are strong, able to carry tremendous loads, and they can go on carrying them for days and days over the scorching desert sands without eating or drinking anything at all. But there's a limit even to what a camel can bear. So we say, 'one straw too many will break his back.'"

"And the one straw too many?"

"For your brother? Being robbed of his life's purpose, I would guess. It was the one thing that made the rest of it bearable. He was an astonishing child, Teo. Like the camel, it seemed that he carried the weight of the world on his back, but he never left off striving. Even his illness and the damage to his legs could not destroy his spirit for long. His only fear was that if he wasn't able to be a warrior, he couldn't be a proper king."

"And has he been?"

"A good king? Oh, yes—far better than Ektor ever was, if I may be so bold as to say it. And he is greatly loved by his people. He is leaving you the kingdom in much better shape than he found it."

Teo is still fiddling with the wreath.

"I thought I had killed him, you know," he says.

"Who—Alexos?"

"Yes. I pushed him so hard and his head slammed into the ground. The sound . . . it was horrible. And then"—he sucks in breath—"I kicked him over and over."

"I know. I was there."

"I wanted to kick him in the face. If Papa hadn't stopped me, I might have killed him."

"Well, you didn't."

"I know that now. But as I was running up the path, I heard Papa screaming, *'He did not have to die!'* and I thought he meant Alexos. I lay here in the dark for hours believing it."

"That must have been hard."

"It was horrible. I've never killed anything in my life—not a lizard, or a beetle, or a worm. Yet this very morning I wanted to kill my own brother. And if I'd been stronger and no one had stopped me, I might have."

"What does that tell you?"

"I'm not sure I know."

"Oh, I think you do."

Teo tilts his head thoughtfully. "It's not as easy to be good as I thought."

Suliman nods.

"I didn't know I could have such feelings. I felt like a whole other person."

Another nod.

"Will he see me, do you think?"

"Alexos? Of course!"

"I'd like that."

"Shall I take you to him?"

"Teo, no!" Aria cries, appalled.

"Leave him be," Claudio says, touching her arm in warning.

"But he can't, Papa! It's wrong!"

"I said, *leave him be*!"

Teo looks at Aria, wounded but resolute. "I wish you could understand," he says. "I'm sorry you don't." Then, to Suliman, "I want to go."

32

THE OFFICERS HAVE SHIFTED themselves to free up a tent for Alexos. Suliman and Teo stand a few paces away from it now, speaking in whispers.

"Should you to go in first and tell him I'm here?" Teo asks.

The physician considers this, then shakes his head. "I think you should just walk in. Does that frighten you?"

"Yes."

"It will frighten him too, but it will be a more honest encounter that way. I *will* make sure you are alone, however. Wait here." Suliman goes to the tent, raises one of the flaps, and peers inside. "Peles," he calls, "I need you for a moment."

Peles appears almost instantly. "Oh, I'm glad you're

back," he says to Suliman. "His legs—"

"We'll see to that later. For now I want you to keep away from Alexos. I'll let you know when it's safe to return."

Peles cocks his head like a curious bird. "Is something amiss, my lord?"

"Quite the contrary." Suliman glances significantly over at Teo, who raises a hand in a shy little wave. Peles waves back with an enormous grin. He has a wide, thin-lipped mouth, all out of proportion with his face, which makes him look rather peculiar—except when he smiles. Then all the features fall in together and he is transformed into something near to handsome.

Suliman leaves Peles to his grinning and nudges Teo closer to the tent. "My philosophy has always been that when the water is cold, it's best to dive right in. What do you think?"

Teo doesn't think. He just nods, takes a breath, and dives.

The flaps fall closed behind him but Alexos doesn't look up. He's sitting on a low stool, dressed only in his underclothes. The iron cage is off, both legs stretched out in front of him, a basin of water at his side. With a wet cloth he's bathing the gashes and abrasions that cover his legs. Presumably Peles was helping with this before he was called away.

Teo holds his breath. It's startling to see his brother like this, exposed and vulnerable. Alexos' face is solemn and beautiful, as it always was. His chest and arms are tightly muscled, the skin smooth and brown: an athlete's body in the full perfection of youth. Then Teo's eyes slide down to the legs, pale and shrunken, legs that were once as perfect as the rest of him. He is a chimera now—half one thing, half another: strong and weak, wise and foolish.

Alexos senses that something is off: Peles wouldn't just stand and stare; he'd come and help. He looks up and is turned to stone.

But his eyes are still alive with expression: hungry, desperate, amazed. And somehow it doesn't seem strange for Teo to go on standing as he is, the two of them just looking at each other. Because this is a full conversation they're having, better than any with words. It goes on for a very long time, both afraid to break the spell, afraid they'll never again share such an intensely intimate connection.

Then, the slightest movement. Alexos closes his eyes. His shoulders drop just a little. And his face is working in small ways, the release of pent-up sorrow.

"I brought you this," Teo says, half surprised his voice still works. Two steps bring him to his brother.

He squats down and hands Alexos the wreath.

"I'm sorry it's not the real crown; you shall have that later. This is only a symbol, an acknowledgment that you are king."

"No, that's not it. I don't *want* it, you see. I don't want to be a king."

"But you already are. You were Ektor's heir."

"Then I renounce it, or abdicate, or whatever it's called. That was always your destiny, not mine. I thought it sounded unbelievably tedious. I wanted to be"—his voice catches and he stops to clear his throat—"the royal fisherman."

Alexos crumbles, all his defenses gone. "Oh, Teo!" he says. "You can be anything you want. Anything at all."

"Suliman says you are a very good king."

"He is overfond. His judgment is suspect."

"No, I think his judgment is probably sound."

Teo sits now, settling in, making himself more comfortable.

"May I?" he asks, reaching for the wet cloth Alexos still holds in his hand. Alexos gives it to him, puzzled. Teo dips it into the basin, squeezes out the excess water, then gently presses it against a particularly nasty gash on the shin, all too aware that he made that wound, along with many others, though this one is the worst.

"I didn't mean to do it," he says, looking down now, abashed, still dabbing at the wound. "I'm very sorry."

Alexos gasps. *"You're* sorry?"

"Yes. I beg you to forgive me."

"Oh, Teo—there is nothing to forgive!"

"Yes there is. I did this to you. And this. And this." He touches the marks of his anger with the cloth.

"But that's nothing. I deserved every blow."

"No, it wasn't 'nothing.' I wanted to kill you."

"I deserved that too."

"Please, Alexos, *listen to me*! If I had been stronger, if I had been wearing heavy boots instead of sandals, and if I had not been stopped, I might have killed you. For a while after I left, because of a misunderstanding, I actually thought I had. And I didn't know how I could go on living with that on my conscience. Later I found out I was mistaken; it was Pyratos who'd died, not you. But there's no going back to how I was before, knowing that I am capable of willfully doing murder—"

"Not willfully, Teo; you were wild with grief and rage."

"But capable of it all the same. So I'm asking you to forgive me. I need you to say it so I can be at peace."

Alexos slides off the stool; it tumbles over and upsets the basin of water. He is on the ground now, his legs awkwardly bent to the side, and he pulls Teo into his arms, so hard it almost hurts. Teo leans into the embrace, feels his brother's hand stroking his hair, touching his face.

"I forgive you, wholeheartedly and completely, though you are innocent of any harm. *I* am the one, Teo. *I* am the one."

Alexos releases him then, and with one hand on Teo's shoulder, he touches his brother's chest, just over his heart. "I hurt you *here*," he says. Then he touches Teo's forehead, where his mind and spirit are. "And I hurt you *here*."

Teo nods, understanding.

"For eight years I believed I had killed you. I walked through my days being the person who sent an innocent child to his death, my sweet little brother who loved and trusted me. So I cannot simply say to you, 'I'm sorry,' because it isn't nearly enough. Nothing could ever be enough."

"I forgive you anyway. See? Now it's over."

There is a long, long silence.

"You are astonishing," Alexos finally says. "You are the finest creature the gods ever made."

"You accept my forgiveness?"

It seems impossible to Alexos that this is happening. But he doesn't question it. He takes it as a blessing, a rare gift, and he thanks Athene for it. "I will accept anything you choose to give me," he says.

"Alexos?"

"What?"

"Doesn't it hurt, sitting all twisted up like that?"

Alexos laughs out loud. "Of course it does."

"Can you get back up on the stool by yourself? Or do you need help?"

"I can do it. But if you would hold the stool while I settle myself, that would be a kindness. There. Thank you."

"Shall I get some more water? This is all spilled."

"No. I'd about finished anyway. I'll put the bandages on now."

"Can I help?"

"If you want."

Alexos shows him how. There are bandages for the wounds and thicker wrappings to protect his skin from the pressure of the brace. Alexos is meticulous in the way he puts them on. Teo helps by cutting strips of cloth with a knife and holding the bandages taut while his brother tucks in the loose ends.

"Does Aria know you're here?" Alexos asks as they work, not meeting Teo's eyes.

"Yes. She knows everything."

A head appears between the tent flaps, one of the soldiers come to ask a question. *Go away!* Alexos snaps, and the head disappears.

"Does she approve—of your coming here, I mean?"

"No. She's angry about it."

"Of course she is. She loves you and wants to protect you. How could she not hate the person who did you harm?"

"That's part of it."

"What's the rest?"

Teo looks up at his brother, studying his face. "She thought very highly of you. She was quite overcome with admiration, in fact. More than that, even—well, you know how girls are."

"I don't, actually."

"Really? I'd think, being king, you'd know a lot of girls. And oughtn't you to be married by now? That's how it is in stories: the ruler must get a wife and produce an heir."

"No and no. Please continue, Teo."

"Well, because she was so very fond before, finding out that you were the one . . . well, that made it worse."

"The handsome prince is revealed to be a warty toad."

"Sort of like that."

"Well, I'm honored that she liked me once and I admire her for hating me now. It shows how loyal and loving she is. I'm glad you have her for a sister."

Teo brings the brace and helps to put it on. Alexos

explains the drill—the thigh and ankle straps must be fastened first, then the ones at the knee, followed by the others; not too loose, not too tight. The wrappings have to be checked to make sure they lie smooth, with no wrinkles to press into the skin.

"Alexos?" Teo says when they have finished. He's been waiting to ask this, waiting till he has his brother's full attention.

"Yes, Teo?"

"Everyone seems to think we'll leave the island soon, that a rescue ship will come."

"Yes, I expect that is so."

"Then what happens? Papa is king of Ferra, and you are king of Arcos, and they are at war with each other."

"Ah," Alexos says. "I understand. Well, I think things may be different now."

"Do you really? That's what Papa said—that this is the great moment everyone's been waiting for, and soon everything will change."

"Did he say anything else?"

Teo hesitates. "He said you were chosen to be the champion of Athene."

"That is true."

"But Aria was chosen, too. And then I was. There are three of us."

Alexos stares at his brother, astonished. "Oh,"

he says, thinking hard. "That changes everything. It makes sense to me now: this is all about forgiveness. We cannot ask from Zeus what we are unwilling to give to each other. Shall I tell you what I think Athene has done?"

"Yes!"

"She chose you and Aria because, even on the day of your birth, she could see the goodness of your souls. Then she put you both in great peril. But it had to be a particular kind of danger—I mean, you can't forgive an avalanche, an earthquake, or a flood. It had to be a person, someone very close to you, who did the harm.

"But the goddess never meant for you to die; she wanted you to grow up and, in the fullness of time, forgive those who committed unpardonable crimes against you. So she brought you here, gave you a wise and virtuous father to guide you, and made you a family: one child from Arcos, one child from Ferra. Even *that* is a kind of symbolic forgiveness—don't you see?"

Teo nods eagerly. He does.

"Then, when the moment had arrived, she brought the transgressors here—again, one from Arcos and one from Ferra—so we could be forgiven. Things didn't go exactly as planned: Claudio forgave Pyratos, not Aria. But since Claudio suffered far more at the hands of Pyratos than Aria did, I expect Zeus will forgive the substitution. As for you, Teo—you played your part with such courage and generosity, it would surely melt the hardest of hearts.

"Now it is done. Athene can say to her father, Zeus: Behold King Claudio of Ferra! Behold Prince Matteo of Arcos! See how dreadfully they were wronged; yet see how merciful they are! Will you not do likewise and forgive the people for their ancient crime?"

"That is very good," Teo says. "I think it's mostly right."

"Mostly?"

Teo gets up and paces, his brow furrowed in deep concentration. "But there's a flaw."

"Show me where it is."

"*You* are the flaw, Alexos. You are a champion, too, the first to be chosen. What was your part?"

"Oh, Teo! How can you ask? *I* was the transgressor! I sent you—"

"No, wait. It's not that simple. Yes, you did what you did; but you and Pyratos are not the same."

"We are the same in every way that matters."

"No, Alexos, that's not true. Let me tell you why. Pyratos wasn't chosen by Athene, was he?"

"No. He was, by all reports, very soundly rejected."

"As I thought. So that's the first thing. Here's another. Pyratos was given everything—beauty, intelligence, wealth, rank. He had Claudio by his side as he grew into manhood. Yet he still became a wicked man.

Athene must have seen that in Pyratos, the darkness of his spirit.

"But you were altogether different. She chose you to be her champion. Then she tested you over and over, threw one obstacle after another in your way."

"You heard that from Suliman."

"And I also observed it. I'm not a little child anymore, Alexos. I can think for myself."

"I apologize. Please go on."

"All right. So Pyratos had an easy life and should have been a better man. Whereas you had a life of suffering and loss, yet still became a good one. *Stop*, Alexos! I know what you're going to say. You *are* a good man—not perfect, but remarkably good. Now let me finish.

"Like Aria and me, Athene chose you as her champion, so you were also given a wise father to—"

"What, *Ektor*?"

"No! Suliman."

Alexos laughs and shakes his head. "Of course."

"Now, Pyratos and Claudio were so fixed in their character that Athene could depend on them to play their parts to perfection. But you, Alexos: I don't know *what* she wanted from you. You are not just a transgressor. For that, the goddess could have found another Pyratos."

"What then?"

"I don't know. It's something different, something more complicated. But I'm pretty sure this isn't over yet. I think there's more to come."

"Yes," Alexos says, "you're probably right."

Also, Teo is thinking, but does not say, *Aria hasn't forgiven anyone yet.*

33

ARIA KNEELS ON THE smooth stone floor, hugging herself against the chill of her sadness. Never has she felt so alone.

Teo has gone off with Suliman, down to the soldiers' camp to make amends with Alexos. The very thought had repulsed her, and she'd spoken against it (as much as Papa would allow). But it hadn't changed Teo's mind. He'd just given her that hurtful look, full of disappointment and regret. When he left, it had felt like they were parting forever.

Then as soon as Teo and Suliman had gone, Papa had fixed her with one of his fatherly stares and, in that new, firm voice he'd recently adopted, announced that they needed to have a little talk.

It hadn't gone well. They were both exhausted

and overwrought by the events of the past two days. Emotions had become heated and before very long they had arrived at something close to anger.

He had used words like *disappointed*. He'd said she was *rigid in her moral judgment*. He may even have said *pitiless* and *hard-hearted*, though she couldn't swear to it now; she was too stung by his disapproval to pay proper attention.

But far worse than the words and his stern disapproval was how completely he had misunderstood her. Aria can't forgive Alexos or be sorry that Pyratos is dead—*not* because she's heartless, but because she feels too deeply! What those men did to her father and brother isn't just some abstract notion; it's hauntingly real to her. Worse, they did it for the basest of reasons: Pyratos didn't want to be meddled with; Alexos wished to be king. How could she brush that away with quick forgiveness? Isn't justice as important as mercy?

The argument had finally come to an end, burned out like a dying fire. Her father had said, "Well!" and heaved a sigh. Then he'd pulled out a bowl and started washing his face and hands. He'd run his fingers through his hair and beard, dusted off his robes.

"Are you going somewhere?"

"Down to the camp. There's some heavy business I must attend to there."

"What heavy business?" It seemed to Aria that everything was already resolved.

"Those soldiers are my men now. And they must atone for what they've done: not only murder, but oath breaking too, for they were sworn to protect and defend their king. But it's more complicated than that, as of course you know. Pyratos was an evil man. And had he been properly tried for his crimes, there would have been more than enough to convict him. So somehow I must find a way to balance it all out: get them to admit their wrong, while at the same time healing their spirits and restoring order."

"Is that what kings do?"

"Among other things. Now listen to me, Aria: I don't want you to sit here and mope while I'm gone. I know you're sad, and hurt, and confused, but you have urgent business of your own. Athene has called you, and things out there are changing by the hour. The time is *now*, and you must do your part. That is why I spoke to you so strongly about forgiveness. If we ask it from the gods, we must first model it ourselves."

He was right. She *was* sad, hurt, and confused; she was also tired of being scolded. "Just tell me what to do," she'd said, her voice flat and cold.

Claudio was standing in the doorway then, looking down at her. He'd drooped a little when she said it, and gave one of his expressive sighs. "You already know," he said.

So here she is, on her knees before the goddess, praying for enlightenment: *O great Athene,* she whispers in the silence of her mind, *bless me with understanding. Teach me your will. Give me the courage and wisdom to do as you command.* She has continued in this way for a long time, but there has been no response of any kind.

And the more she gazes at the stone figure, pale and smooth against the slick, black wall, the less it seems like a goddess. The face is flat and expressionless. Only the eyes have any life at all, because Claudio made them so large, giving her a look of perpetual sorrow. But that's just an illusion. The statue has no feelings. It isn't Athene. It's an ordinary sculpture— not even a very good one.

Aria has been talking to a stone.

Stiff from kneeling so long, she rises, puts on her sandals, and steps out of the dimly lit temple into the bright afternoon. Dazzled by the light, she waits for her eyes to adjust. But even when they have, she continues to stand there, squinting and blinking. There must be something wrong with her vision. The sacred grove and the landscape beyond seem to have faded to drab. It's like the world is dying, all the life and color bleeding out of it.

But no, her eyes are fine. Her hands, her tunic, are exactly as they were—it's everything else that has changed. The trees are almost entirely bare, their branches bleached bone-white. The fallen leaves lie in heaps on the ground, dark and wet, rotting.

Was her father trying to warn her when he said things were "changing by the hour"? If so, she'd misunderstood, assuming he was referring to *events*, not changes to the island itself. She should have listened more carefully, or maybe she should have asked, or maybe he should have explained himself better. Then she might have been prepared.

But wait—could this be just another example of Athene's protection, like the overgrown path and their weed-choked garden? Aria likes this theory, though she knows it isn't logically sound: her family doesn't need protecting anymore. Pyratos is dead, Claudio is king, and their presence on the island is hardly a secret. And another thing: these dying trees feel altogether different from the changes to the garden and the path. It isn't just wild and weedy; the sacred grove feels polluted, sickly. It frightens her just to be there, as if the ruin were contagious and to stay too long would mean her own destruction.

Suddenly she is desperate to get away. Already

something inside her is curdling. So she runs.

She will go to the waterfall. It's where she and Teo always went to bathe, but also to lie in the grass and talk. It's a healing place, full of warm and happy memories. She will go there now. She'll stand on the smooth stone platform under the cascade of fresh, cold water and let it wash away the dust and her misery both. She hadn't realized how troubled she was till she thought of the waterfall. Now it's like something to drink when you're thirsty, food when you're starving: exactly what she needs. And the anticipation of this small, sweet comfort grows so vivid in her mind that Aria grows almost sick with yearning.

She runs and runs—away from the dying trees, toward hope and beauty and healing—but things don't get better; they get worse. In the orchard, rotting fruit and nuts lie scattered on the ground, half-covered with a blanket of shriveled leaves.

In her agitation, Aria is not careful where she steps. She slips in the muck and falls hard, landing on a mound of decomposing scarlet perrums. They are gooey and black, turning to mush; they smear her arms and legs with the sticky mess. The smell of decay is in her nostrils, musty and overripe, and her stomach heaves. Tears sting her eyes.

She forces herself to rise and keep on going, but

she's losing hope with every step. Everything everywhere is in decline: fading, moldering, cracking, shriveling, rotting. And though she's almost there, certainly close enough to hear the roar of a rushing stream, the only break in the silence is the crackle of dry leaves under her feet. *The waterfall has run dry.*

But this knowledge does not prepare her for what she sees when she gets there, for however dark her expectations, the reality always seems to be worse. The waterfall has not merely dried up; the cliff itself is crumbling away. A dusty pile of rocks spreads out from the base, half filling the pool. And what water remains is dark and cloudy. Noxious scum floats on the surface. The air is thick with a putrid smell, worse even than the rotting fruit.

Aria drops onto the dry and matted grass, utterly defeated. There's no point in resisting the obvious: her beautiful home is dying. It will be like this wherever she goes. There is nothing left to eat anymore, no fresh water to drink. Athene, who made this island in all its perfection, doesn't need it anymore. Now she is shrugging it off like an old, worn cloak.

It shocks Aria down to the marrow of her bones.

She wanders randomly from one ruined place to another. She knows there's nothing new to learn; she fully understands what's happening. But she feels the need to mourn. That's what you do when something or somebody dies: you take a last look, you remember the good things, you give yourself permission to be sad.

At some point she becomes aware that her feet are carrying her down the mountain slope toward the great stand of pines that grows at the edge of the sea. Aria has always loved that particular forest. The air is so fresh and briny there, the trees so tall and straight, their trunks like the pillars of an enormous temple. It always felt to her like a holy place.

The old path has disappeared under a wild tangle of thick growth, but Aria knows the way. She plows through the thorny underbrush, her bare ankles stinging from the countless little scratches. Most of the time she is looking down, watching for hidden rocks and ruts, stepping carefully over trailing vines. But now and then she raises her eyes to make note of landmarks and stay on course. Before long she begins to hear the rhythmic sounds of the sea, the *hussssh, hussssh, husssh* as waves crash against the rocks below.

All her life she's wondered what lay beyond that shore, beyond the sea and the fog. She'd asked her father about it many times. "It's not like this," is all he would say. "People must struggle just to eat. The weather is foul. There is suffering and disease. It's better here."

But Aria couldn't help being curious. On lazy afternoons she would lie in the grass, her fingers busy making flower crowns, trying to imagine that faraway land and all the strange things she'd read about, but never seen: wolves, chariots, bread, cities, snow.

Soon she will see it for herself. A ship will come, everyone will climb on board, and they'll sail across the dark waters to a strange and foreign place. Aria will go because she cannot stay. The island will be gone.

She's been so occupied with these troubling thoughts that she's surprised to look up and see tall pines ahead. They are dying, too, of course, their branches mostly bare, and the few needles still clinging to the bark are an angry, ugly brown.

But—she blinks, squints, and is half convinced that she sees a faraway patch of green. Her heart pounding with hope now, she leaves the scrub and enters the forest. The ground is soft and spongy here, the air still sweet with the fragrance of salt and pine. The deeper she goes, the surer she is that she was not mistaken. Those are living trees up ahead, as grand and majestic as ever they were—only more so now, stage lit as they are by that inexplicable stream of light cutting through the mist.

She reaches the circle of light and stops at the edge of it. It's as if the fog has swallowed the sun, each tiny droplet of moisture catching and reflecting its light. Everything is alive with brilliance and color, like being inside a diamond.

Suddenly Aria is struck by a force of such immensity that her knees grow weak and she sinks to the ground in awe. There is no doubt, none at all, that she is in the presence of the goddess. Athene is not a statue; she doesn't need a temple. She is light and air, things you cannot touch: wisdom, goodness, power.

There are things Aria ought to say at a moment like this: words of praise, words of thanks, and all those other words her father uses in his prayers— ancient and mysterious, appropriate for addressing the immortals. But they have all flown out of her mind. So she stays as she is, knees resting on a soft carpet of pine, the sound of her labored breaths filling the silence, tears streaming down her cheeks.

And as slowly as the dawn, it comes to her: Athene doesn't want her thanks or praise right now. She wants something very particular, something important, something only Aria can give.

"I am here," Aria says. "I give myself to you. Guide me and I will do whatever you ask." The light swells, blindingly bright. At the same time the air seems to compress around her. Dense and warm, it seems to hold her. It feels like an embrace.

Aria is bent over now, her forehead resting on the forest floor, her arms reaching out to the circle of light. She has committed herself, made her offer. The answer is not long in coming.

She is standing in a beautiful room. There are tapestries hanging on the walls; the furniture is finely carved, the wood dark. There are tables, scrolls, carpets, silver lamps on silver stands. The floor is a cunning pattern made from countless tiny stones—black and creamy white, russet, green. The shutters are open, but there is no breeze. It's hot in the room, hot and damp.

She is standing in front of a man, her hands behind her back. He is sitting at a desk, looking up at her: a burly man, broad of shoulder and brown of face, and richly dressed, like someone important.

Aria is afraid of him.

"You may sit," the man says, so she does. And in the process, she notices the fine tunic she's wearing, the strong, slender legs, the beautiful long-fingered hands. None of them belong to her. It's as though she has become another person altogether—a different person in a place she's never been; and somehow she knows that the man with the hard eyes is her father.

"I have good reports from all your masters," he says. "That's as it should be, of course. Much is expected of you. You cannot afford to fall behind."

She has heard this before many times and it's always the same: good work, now do better. Her spirit shrivels a little. The way he looks at her makes her cringe.

"I won't, Father," she says. . . .

34

THEY ARE SITTING ON the camp bed when Suliman comes in. They have leaned in close as they talk, their heads almost touching; Alexos is holding Teo's hand. At the sight of them, the physician seems to melt: soft folds form around his eyes, which somehow grow darker and brighter at the same time.

"Please excuse the interruption, my lord," he says.

Alexos sits up a little straighter. "Is there something the matter?"

"Not at all. I have only come to say that Teo's sister is waiting outside."

There follows a weighty pause. Then, tentatively, "What does she want?"

"To speak with you, Alexos. Alone."

They exchange a long and meaningful look. All of

this makes Teo nervous. His eyes dart from one to the other, trying to make sense of it.

"All right," Alexos says, but he doesn't move.

"Shall I help you dress?" Suliman seems to be stifling a grin.

Alexos looks down at his bare chest, his underclothes, his uncovered legs. "Oh. Yes. That would be good."

"Is she angry?" Teo asks.

"No, my prince." Suliman fetches the king's tunic, now ruined with damp and dirt, and helps him pull it over his head. "I believe it would be more accurate to say that your sister is terrified."

"Ah," Alexos says. "Well, that makes two of us, then."

"Would you prefer to stay seated as you are? You will have the advantage of height if you are standing." Suliman is actually chuckling now. Alexos points to the cane and Suliman brings it. Then he rises and positions himself in the middle of the tent. He can feel all the color draining out of his face.

"I hope she's nice to you," Teo says, looking up at him.

"I hope so too, little man. Give me your hand for luck." Teo does. "Will you come again soon? Please say yes."

"Of course I will."

She slips in quietly and stands by the entrance. It seems to Alexos that she has brought her own light—it's that astonishing white-gold hair; the perfect, radiant skin: pink, like the blush on a peach. A shiver runs through him and all he can do is watch her: the subtle hint of emotion playing over her face; the way she looks down at her feet, dirty and covered with scratches, then up again; the strand of hair that falls across her eyes; how she brushes it away.

Is she waiting for him to say something? Is he supposed to begin? Yes, probably. But what can he say?

"Thank you for coming here," he tries. "Though of course I understand it is not something you would . . . that is to say, that you might . . . I mean . . ."

He gives it up.

She is studying her fingernails, as nervous and tongue-tied as he is. And she's so small! He hadn't noticed that before. Now he positively looms over her, not at all what he'd intended. He wishes he hadn't chosen to stand, but now it's too late.

He really needs to say something. This silence is dreadful. Frantically, he works it out in his mind, numbering and arranging the things that need to be said. Finally they fall into place. He has it now. He can do this.

"May I tell you something?" he begins.

She looks up with interest.

"When we spoke those two times, while I was still a prisoner and you came to me in disguise, I told you I had dreamed about this island, but I thought it was the death-world. Do you remember?"

She nods, so serious.

"I have had those dreams many times. I was twelve years old when they began. You were even younger; Teo was only four. I watched you grow up. And in a strange sort of way, I shared your childhood—your lessons, your games, your adventures. I saw you tame a fox."

Still she doesn't speak.

"But those weren't common dreams; that's what I'm trying to say. Athene sent them to me, first in the temple on the day she called me out of childhood and into her service, then again as I lay dying from despair over the terrible thing I had done. It was only because I saw Teo here, in what I believed to be a blessed afterlife, with a loving death-father and death-sister to comfort and care for him—" His voice breaks. He swallows, clears his throat. "That's the only reason I was able to go on living, to finish the task the goddess had set for me. Those dreams were my one great consolation."

His neck is flushed; beads of sweat have formed on his brow and cheeks. Trying not to be too obvious, he wipes the sweat away.

"The point is, I feel that I *know* you, that I've known you all my life. And there has to be a reason for that. The goddess could have shown me happy visions of Teo if all she'd wanted was to keep me together so I could finish my task. But you were in every dream; I saw you even before Teo came to the island. So I think there is a reason you and I are here, exactly as we are now. Whatever we say to each other, there is purpose in it. I'm sorry if that disturbs you."

"Maybe we should sit," she says, pointing to the cot, then taking a stool and settling herself upon it. There's something so natural about the way she moves, graceful yet boyish. She doesn't watch herself being watched, as the court ladies of Arcos do.

"All right," he says. "But you will have to excuse me if this is a little indelicate." He stands by the camp bed, raises the hem of his tunic, and releases the catch so the brace can bend at the knee. Then, supporting himself with the cane, he sits down with all the grace he can manage.

"I believe what you just told me," Aria says, "because I have seen you as well."

"You have?"

"Just today; not before. But the goddess made up for the delay, I assure you." Her brows shoot up, green eyes wide. "She gave it to me all at once."

"And that's why you are here?"

"Yes. I wasn't willing to come before. In fact—well, it doesn't matter."

"How can I make it easier for you?"

She isn't expecting that. "I don't know."

"Then let me try?"

She nods.

"I know how you feel. I really do. You love Teo very much. And ever since he came here, you've wondered about his past—how he came to be alone at sea in that little boat. You couldn't imagine that anyone would intentionally harm a child. The thought would be repellent to anyone, but more so for you, since you've had no personal experience with evil. Until Pyratos came, no one was ever cruel to you. Teo is an angel, your father is wise and kind, everything a father ought to be—"

"Not like yours."

That stops him. "You're right. My father was not at all like Claudio. But my point is that for you to confront evil for the first time—and not just evil of a general sort, but a very particular, personal crime, committed against someone you love . . ." He throws wide his arms as if to express the enormity of the disconnect. "I can only imagine the horror you must have felt when you discovered that *I was that person*. And yet, when Athene told you to come here, as I assume she did, you obeyed. I believe that's more than enough to complete her circle of absolution and satisfy the gods."

This feels incomplete to Alexos. The conclusion is only implied. But what is he supposed to say, *you're done now; you can go*?

Aria rocks on her stool, staring off into the middle distance, her chin in her hands. "No," she says. "Listen."

Of course he will listen!

"When the goddess showed me your life today, I wasn't watching you as I am now, from the outside. I was in your skin. *I was you.* I saw what you saw and felt what you felt."

"How terribly unpleasant."

"It was, yes—and to such a degree that after a while it seemed *intentional*. Oh, I'm afraid I'll get this wrong."

"Please try."

"All right. The goddess chose me, and she chose Teo, too—did you know that?"

"Yes. He told me."

"But you were different. She chose *you* especially."

He waits.

"The whole time I was living your life, except when I was running and when I was with Teo, I was wretched. No matter how hard I tried, it was never good enough. And no one but Teo really loved me—" She looks up then, as if she's had a new thought. "Except for Suliman, and Peles, and Leander."

He flushes and looks down. She notices.

"Can I ask you something? I don't mean to intrude—"

"That's all right. Go ahead."

"I know Suliman loves you still. But what about the others—Peles and Leander? Have they abandoned you now that they know what you did?"

Alexos plays with the folds of his tunic, frowning. "Peles is under the impression that I saved his life, which I suppose I did, and he is firmly convinced that I have a noble heart. So he refuses to believe I could do anything vile, though he heard me admit it myself. He thinks there must be some missing piece that would explain it all. If anything, he is kinder to me now."

"That is amazing."

"Yes. Peles is an amazing man. Saving him may have been my greatest achievement."

"And Leander?"

"Ah. Well, that's a different case. We have been friends since childhood. He knew Teo, or at least knew of him. He saw him once."

"At the race."

She *has* seen his life. "Yes, at the race. And after I was sick and Teo disappeared, Leander comforted me. Everyone did. *Poor Alexos, on top of all he has suffered, now he has lost his beloved brother.* So you can imagine how repulsive Leander finds me now. He can't even look me in the eyes."

"Yes, I understand him. I felt the same."

Alexos blinks. Did she *mean* to use the past tense?

"I have released him from any obligation to attend me. But it's hard for him because we are here on this small island. He can't go back to his father's house or ride down to the borderlands. So we just avoid each other. That's the best we can do."

"Did you love him—Leander?"

Alexos doesn't have to think. "Oh, yes."

"And he loved you?"

"I believe he did. He was uncommonly attentive and kind. He anticipated my needs, eased my way, made me laugh. But it's hard to know with Leander. He's all sunshine and no shadow. I wonder sometimes if a person can truly love if he has no sorrow in him at all."

"Oh, I hope that's not true," she says. "For, like Leander, my life has been easy. Maybe that's why we reacted in the same way. He will feel differently, though, after I have spoken to him. For Peles was right, Alexos. What a clever fellow he is!"

"I'm afraid I don't follow you."

"I'm sorry. Let me go back and tell it all in order; then it will be clear. Do you remember where we were?"

"The suffering was excessive and no one loved me."

"Yes. Well it *was* excessive, just one thing after another. *Dear gods*, that dreadful race, and the illness, and then you were disinherited—incredible!"

"I'm sorry you had to go through it."

"Those weren't just things that happened, you know. They were carefully arranged. Athene wanted—no, that's wrong—she *needed* you to suffer. Would you like to know why?"

His hand goes to his mouth, then to his chest. *"Yes,"* he finally says, a little too heartily.

"Teo and I were chosen, as you know, and what Athene needed from us was forgiveness. But *you* were a different sort of champion. Zeus demanded a sacrifice—and you were it, Alexos.

"So the goddess made your life a misery. She drove you beyond your limits, then robbed you of your few consolations. You were strong and fast, you found peace in running, so she damaged your legs. You had purpose in your life as heir to the throne, so she took that, too. And finally, there was Teo."

She stares at him for a moment, her shoulders slumped, her head at an angle. "She did that to you, Alexos—also to Teo, but mostly to you. She rescued him and gave him a family, love, and forgetfulness. But she left you to suffer."

Alexos is bent over now, his face in his hands. Aria moves the stool closer and lays her hand on his knee. The touch is light, as if she'd laid a flower there.

"Suliman told us about your life. He said you were 'broken' and that's why you did what you did. Somehow that made sense to Teo, who is clearly a better person than I am, since he was able to forgive you and I was not. Even after Athene showed me how it felt to be you—oh, my heart was softened, I felt pity, but still I would not have come."

Alexos sits up now. He is trying to imagine what could possibly have made her change her mind. "Then why are you here?" he says.

"Because Athene had another task for me—besides granting my forgiveness. I am the messenger, Alexos. She gave me the key. I don't know why; it should have been Teo."

"What key?"

She takes a deep breath. "Peles' missing piece. Alexos, when I came to the scene with Teo in the skiff, and he was sitting there begging me to come fishing . . . Alexos, *I know it wasn't me* who pushed that boat away. Yes, my hand untied the knot and gave the bow a shove—but I was not controlling it."

"I don't understand."

"Let's say I was standing behind you and a great

wind came along and blew me over, and as I fell I brought you down with me. Yes, I made you fall; but it was really the wind that caused it. And there is no doubt in my mind: *I didn't push Teo away.*"

Alexos just stares at her, incredulous.

"To truly be the sacrifice that Zeus required, your suffering had to be brutal. Just taking Teo away from you was not enough. It had to be worse than that. *So she made you do it, and made you believe that you had killed him.*"

He cries out suddenly and it startles her. But he doesn't hide his face. He just stays as he is, looking at her, showing everything he is feeling. She gets off the stool and kneels before him, reaching up to grip his arms. Her face is inches away from his, her eyes very wide.

"And then I understood. The life Athene gave you would have broken anyone. But as hard as she tried, she failed—because you could *never* be damaged enough to harm your brother. So she *had to do it for you.* She gave you the guilt without the crime. Surely you must have wondered. Surely it must have seemed impossible to you—what happened."

"*Yes.*"

"Athene didn't want to do it. She loves you above all mortals. But she *had* to have the sacrifice to save her people." She stops for a moment, quivers all over like a dog shaking off water.

"I have learned a lot today, Alexos, enough to last a lifetime. Teo said, 'It's not as easy to be good as I thought it was,' and I didn't understand. Now I do. I believe I will spend the rest of my life trying to be like my brother, like Peles, like Suliman, generous and merciful. We must be careful how we judge one another in this life. There is always a missing piece. Oh, Alexos, I am so ashamed."

"No."

"Yes. Because you did not deserve my cruelty. You thought you did, and I thought you did, but we were both wrong. You have given more and asked less, have worked harder and thought more of others—"

"Please stop. You have broken the chains that have bound me since I was twelve years old. You don't have to say another word."

"Yes I do. I haven't completed my task. Alexos, whatever needs forgiving, I forgive you."

"And I accept your forgiveness." She is still gripping his arms, rather firmly for such a small person, and looking up at him in a way he doesn't quite understand. He just knows that the hair is rising on his scalp and he is dizzy from forgetting to breathe.

"Now I must ask you to forgive me," she says.

"Don't be ridiculous."

"Please, Alexos. Forgive me, as I forgave you. Do it, and then we are done."

"All right. I forgive whatever needs forgiving."

She is nervous, breathing hard. "And I accept your apology. Now, to show that we are friends, and to dazzle the gods, and because I find I want to very much—would you mind if I were to kiss you?"

"No," he says, his heart slamming against his chest, cold chills running down his neck and arms. "I wouldn't mind." He leans down a little and she rises to meet him, gently pressing her lips to his cheek. It's the way she used to kiss Teo when he was little.

"Thank you," he says, with an involuntary shudder. "But would you come and sit beside me? It would be somewhat more awkward for me to come down to you."

"Oh, of course."

"Thank you. And now, I wonder if we might try that another way. Like so." He cradles her face in his hands and gently presses his lips to hers. He lingers there, softly. Then he pulls back a little to look at her. *Please don't be offended!* "Was that all right?"

"Oh," she says. "It made me rather out of breath."

"Me, too—in a very good sort of way."

"Alexos, why is it so bright in here all of a sudden?"

The canvas is glowing and the tent is full of light.

"The fog has lifted, I expect. The sun is shining."

"But that never happens. There is always fog."

"I think Athene is ready to show her handiwork now; no need to keep us hidden any longer."

"You mean the gods are watching us?"

Delicately, with the third finger of his left hand, he's tracing the contours of her face: across the forehead and around the brow; down the slope of her nose, touching her mouth and her chin.

"I think so," he says. "I hope they like what they see."

"Oh yes, I hope so too."

He kisses her cheek, just to the side of her nose, then her lips again.

"Have you done this before, Alexos?"

"No."

"Nor have I. But I must say, you're uncommonly good at it."

"I'm relieved to hear it. How would it be if I took you in my arms?"

"I think that would be very nice." She leans her head against his chest. He kisses her hair. He thinks any moment now he is going to burst into flames.

"What is all that shouting outside?"

"I believe they have spotted a sail."

"A ship?"

"Yes. But there's no hurry. It'll take some time to get here."

"We can stay a while longer, then?"

"I thought we might."

And then it washes over him, and for a moment he is near to drowning in a wave of high emotion. It feels like desperation or unspeakable pain. But he's pretty sure it's neither one. "I never expected this," he says, a sort of gasp. "I did not think it possible."

"What—kissing?"

"A happy ending."

"Oh, Alexos, wouldn't you rather think of it as a happy beginning, which will lead to a very long, happy middle, and finally, years and years from now when we're aged and crotchety—*then* we can have our happy ending?"

"I quite agree. A much better way to look at it."

"Would you like to kiss me again?"

"Oh yes, Aria. I would."

Coda

THEY STAND TOGETHER, THE two old men, on a rise overlooking the harbor. Three ships flying the flag of Ferra are anchored offshore. The men and their gear will have to be ferried from the island to the ships in small boats. It will take the rest of this day and much of the next to get everything and everyone on board. But there's no sense of urgency. The weather is fair and looks to remain so.

The tents, already taken down and neatly folded, are piled up on the beach along with the cauldrons, trunks, barrels, boxes, and casks. Everyone will sleep under the stars tonight. The fog has gone for good.

"It's past believing," Suliman says, gazing down at Alexos and Aria, standing apart from the others, arms about each other's waists, while Teo turns cartwheels in the sand. Every now and then he runs back to his brother and his sister to hug them in the wildness of his joy.

"Indeed," Claudio says. "Here I am, sniveling like a child."

"Will they marry?"

"Oh, yes. They'd do it tomorrow if I'd allow it. But Aria has lived a simple life here; it's all she's ever known. Now she's going to a brave new world, full of wonders and terrors. There will be so much to learn about—dressmakers, banquets, court manners; only imagine! She'll need time to adjust."

"He'll wait however long he must. He's loved her since he was twelve."

"Oh, I don't intend to torture them. It will happen soon. But it'll be a busy time—so much to do, so many changes. That should distract them for a while."

"Yes," Suliman says. "It'll be a brave new world for us all. Both armies disbanding, men going home, which of course will mean more hands to work the farms. If the old stories are true, we'll have fine weather once again, bringing rich harvests and prosperity. Good changes, all. But of course there will be decisions to make as to how Arcoferra will be governed."

"Since we seem to have one king too many?"

"Well, yes. That is one of the complications."

"I have given the matter some thought, Suliman."

"I rather imagined you had."

"To wit: I have grown weary of the heavy burdens of

great office, have become old and worn with care . . ."

"In two days?"

"Yes. Positively exhausted. See the lines in my face and the bags under my eyes?"

"Claudio, I believe you are quite demented with joy."

"True. I have not been sleeping well. I wake in the night, laughing."

"That *would* wear a man down."

"Oh, it has. And so it has occurred to me that I might, as my nephew did, abdicate my throne."

"In favor of Alexos?"

"No, Suliman. In favor of my daughter."

"Oh. That is original—a queen!"

"I know it goes against custom—and possibly against the laws of Ferra—to choose a daughter as my heir over a son. But I can't claim Teo, not in any dynastic sense. He belongs to Arcos. And he has already refused that throne."

"I understand you completely, Claudio. A very neat and generous solution: the queen of Ferra marries the king of Arcos, and just like that"—he makes an extravagant sweep of the hand—"we are one kingdom again, jointly ruled by a united royal family. And Teo will not have to part from father, sister, or brother."

"You have it exactly."

"Where will they live—in the north or the south?"

"I would think they'd spend the summers in Arcos and the winters in Ferra."

"And with us around, they'll never lack for advisers!" They break into laughter at the same moment.

Down on the beach, Teo bounds up the slope and comes close to knocking his brother over. But Aria has such a firm grip on Alexos that the accident is averted. Now Alexos has the boy around the shoulders and they are linked, the three of them. It's a beautiful sight. Even from this distance, the men can feel their happiness, that much greater for being so unexpected.

Claudio looks over at Suliman and sees that he is weeping. He turns away, not wanting to intrude on a private moment. But Suliman knows he's been observed and he doesn't mind. He welcomes it, in fact, the long-missed opportunity of sharing his deepest feelings with a friend. He opens his heart.

"I had a wife once—long ago, before I came to Arcos."

Claudio turns but does not speak.

"We had a beautiful son. He was three years old. I loved my wife very much and I doted on my boy. I was a prince, though a minor one, the youngest of seven. I had everything a man could desire: wealth and position, love and purpose. I am glad to say I knew at the time how fortunate I was.

"But then, when I had been away on some business

for my brother, I returned to find that there had been a fire and my family had perished in it."

"Oh, Suliman!"

"I need not tell you what I felt. You have lost your own wife, so you will know. But after a time, those around me grew impatient with my mourning. 'Find yourself a new wife,' they would say. 'She will give you a new son.' But I had loved *that* woman and *that* child, and they were not replaceable. So I took my grief and withdrew from court and pursued my studies— medicine, languages, philosophy.

"Then, restless still, I decided to see the world. I eventually settled in Arcos and made a new life for myself. But I never spoke of my past. King Ektor knew who I was, of course, who my brother was, and where I'd been trained in medicine. But the most important things, the true and personal things, nobody knew. Not once since leaving my country have I spoken the names of my wife or my son."

"Will you speak them now, to me?"

"I will. My wife was Laleh; that is also the name of a flower in the language of my people. We called our son Hami, which means protector, defender."

"Laleh," Claudio says. "Hami. I will remember."

"It must already be obvious to you that Alexos has become my second son. I did not seek it, nor did he. It grew over time and we never gave it a name. But he is my son and I am his father.

"It has been difficult, of course. His pain became my pain. And while there were times when I was able to ease his way and calm his fears, the very nature of his destiny meant that he must walk alone. As the long-awaited chosen one—we didn't know then that there were others—a lot was expected of him. It became clear over time that he was being tested."

He pauses thoughtfully, takes a deep breath; his shoulders droop as he lets it out.

"There are words often used when speaking of the promise Athene made and the role her champion must play: dedication, selflessness, sacrifice. But no one really knew exactly what the boy was supposed to do.

"And so, being a scholar—as you are, Claudio—I made a study of the ancient scrolls that are kept in the sacred archives. They are written in an archaic form of your language, not easy to decipher. But I have been a student of languages all my life. With time and effort I managed to learn it."

Claudio leans in closer now; Suliman's voice has dropped.

"I read the scrolls from beginning to end. And then, hoping I was mistaken in my translation, I read them again and again. But it was not a mistake. Claudio, the word *sacrifice* was literally meant—not merely in the sense of doing without or giving something up, but in the same way we sacrifice a bull or a goat."

"He was meant to die?"

"Yes."

"When did you learn this?"

"He was very young, five or six years of age. Since that time I have waited and wondered—how and when would it happen? I prayed to Athene, *Let it be easy; let it be quick.* Then he was captured by Pyratos, and I understood. His death could not be easy and quick: this was a *sacrifice*; Zeus required suffering on an epic scale. Thus the false accusation, the prospect of a shameful trial and a public execution. It had to be horrible."

Now he looks at Claudio with amazement in his eyes. "Yet now I see that Athene has managed, with the exceptional cleverness for which she is so famous, to put on such a stirring display of noble suffering and generous forgiveness that Zeus failed to notice that the ultimate price was never paid. Then, once absolution had been granted and the immortals had moved on to other things, she . . ."

He can't go on. So Claudio finishes for him. "She restored Alexos to life."

"Yes. And so I weep with joy and gratitude, you see."

They are silent now, thinking of their children,

thinking of the future, gazing out at the tender blue of the summer sky, the calm waters sparkling in the sunlight, the ships rocking gently, their sails ruffling in the breeze, and the little boats coming and going.

More magic, fantasy, and adventure from
DIANE STANLEY

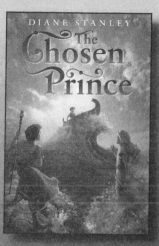

The Silver Bowl Trilogy

HARPER
An Imprint of HarperCollinsPublishers

www.harpercollinschildrens.com